MICHELLE FINCH sticks TO THE PLAN

RITA HARTE

Copyright © Rita Harte, 2023

First published 2023

Email: ritaharteauthor@gmail.com

All rights reserved. Without limiting the rights under copyright reserved above, no part of this publication may be reproduced, stored in or introduced into a database and retrieval system or transmitted in any form or any means (electronic, mechanical, photocopying, recording or otherwise) without the prior written permission of both the owner of copyright and the above publishers.

Cover by Cover Ever After

ISBN: 9798393613174

Imprint: Independently published

For my lovely dad, who knows exactly how life-changing learning to read can be.

Michelle Finch Sticks To The Plan

Rita Harte

1 Michelle

"**M**ichelle!"

I scanned the crowd, searching for familiar faces.

"Michelle! Over here! Michelle!"

I rubbed my eyes, gritty with recycled air, and blinked rapidly. Nope, I still couldn't see anyone whose face I knew, though a man with a combover and too many shirt buttons undone gave me an unsettling smile when my eyes caught his. Yuck.

"Michelle! Seriously, you need better glasses or something!"

That last comment was accompanied by a tight double hug that squeezed the breath right out of me.

"I swear you were looking right past us!" My sister Abby's familiar voice was in my ear. The hug wasn't over yet.

Knowing my sisters, the hug was just getting started. "I should have made that sign!"

"You wanted the sign to say, 'Welcome home from prison!'" Tessa, my other sister, objected. "And I vetoed it. You owe me one, Michelle."

"Much appreciated." I extricated myself from my two grinning sisters. "It's so good to see you!"

"I'm so glad you're finally here!" Tessa gave me one more squeeze as Abby grabbed my suitcase.

"I can do that." I reached for the handle, but Abby pulled it out of my grasp.

"Nope!" She shook her head. "You look exhausted; I'll do it."

"And I'm taking your carry-on," Tessa added, eager fingers stealing it right out of my hand. "All you have to do is make it to the van. Reckon you can manage that?"

"I'm sure I can muster up the strength somehow." I let out an exaggerated sigh. "But you'll have to carry me if I pass out on the way."

"I should have brought Dylan," Tessa said. "He could carry you, no problem."

"Absolutely not!" Abby was adamant. "This is sister time! No dudes."

"But I want to meet Dylan!" I was curious to meet Tessa's boyfriend, especially given all the time we had spent analysing his personality, behaviour, and intentions in our group chat.

"You will," Tessa assured me. "Tomorrow, maybe. But right now, we want you all to ourselves."

"Exactly," Abby agreed, striding ahead and dragging my suitcase behind her in a way that couldn't be good for the little wheels. "I wasn't sure you'd make it until you sent that selfie from the plane."

"Ouch," I said, forcing a smile, but her words hurt. "Of course I was going to come! I've been dying to see you two."

"It's just that you cancelled the last three times," Tessa sounded almost apologetic. "It's okay. I know how busy your job gets and how important it is to you, but—"

"But that job has totally taken over your life!" Abby declared. "Ever heard of work-life balance?"

"There were extenuating circumstances!" I wanted to defend myself. "First, share prices crashed across the resources sector, then a Senior Partner quit just before the end of the financial year, then there was that scandal where the Finance Minister was accused of doing something inappropriate with a whiskey bottle on Snap Chat, and then—"

"Excuses, excuses!" Abby waved a dismissive hand. "You're here now. That's what matters."

As we stepped through the sliding doors of Kingsford Smith International Airport, the sound of honking horns and the smell of exhaust fumes hit my nostrils. Still, I couldn't help gasping in delight at the sudden sunshine that warmed my sallow, plane-dehydrated skin. "It's sunny!" I said, sticking out a hand to catch the rays. "Like Sydney is supposed to be!"

"You've got way better luck than me," Tessa told me. "When I first landed in Sydney, it rained for a week."

"Maybe the universe is rewarding you for finally taking a break," Abby said, unwilling to let the topic go.

But I just shrugged. "Maybe," I said mildly. I knew better than to argue with Abby when she was insistent on making a point. We crossed a busy walkway and began to make our way up a winding ramp, Abby taking a panting breath as she tugged my suitcase over the concrete.

"We could get the lift," Tessa suggested. "If you're struggling with that suitcase."

"No way!" Abby turned to shake her head at us. "The lift is for losers. And I am not," she drew herself up to her full height, "struggling with this suitcase. See these arms? Strong enough for two suitcases. Probably four!"

"Of course they are." Tessa shot me a wink, and I had to cover my mouth to stifle a giggle.

As I followed my sisters up the apparently much quicker ramp, I pulled my phone from my pocket, relieved when it showed that, yes, it had connected to Australia's 5G network. My relief dissolved when I clicked my email icon; it was like unleashing a tsunami.

"Shit," I murmured, scrolling through the sea of emails. It didn't seem like anything too crazy had happened in the finance industry since I had left Glasgow, but—

"Oh no, you don't!" Abby whipped the phone from my hands. "You're on holiday, Michelle! No checking your work emails."

"You don't know I was doing that!" I protested. "I could have been updating my Tinder location."

"Were you?" Abby raised her eyebrows, making full use of the fact that she was the tallest of the three of us to look down her nose at me.

"No," I confessed. "It was work emails. You know I'm not on Tinder."

"Just as I thought." Abby nodded with satisfaction. "Seriously, Michelle, I'm not going to battle it out with your phone all week for your attention. You said you needed a break and wanted to see us."

"I do," I said. "I was just—"

"Give her back the phone, Abby," Tessa intervened, taking it from Abby's hand. "Michelle's a big girl. She can decide how unplugged she wants to be."

"Fine!" Abby huffed. "I just want you to have a proper break," she added, looking at me with the kind of genuine concern that made me instantly forgive my big sister for being so irritatingly overbearing sometimes.

"I know," I said. "And I do too. Look, I'll delete the app and just check my emails on the web version. Sometimes. How does that sound?"

"Like an excellent compromise," Tessa cut in before Abby could protest and handed me back my phone.

"How many more levels up is the van?" I asked as Abby began to march off again with my suitcase, an even more determined bounce in her step.

"Six." Tessa rolled her eyes. "Think you can manage it?"

"Oh, I'll be fine. It's Ms Muscles there I'm worried about."

"I heard that!" Abby flipped me off as she pranced up the ramp at an even greater speed. I couldn't help but chuckle. It was good to be back with my sisters.

"So, apparently, my Air BnB has ocean views." I pulled up the listing on my phone. "Wait. Make that 'ocean glimpses'."

Abby scoffed. "If you stand on the roof on your tiptoes, you might catch a glimpse of blue? What a rort!"

"What's the address?"

"Twenty-Six South Side Road," I read out. "Newly renovated two-bedroom cottage, just a short walk from picturesque Brekkie Beach."

"South Side Road *is* pretty near the beach," Tessa said evenly. "You might get more than a glimpse."

"So long as it's clean and convenient, I'll be happy," I said with a firm nod. "It looked like a good location. Three minutes' walk to that coffee shop you're always talking about. The one with the weird food?"

"Nick and Nikki's?" Abby supplied. "Miss me with the goji berry and wheat grass muffins, but their coffee is great."

"Wheatgrass is the devil's work." I wrinkled my nose. "I used to work with this guy who had a wheatgrass shot in his smoothie every morning. He made sure everyone knew about it, too. He smelled like lawnmower clippings."

"Ugh, those guys are the worst." Abby nodded vehemently. "Rattling their protein shakers, talking about their one rep max non-stop, finding any excuse to lift stuff..."

"Doesn't stop you checking them out at the gym," Tessa teased from the back seat.

"Well, I've got eyes!" Abby shrugged. "Hey, look!" She pointed to a sign that read 'Welcome to Brekkie Beach'. "You're finally here!"

"I sure am." I looked out the window eagerly, taking in streets full of sun-bleached weatherboard cottages, modern architectural masterpieces, squashed-looking duplexes, and a few square mansions with imposing electric gates. In the sparkling sunshine, it looked nothing like the terraced rows of Birmingham where I had grown up. It looked even less like Glasgow, where I had lived the last six years. I had applied for a transfer to the Sydney office more than once but had always been denied. I'd just have to enjoy Australia for the brief time I was here.

"And the sun's out for you," Tessa said. "Should be an amazing sunset tonight over the water."

"What's the plan for tonight? Please tell me it involves alcohol."

"We thought you'd be tired from your flight and would just want an early night—" At my stricken face, Abby burst out laughing. "Okay, that's a total lie. But I had you for a minute there!"

"What's the real plan?"

"Pub," Abby and Tessa answered together.

"It's not exactly a glittering nightspot," Tessa went on. "But there's decent live music, two kinds of rosé, and the view of the beach from the terrace is amazing."

"Perfect," I said, sighing in satisfaction. A night of wine and catching up with my sisters sounded *good*. It had been too long. So long, in fact, that I was choosing not to calculate the exact number of years and months since I had been with both my sisters.

"And here's your new home!" Abby said, pulling her van to a stop outside a weatherboard cottage that looked—

"Maybe the interior is the bit that's newly renovated," Tessa sounded like she was trying to be optimistic. "Like, maybe it's got a really nice bathroom."

"It would need to." Abby curled her lip. "How much are you paying for this place? They're ripping you off!"

"I'm sure it's fine," I said, unclipping my seatbelt and yanking open the door of Abby's van. Immediately the delightful smell of salt and fresh, crisp sea air hit my nostrils. The house, however, looked like something from a movie. A horror movie. With its overgrown garden, peeling paint, and crooked wooden steps, it looked like the sort of place a group of plucky teenagers would break into, only to be tormented by a vengeful ghost.

"Do you need to call someone to let you in?" Tessa asked, following me and still clutching my carry-on bag.

"Nope, they said the key was under a flowerpot," I said, scanning the email confirmation I had received.

"I bet it is." Abby scowled. "No one's going to break into this place."

"It's not that bad!" I protested, even though the gate creaked ominously as I made my way into the front yard. There might once have been a path up to the door, but it was so overgrown with weeds it was now impossible to tell where the path might once have been. "It's...rustic."

Tessa laughed. "Rustic is right," she said but then lowered her voice. "You know, if it's really horrible, you can stay with Dylan and me. The kitchen is still being renovated, and we've only got one working bathroom, but—"

"You're lovely," I said. "But I like my space, and I'd hate to intrude on your love nest. Especially when it's being renovated."

There was a single chipped flowerpot on the creaking front porch, containing something that had died around the same time as low-rise jeans. When I lifted it, I found a rusty silver key. With a bit of effort, I managed to fit it into the lock and pushed the front door open.

I went inside, followed by my sisters, who were toting my luggage like porters seeking a large tip. The three of us stood there, looking around in all directions.

"It could be worse," I said finally.

"How could it be worse? The pictures on the listing were a total lie!"

"You can do a lot with angles," Tessa said. "And lighting."

"You can do a lot with photoshop," Abby said darkly.

The weatherboard cottage was, to put it mildly, a dump. Scratched vinyl was stretched over the concrete floor and didn't quite meet the battered skirting boards. The walls were an unappealing shade of yellow, and a haphazard assortment of framed IKEA prints didn't improve them. A faded sectional sofa and a bulky TV that clearly predated the digital era dominated the living area, while a galley kitchen was squashed against the opposite wall.

"It doesn't smell," I said, trying to find positives. "And the kitchen looks clean." I bent my head to inspect the sink and was relieved that none of Australia's famed terrifying arachnids came up through the plughole to greet me.

"This bed is like a rock!" Abby called, clearly having taken herself on a tour.

"The bathroom is...functional." Tessa poked her head out from behind a door. "The plumbing works!"

"Look, it's not like I'm going to be spending much time here. It's just a place to keep my luggage and sleep, right? And the location's great."

"You always see the bright side," Tessa said warmly, wrapping me up in a half-hug.

"Are you sure you read the listing right?" Abby joined us, looking disgusted. "I can't believe you booked this place!"

"Yes, I read the listing right." My temper flared. "I can read these days, you know!"

"I'm sorry," Abby said quickly. "I didn't mean—"

"I know you didn't." I sighed. "Just, you know I'm sensitive on that one."

"You can come and crash on my couch," Abby began, by way of reconciliation. "Or I could get an air mattress, and maybe—"

"It's fine," I said, forcing a bright smile. Inside, I was disappointed. I had imagined a cute beachside cottage with a Hamptons vibe. I had seen myself stepping out onto an expansive wooden deck and drinking in the smell of the fresh, salty air every morning. That seemed unlikely, especially given the complete lack of a deck. But I was finally here, wasn't I? Reunited with my sisters, about to enjoy a much-needed break from work, and I had the prospect of sunset on the water and plentiful wine to look forward to.

"Are you sure?" Tessa looked concerned. "You don't have to stay here; we can—"

"It's definitely fine," I said again, with a determined nod. "Anyway, I'm going to brave that bathroom because I need a shower. You two promised me a beachside pub, and I am not going to attract hot surfers smelling like four hundred people's recycled sweat."

"Atta girl!" Abby pumped her fist. "Looking for a holiday fling, then? I'll be your wing woman!"

"Honestly?" I said. "All I want right now is a drink. Hot surfers are way less appealing than a nice glass of wine."

"Amen to that!"

"You left your phone at the cottage, right?" Abby nudged me as we walked down the footpath towards the strains of loud conversation and classic rock that indicated we were nearing the pub.

"Yes," I said, feeling ever so slightly annoyed. "After you insisted. Three times."

"I just want you to switch off for a night!" Abby scrunched up her face. "Enjoy the ambience, you know."

To be fair, the night *was* ambient. Across the street, I could see crashing waves breaking onto golden sand under the setting sun. A deliciously refreshing breeze came from across the water to break the sticky summer evening air, and I felt a thrill of excitement that I was somewhere entirely new, somewhere I had never been. After months – no, make that years – spent going from work to my apartment to work, I was more than ready for a change.

"I've got mine," Tessa said. "For selfies. We haven't got a photo together in ages."

"Oh, she's allowed a phone?"

"For selfies only! And if I catch you checking your emails or texting Dylan, I'm confiscating it, Tessa."

Tessa, for her part, stuck her tongue out at our older sister, and I laughed, feeling a little of the tension that the long flight and disappointing murder shack of a cottage had put in my shoulders disappear.

"So, this is it?" I said, entirely redundantly. There was only one pub in Brekkie Beach, and the whitewashed building in front of us bore the words 'Brekkie Beach Hotel'.

"This is where the magic happens," Abby told me. "And keep your eyes out; I'm sure we'll find you some local hotties."

But as we stepped into the crowded and cheerful pub, all I could see were couples. It seemed like every table was occupied by people holding hands, sharing burgers and chips, or sitting together while each stared at their phone. The few single men I saw looked like they'd qualify for the old age pension.

"Don't think about looking for men," Tessa said to me in a low whisper. "Let's just get a drink."

"I'll get the wine," Abby decided. "You two get a table on the terrace before they all fill up."

"I'll pay," I said, fumbling for my wallet, but Abby stopped my hand.

"We all know you're the financially successful one," she said with a roll of her eyes. "But I can afford a bottle of rosé at the local pub."

I winced. My sisters and I were happy to share the details of potentially infected ingrown hairs, dreams involving highly inappropriate sexual partners, and the effects of too much fibre on the digestive tract. But money was one thing we did *not* discuss.

"You can get the next one," Tessa said, patting my arm. "Come on, let's get a table. The view is seriously amazing."

I followed Tessa through the crowded tables of couples and onto a wide terrace, where shade cloth hung in heavy strips. The cane chairs were battered, the floor was sticky, and the acrid smell of cigarettes was escaping the smokers' area, but—

"Damn, that is an Insta-worthy sunset right there," I said, my mouth hanging open. And it was. The sun was low above the water, just starting to melt into the undulating waves. The beach was stretched out beneath us, the headlands protecting it from the harsh ocean.

"I know, right?" Tessa looked pleased. "We can go to the beach tomorrow. But you have to promise me you'll be more thorough with your sunscreen than I was my first time at the beach. I turned into a lobster!"

"But didn't that end in Dylan rubbing aloe vera into your shoulders in a very sexy way?" I said, sinking down into one of the chairs. The cane was unravelling from the armrests, and I wouldn't have wanted to examine the stains on the cushion with a black light, but I was too comfortable and happy to care.

"It was kind of sexy," Tessa admitted, sinking down beside me with a sigh of satisfaction. "In an incredibly embarrassing way. But you don't need to turn into any kind of crustacean to get a man to touch you."

"Maybe I do," I confided. "It's been a while."

"Well, you're very busy with work. I guess that makes it hard to meet the right guy."

"You know I'm not looking for the right guy," I said. "At least—"

"What are we talking about?" Abby interrupted, squeezing into the sofa beside me and putting a glass into my hand, which she quickly filled with rosé.

"That Michelle doesn't have time for men," Tessa said promptly. "And so it's been a while since she's...you know."

"All the more reason for a holiday fling!" Abby filled up Tessa's glass and then her own. With the way Abby poured, the bottle was empty once she had finished. "We just have to keep an eye out for someone worthy of you."

"I wouldn't mind a little holiday fun," I said, taking a big gulp of rosé. It wasn't the best rosé I had ever tasted, but it was so welcome that I made a sound close to orgasmic as I drained half the glass. "It's not like I have time for a real relationship. Not yet."

"I know, you've got your whole plan." Tessa pursed her lips. "No serious men until after you make Partner."

"That's right," I said, setting my glass down and rolling my shoulders. "Once I've done that, I'll find someone appropriate – or better still, he'll find me – and we'll have a fabulous whirlwind romance and be disgustingly happy."

Abby snorted into her glass. "That's how it's going to go, is it? What if Mr Right walks into the pub tonight? Are you just going to ignore him?"

"It's impossible," I said, shaking my head. "He couldn't be Mr Right if I met him now because it's the wrong time."

"For someone who reads as many romance novels as you, you're not very romantic." Tessa nudged me. "I thought that the workaholic career woman gets swept off her feet by the hometown hunk, and they end up running the cupcake store of her childhood dreams."

"My childhood dreams involved spreadsheets and client presentations," I scoffed. "I don't like it when the woman has to give up her career to get the guy. Any guy who expected me to do that is the wrong kind of guy."

"Now that I agree with," Abby said warmly. "So, we won't be on the lookout for your Mr Right then. Just Mr Fling, yeah?"

"Look, if there's a single guy here with an Aussie accent and nice arms, I'm down," I said, finishing the rest of my drink. "But what I really want is to hear about everything that's been happening in the lives of my beautiful sisters."

"To sisters!" Abby raised her glass, and I held up my own, which was now empty.

"Sisters," I repeated. Sisters were *way* more important than men.

We were well into our third bottle of rosé and had consumed two enormous bowls of chips covered in chicken salt, which I was rapidly coming to believe was Australia's greatest invention, when Abby nudged me.

"Look, the band's setting up," she said. "We might get a bit of a dance floor going."

"I hate dancing." Tessa wrinkled her nose. "Unless I've been drinking."

"But you have been drinking," I reminded her, and Tessa's face broke into a relieved smile.

"Well, in that case, dancing sounds like an awesome idea."

"Just us and fifty couples," I said with a grimace.

"It does seem to be date night in Brekkie Beach," Abby agreed. "We were probably lucky to steal this one away from her honey bun love bucket."

"Ew!" Tessa stuck out her tongue again. "And, of course, I'm here! I see Dylan every day, but I only get Michelle once in a...how long has it been?"

"Too long," I said, and then let out a groan as the band – all of whom looked too old for the man-buns they were rocking – began the far-too-familiar opening bars of *Wonderwall*. "Is every pub band contractually obliged to play this? Everywhere I go, it's bloody Oasis!"

"I like it," Tessa shrugged. "It's familiar, you know?"

"If they do any Bon Jovi, I'm leaving." But it was an empty threat. I was enjoying myself too much to mind that the music wasn't exactly creative.

"Oh, I wouldn't do that," Abby said, her eyes on something behind my head. "I think I've just spotted a contender for your holiday fling."

I couldn't help myself. I looked around instantly – and completely obviously – in the direction of Abby's gaze. And wow, I didn't need her to point out who she was talking about.

"Oh," I said, my mouth gaping like a fish. "Huh."

Leaning against the wall and chatting lazily to a (thankfully male) companion was precisely the sort of man I had hoped Australia was full of. He was tall and tanned, with scruffy blonde hair and bright green eyes. Dressed simply in a black t-shirt and jeans, I could see that, yes, he did have *good* arms. Very good arms indeed. But what really made me stare was his smile. He had a seriously dazzling smile, and I could only imagine how it might feel to have that smile turned on me.

"Oh wow," Tessa said, following my gaze. "He's so your type."

"Even if he's not in a suit with a briefcase," Abby quipped, nudging me again.

Mr Handsome's eyes wandered over to our sofa, and I furiously busied myself with my half-empty glass, not at all eager for this dream boat of a man to see that all three of us were staring at him.

"No way could a man like that be single," I said into my wine glass, trying to convince myself.

"No ring."

"How on earth can you tell from here?"

"Because I have great eyesight, unlike you," Abby said. And that was true. At work, I donned thick black-framed glasses, partly to see my colleagues and partly to look older and more authoritative. It was tough being a young woman in a male-dominated industry, and I'd use any and all props I could to help myself out. Tonight, though, I was wearing my contact lenses. My eyes, still gritty from the plane, weren't entirely pleased by this.

"No ring doesn't mean single."

"But it's a good start," Tessa said encouragingly. "I bet if we get up and dance, he'll come over to you."

"As if he's going to notice me."

"He's been looking over here," Abby reported.

"Probably because we were all staring at him!" I said. "Or he's looking at one of you. Why couldn't I be like Cinderella and have two ugly sisters?"

"You hate housework," Tessa pointed out. "And I've never seen you sing to mice. That seems like part of the job description."

"True," I said. "But I seriously doubt he's looking at me."

"Why wouldn't he?" Abby demanded. "You're freaking gorgeous! If I do say so myself, as someone who shares your DNA."

"I just came off a twenty-eight-hour flight; I'm not exactly looking my best."

"Your worst is stunning," Tessa said loyally. "Come on, if the band plays a decent song, let's dance and see what happens."

"What counts as decent?"

"Anything I heard being blasted out of your bedroom between the ages of ten and eighteen," Abby said promptly.

"Deal," I said, shaking my sister's hand. "But I don't think anything will happen. Or that this band will play anything—"

But then the singer crooned out the opening notes of Pink's *Get This Party Started*, as if the band had somehow hacked into my teenage playlist and selected one of my all-time favourites.

"Oh, come on," Tessa said. "We have to dance!"

But I was already on my feet. "You don't have to convince me!" I told her, weaving my way to the dance floor. "Forget the dude; nothing could stop me from dancing to this!"

"Yes!" Abby pumped a fist as though in victory. "Get it, girl!"

A sticky pub floor, surrounded by couples with arms around each other, wasn't exactly the ideal location to throw moves that would attract the attention of Australian hotties. But as the singer began the chorus, I had almost forgotten about the hottie in the corner. I was too busy laughing at my sisters as we tried to remember the choreography I had once invented for this very song.

"No, it was two hip pivots and then the hair toss!" Tessa laughed, clutching my arm. "You forced me to practice for hours!"

"What, like this?" Abby bopped to the music, tossing her admittedly glorious head of hair.

"Yes!" Tessa clapped her hands together as I laughed so hard that I almost choked. I couldn't resist glancing over at the corner again, and when I saw that the hottie was looking right at me, that lazy grin on his face, I completely stopped in the middle of my choreography, and Tessa trod on my foot.

"Ow!" I hopped painfully, gripping Tessa for stability.

"Sorry!" she said. "I thought we were doing the thing!"

"Someone got distracted." Abby gave me a knowing look. "Making eyes across a crowded room."

"Well, I doubt I impressed him with my moves."

"That routine is killer! We didn't even get to the slut drop!"

Reluctantly, I let out a laugh. And once again, my eyes moved to the corner where Hottie McHotterson had been laughing with his friend. But he was no longer there. I was surprised by the jolt of disappointment in my stomach. After all, I hadn't even spoken to the guy, and I couldn't have made a good impression so far with all the staring and my rosé-impaired dance routine.

"I like your moves," a deep Australian voice said from behind me, and I whirled around to see the man I had been very obviously staring at standing right there, his friend beside him. "I don't think the dance floor has seen that kind of action before."

"Definitely not from this guy," his friend, dark-haired and sporting a scrubby beard, said. "I'm afraid Patrick here's afflicted by the curse of heterosexual white men," he announced sadly, shaking his head. "He's dance-lexic; there's no treatment."

"Is that so?" I asked the handsome Australian, who I had just learned was called Patrick. "Sorry to hear that."

"It's true." Patrick put on a rueful expression. "But you're clearly an expert. Maybe you could give me a private lesson."

"I—" my mouth went suddenly and inexplicably dry because he was even more handsome close-up. There was a little dimple in his left cheek, and I could see his nose was slightly crooked like he had broken it at least once. But that didn't diminish his appeal. Not one bit.

"Michelle's an amazing dance teacher!" Abby pushed me forward with so much force that I stumbled right into Patrick, who caught me with impressive reflexes. "Seriously, practically a professional."

"Well, I need a lot of help," Patrick said, looking down at me. "Michelle, was it?"

"Uh, yeah," I said, looking up into those green eyes and taking a moment to remember that Michelle was indeed my name. His big hands were strong on my bare arms, and I felt a spike of electricity go through me at his touch. *Please let this man be my holiday fling*, I thought. *Oh please, please!*

"We'll leave you to it," Tessa said, turning away and leaving me in the arms of Hottie. No, not Hottie. Patrick. His name was Patrick.

I wasn't usually the blushing type – that was Tessa – but now, it took a surprising amount of mental fortitude to force myself to look up at him as our bodies swayed slowly to the music.

"You don't really want me to teach you that routine, do you?" I asked finally, my voice a passable imitation of flirtatious.

"Nah, that was definitely just a line to ask you to dance with me," Patrick said, blessing me with that lazy grin.

"Oh, that's a relief," I said, relaxing into his arms and letting my body move just a little closer to his so I was almost – but not quite – pressed into him. "Because my sisters will tell you; I'm an absolute tyrant. It would end in tears."

Patrick laughed, throwing his head back and exposing the line of his throat, his Adam's apple bobbing. I had a sudden urge to lick that throat right down to the collarbone. Maybe, just maybe, I could do that if I was lucky enough to take this man home. But licking his throat would be inappropriate in the middle of the pub, minutes after meeting him.

"Well, you've given me fair warning," Patrick said. His Australian accent was doing things to my nether regions that would necessitate a change in underwear if this went on much longer. "You're English, right? Are you on holiday?"

"I am," I said. "Originally from Birmingham, but I work in Glasgow. My sisters are locals, though," I added quickly, as though wanting to prove I had a right to be here. "You?"

"Well, I was born in Queensland, but I've been living in Sydney long enough they've almost accepted me as one of their own," Patrick told me with a grin. "At least until it's time for State of Origin."

"Is that a sports thing?" I wished I had read up on Australian sports; I should have known it would come in handy for seducing handsome strangers.

"Rugby League," he clarified. "But you're English, so you'd be into the Premier League."

"Am I going to disappoint you if I tell you the only footballer I know is David Beckham, and that's because he married Posh Spice?"

But Patrick just laughed again. "Not at all." As he said it, he moved one hand from my bare arm to my lower back, pulling me a little closer. I gasped, pressing my body into his and almost moaning at the heat of his firm chest pressed against me. He smelled good, too, I thought distractedly. Not of cologne, but of laundry dried outside in the salty air, clean soap, and—

"So, I should probably tell you that your sisters and my mate Khalid are watching us right now like we're chimps at the zoo."

I let out a groan then that was definitely not sex-related. "I'm sorry," I said. "My sisters have zero concept of boundaries or privacy."

"Neither does Khalid," he confided. "He thinks he's the best ever wingman, and that makes him entitled to watch me like I'm performing for his personal entertainment."

"Oh, he's going to get along great with my sisters."

"Maybe we should give them something to watch," Patrick said, and he swiped his thumb ever so gently over my lower lip. I shivered at his touch, feeling almost faint and letting myself lean into him. For safety, if nothing else. "Can I?"

"God, *yes*," I murmured, not caring how hopelessly eager I sounded. I was pleasantly tipsy, I was having a wonderful night, and I was finally on holiday – what better way to cap it off than to kiss a handsome Australian on a sticky pub dance floor?

Patrick's lips captured mine in an instant. We were pressed together, jostled by the increasingly busy dance floor who couldn't get enough of the band's rendition of *Khe Sanh*. But *damn*, it felt good. I didn't want to calculate how many days, months, or years it had been since I had been kissed, but it had been way too long, and I was sure – absolutely sure – that my last kiss hadn't been this good. Not even close. Patrick's mouth moved over mine with a certain confidence, like he wanted this to be just a taste of what was to come. I wrapped my arms around his neck, pressing into him, incredibly aware of the needy heat between my thighs.

If this man didn't ask me to come home with him, I was going to be seriously disappointed. Not to mention sexually frustrated.

The combined whooping of my sisters and Patrick's friend Khalid broke us apart. He pulled back, grinning sheepishly. "Our audience approves."

"They do." I wished my beloved sisters would disappear off the face of the earth. "Maybe we could get a drink, then go and find somewhere more private to chat?"

"Now that's an idea," Patrick said. "I'll go to the bar. You're drinking rosé, right?"

"Rosé would be amazing," I said, disentangling myself from him rather unwillingly.

"Don't you go too far," Patrick whispered, his lips brushing my ear. "I'll be right back to find you."

I watched him weave his way through the crowd to the bar and disappear with a stupid smile on my face before I realised my knees were legitimately weak. I needed to find one of those battered cane armchairs before I melted onto the sticky deck in a sticky mess.

A few minutes later, Tessa and Abby spotted me and made their way over.

"Go away!" I said as Abby made to sit down beside me. "Patrick's coming back with drinks! I don't need an audience; we're hiding from you!"

Tessa and Abby exchanged a look.

"What?" Somehow, I already knew.

"I'm really sorry, babe," Abby began, and then she looked at Tessa.

"We just saw him leave with his friend," Tessa finished, looking almost as crestfallen as I felt.

"Seriously?!"

"Unfortunately, yes." Tessa looked down.

"He ghosted me? I can't believe it!"

"I'm really sorry," Abby said again, but I shook my head and stood up, wiping the taste of Patrick from my mouth.

"We need more drinks," I declared.

My holiday in Brekkie Beach was *not* off to a promising start.

2 Patrick

"Patrick!"

I turned to see Khalid, an unusually serious expression on his face.

"Mate," I said, clapping a hand on his shoulder. "I think I'm in with Michelle. I'm just getting us drinks, and we're going to—"

"Patrick, we've got to leave," Khalid said, pulling me from the crowded queue in front of the bar.

"Leave?" I looked at him in disbelief. "Why would I leave? It's going great! Michelle's bloody gorgeous! And she's funny, too, which is a nice change."

"I'm sure she is," Khalid said, shaking his head. "But your mum has been blowing up my phone; you left yours in my car. And we need to go right now. Your sister is... I don't know, but it's not good."

In an instant, my pleasantly mellow beer buzz, enhanced by the delight of a dancefloor snog with a gorgeous Englishwoman, disappeared.

"Shit." I let out a breath. "What's happened?"

"I'm not sure," Khalid admitted. As we left the pub, the cool night air hit my face like a sobering smack. I needed it, too. "But I've got, like, ten messages saying you need to go down there, right now. Something about how Julia's not well, and you need to take Phoenix."

"I am so not okay to drive right now."

"Lucky your best friend is doing Dry January. I'll drive; just give me the address."

"It's a long way," I warned him. "They're down on the south coast, practically Wollongong."

"Gives you time to sober up." Khalid slapped me on the back as we reached the top of the hill where his car – a bright red Mazda with zebra-print seat covers – was parked. I got into the passenger seat heavily, wincing when I discovered my forgotten phone underneath my arse. When I squinted at it, I could see twenty missed calls and about a dozen texts.

"So, head towards the motorway?" Khalid asked as I began reading through my mother's cryptic messages.

"Yeah," I said distractedly. "Um, I'm going to call Julia."

"Good idea." Khalid nodded, pulling the car out towards the one road that led in and out of Brekkie Beach.

I cast a final look at the pub as we drove past and wondered if Michelle had waited for me to come back. Ghosting someone like that was a serious dick move. But there was nothing I could do about that now. And a woman like Michelle must have men cracking onto her at the pub every five minutes. She wouldn't be too fussed about me, surely.

I tapped my thumb over the icon next to my sister's name and waited, but I wasn't entirely surprised when it went straight to voicemail. I swore again.

"No reply?"

"Straight to voicemail. I really hope Julia hasn't done anything...drastic."

"Don't think like that," Khalid advised, and then he fiddled with the sound system until inappropriately cheerful techno music filled the car. He turned it down slightly at my glare. "You don't know if it's anything really bad."

"It must be pretty bad for Mum to say she wants me to take Phoenix," I said, biting my lip. I already had that sinking feeling in my stomach, that tightness in my chest, that I associated with my sister. That mixture of dread, fear, and utter frustration.

Phoenix was my nephew. He was fourteen years old and a good kid despite having to grow up with a mother like Julia. My sister tried her best, but 'stability' and 'structure' weren't words I'd choose to describe her parenting style. But I hadn't seen him in three years. What was he like now?

"I'll try calling my mum," I said, looking down at my phone again. When I dialled my mother's number, the phone, at least, began to ring.

"Patrick?" My mother's voice was sharp enough to cut glass, or at least a front lawn. "Where have you been? Why didn't you answer your phone?"

"I was out with Khalid," I said, hating how I sounded whiny and defensive like a teenager. "I left my phone in the car by accident. What's happening?"

"Julia's..." There was a pause. "She's not well," my mother, always the queen of the understatement, finished. "You need to get down here right now."

"I'm already on my way," I said, annoyed. "I'll be there in..." I looked at the dashboard where the map was winding its way through the darkness. "An hour and thirty-seven minutes."

"I don't know why you insisted on moving so far away from your poor sister," she said, huffing dramatically. "I suppose you think you're too good to live here."

"That's not true," I said evenly. "What's happened to Julia? Is she drinking again?"

"Patrick, you make it sound like she's an alcoholic!"

"I didn't mean that," I said quickly. "Just, when she drinks, I know it doesn't always go well for her."

"She's not well," my mother repeated. "Things are very hard for her sometimes. She's a single mother, Patrick! She needs rest and relaxation. You need to take Phoenix for a few weeks to give her a break."

"She wants me to take Phoenix? Last I heard, she didn't even want me to see him."

"That boy causes her a lot of stress," my mother said darkly, as though my quiet, polite nephew was somehow the cause of my sister's latest meltdown. "She needs time to be a woman, you know."

I let out a groan. "Has Julia been seeing some guy? And now they've broken up, and she's a mess?"

"Don't you call your sister a mess!" my mother said sharply. "Her personal life is none of your business."

I, privately, thought it *was* my business when it meant I had to take custody of my nephew in the middle of the night, but I decided not to say so.

"Is she safe right now?" I asked instead. "And Phoenix, is he safe?"

"Of course he's safe." Mum made it sound like an unreasonable question when I knew that Julia had left my nephew in plenty of unsafe situations. "He's meant to be watching TV, but he's just staring at his phone. Typical teenager. Julia's upstairs; I gave her something to help her sleep."

I was fairly sure that whatever she had given Julia to help her sleep would not have been endorsed by a doctor but chose not to say that either.

"I'm on my way," I said wearily. "An hour and thirty-one minutes."

"Just get here soon."

"Your sister having boyfriend trouble?" Khalid asked as the call ended, scrunching up his nose.

"Something like that." I sighed. "I don't know why she keeps getting involved with these guys. It always ends like this. She'll be on top of the world for a few weeks, and then it all comes crashing down when he decides that he loves his wife after all and has zero intention of starting a new life with her."

"It's a shitty situation," Khalid said, shifting in the seat. "But you're a good brother. Good uncle, going to get Phoenix like this."

"I don't know about that. It's not like I want to do it. I don't want to be involved in any of my family bullshit. But I don't have a choice."

"You could tell your mother she can look after him," Khalid suggested. "I mean, he's her grandson."

"She doesn't even like the poor kid! I don't have a clue what to do with a teenager, but I can't leave him with her."

"You see, that's because you're a good guy. You're doing the right thing."

"I hope so," I said, allowing myself another sigh. "I mean, it sucks for him, bundled off to some uncle in the middle of the night."

"Better than the alternatives. You're a responsible adult. Well, kind of, anyway."

"Do you reckon we can stop at a petrol station?" I asked, looking out of the window as though one might appear.

"Yeah, sure," Khalid said. "Why?"

"Because the responsible adult really needs to take a piss."

· ♥ · ♥ · ♥ · ♥ · ♥ ·

"Finally!" My mother opened the door, wearing a white fuzzy dressing gown, a hair net, and an impressively fierce frown for someone with that much Botox in her forehead. "I've been waiting for you to get here."

"Hello, Mrs D," Khalid said from behind me. He gave her a winning smile, and I saw my mother soften slightly. "My fault; the Mazda isn't as nippy on the motorway as Patrick's SUV."

"You were kind to drive him here, Khalid," she said, letting us into the house. "Have you been drinking, Patrick? Are you in a fit state to be taking your nephew?"

"I was at the pub, Mum," I said wearily. "I'm sure I'd be under the limit to drive by now; we just wanted to be safe. Where's Julia?"

"Sleeping." My mother frowned again. "Like I told you. Phoenix is in there."

I felt my body stiffen in the stifling walls of my mother's almost clinically clean and hideously decorated house. Adorning each and every wall were photographs. Photographs of Julia and of myself (though there were far more of Julia) back when we were young, photogenic, and on the way to Hollywood stardom. Or at least, that's what she thought back then. Framed headshots covered one wall of the dining room, while the hallway was devoted to enormous publicity posters of *Outback Adventures*.

"This one's my favourite," Khalid nudged me, pointing at a poster where a younger version of myself was lassoing a crocodile, an expression of exaggerated fear on my face.

"Don't." I shook my head, cringing.

"Phoenix?" My mother called out as we went into the living room. I could see Phoenix sitting on the sofa, half-asleep, as some old action movie played on the TV. He looked the same as I remembered; dark hair, dark eyes, and skin brown enough to make my mother mutter about his father's likely ethnicity. My nephew started at the sound of his name, then looked up at me. "Uncle Patrick is here."

"Hi," I said, feeling all kinds of awkward. The poor kid had probably just witnessed his mother having a full-blown breakdown, and now I was here to take him away, and all I could manage was 'hi'. "Uh, this is my friend Khalid; he drove me down. You remember him, right?"

"Hello," Phoenix said quietly. His hair was long, with dark bangs falling into his eyes. I strongly suspected he liked it that way. He was dressed in jeans and a t-shirt that bore the Ralph Lauren logo. My sister was clearly still under the impression that dressing her son in designer labels would make people think she had her life together.

"Hey, Phoenix," Khalid said, giving him a grin. "Up for a road trip? You can sit in the front; we can stick Patrick in the back seat."

"No, it's okay," Phoenix said, stuffing his phone into his pocket and picking up a navy sports bag I remembered my mother giving him for Christmas a few years before. It was a terrible present for a kid, but knowing my mother, he was lucky not to have received a DVD box set of *Outback Adventures*. "Is Mum going to be okay?"

"Your mum needs to rest, have some peace and quiet. Time to herself," my mother said, folding her arms over her chest. "I'll look after her."

"Okay," Phoenix said again, and he dawdled by the door. "Well, um, bye?" He looked at his grandmother as though wondering if he had to endure a hug.

But the hug was not forthcoming. "Don't give your uncle any trouble, will you? And don't do anything that would upset your mother."

"I won't," Phoenix said, his voice so low it was almost inaudible.

"Come on, mate," I said. "Let's get to the car, it's late, and you must be exhausted."

Phoenix just nodded, following Khalid towards the door.

"How long is this going to be for?" I asked my mother in a low whisper. "I mean, until Julia's..."

"I didn't realise it was such a burden, looking after your own nephew."

"I didn't say it was!" I protested. "Just, I know he'll ask me."

"I can't be expected to know these things!" My mother threw up her hands. "She'll be ready when she's ready. Don't you dare pressure her – that could set her back!"

"I won't," I promised. I knew all about not upsetting Julia. "Bye, Mum."

But she didn't look at me as I left the room to catch up with Khalid and the silent Phoenix.

· ♥ · ♥ · ♥ · ♥ · ♥ ·

"Well, this is it," Khalid said, pulling up outside my house. Phoenix, who had been half-asleep in the back seat despite the pounding techno music, stirred and straightened. "Hey, look, there's a light on next door." Khalid pointed out of the window.

There was indeed a light on in one of the windows of the weatherboard cottage next door, which had been empty and increasingly derelict in the four years I had lived in Brekkie Beach.

"I can't believe someone's actually living in that dump."

"The housing market's pretty tight," I shrugged. "And it's a great location."

"It's still a dump," Khalid proclaimed. "Need any help getting your bag in, Phoenix?"

"No, it's okay," Phoenix said. It was the only thing he had said on the trip. Whether he was offered chips and a burger from the McDonald's drive-thru or when Khalid graciously offered to let him change the music, it was always the same response.

I pushed open my door, fumbling for my keys, aware of my nephew beside me in the dark.

"Thanks again for driving us, dude," I said to Khalid, who gave me a wave as he pulled out from the curb.

"So, here we are," I said to Phoenix in a falsely bright tone. "My place."

A light came on automatically as we approached the front door, and I could see how tired the poor kid looked, with dark circles under his eyes. I suspected this hadn't been the only sleepless night he had endured lately.

Unlocking the door, I flicked on the lights, clearing my throat a few times because I had no idea what to say.

"It's been a while, but you remember where everything is, right?" I said finally, climbing up the stairs and pushing open the door of my guest room. "Bathroom's just down the hall, and you're welcome to anything in the fridge. Except for the beer." I tried for a matey laugh, but Phoenix just looked at me.

"I don't drink beer."

"No, of course not," I said. "It was a stupid joke. Um, is there anything else you need? I'll get you a towel if you want a shower first thing."

I busied myself in the linen cupboard, pressing a fresh blue towel into my nephew's hands. "There you go," I said. "Um, did you want to talk about...things? Or are you tired? Either way, we can—"

"I think I just want to go to bed." Phoenix sat down on the guest bed, clutching the towel, and toed out of his sneakers. "I'm pretty tired."

"Yeah, you must be," I said, nodding slightly too hard. "Long day, huh?"

"Yeah," Phoenix agreed, tracing his fingers over the towel as though the pile was deeply fascinating.

"If you need anything, even during the night, you can come and get me, okay?" I said. "I don't mind at all." I was hoping he wouldn't, though. I had gotten used to an uninterrupted eight hours of sleep in my years of living alone. Ten, if I was hungover.

"I'll be fine," Phoenix said, and he raised his chin for a moment, looking at me.

"Well, I guess I'll leave you to it," I said, unsure whether or not to shut the door for him.

"Uncle Patrick?"

I looked up. "Yeah?"

"Thanks for coming to get me." Phoenix was looking back down at the towel again, but his voice sounded hoarse like he was trying not to cry.

I felt something like a sob rising inside me, but I quickly swallowed it down. This was about my nephew, not about me. I wanted to hug him, ruffle his hair like I had when he was little, and tell him everything would be just fine.

"I always will, mate," I said instead. "I'm happy to have you here. You're always welcome."

Phoenix gave me a tiny smile, and then I turned and went down the hall to my bedroom. Shutting the door behind me, I let out a long breath.

"Bloody hell." Poor kid. I wished that I had another sibling. A brother, maybe. Someone older, more responsible, with kids of his own, who would know what to do. Clad in knee-length shorts and Crocs, my imaginary brother would be way better at taking care of Phoenix than I would. "But I'm the only uncle he's got," I said aloud, shaking my head.

I brushed my teeth, pulled on fresh boxers and a t-shirt so I wouldn't be inappropriate if Phoenix did happen to need me in the night, and sank down beneath the covers. All the while, I kept thinking about how I wished that Phoenix had someone better to rely on than his Uncle Patrick.

After the excitement of the late-night rescue mission, I slept *hard*. When I finally blinked awake, I was briefly alarmed by the sound of a kitchen cupboard opening before I remembered that my nephew was in the house and that I wasn't being robbed by hungry burglars.

A glance at my wrist told me it was after ten, and I groaned, pushing myself out of bed and rubbing at my eyes with my fists. I was *not* a morning person. Usually, it took me three cups of coffee and at least an hour of coming to terms with consciousness before I could be even vaguely civil to anyone. But now, I had to be a responsible and mature adult straight away because Phoenix needed me to be. That kid needed *someone* to be a responsible adult in his life. But all he had was me.

"Morning," I said in a passing imitation of cheerfulness as I entered the kitchen, where I found Phoenix, fully dressed, sitting at the kitchen table with a glass of water. "How'd you sleep?"

"Okay," Phoenix said, looking down into his water.

"Do you want something else?" I asked. "Uh, I think I've got tea. And maybe some Milo, but it might have gone a bit hard."

"I don't mind," Phoenix said, and I suppressed a sigh. It had been a long time since I had spent any time with him, which made me feel guilty as hell, even though it had been entirely my sister's choice. It had been three years since I had last seen him, and for a kid, that was a lifetime. I was practically a stranger to him now; the affable familiarity that had previously existed between us was long gone.

"We should go out for breakfast," I said when opening my freezer revealed frozen chicken breasts, frozen steak, frozen vegetables, and absolutely zero bread for toast. I had avoided carbs ever since some paparazzi shots of me, aged nineteen and having enjoyed more sausage rolls than was wise, had done the rounds online with some very unflattering commentary. "We could go for a walk down by the beach, too. How does that sound?"

"Okay," Phoenix said, taking a small sip from his glass of water.

"The coffee shop here does really weird food," I told him, trying to make him laugh. "Last week, they had muffins made out of quinoa and green tea. They looked mouldy, even fresh out of the oven. But there's a bakery that's pretty decent if you don't mind eating down by the beach."

"I don't mind," Phoenix said again.

"Okay then," I said, still forcing cheerfulness into my voice that I didn't feel. "Well, I guess... I'll get dressed, and then we'll head off."

Fifteen minutes, one pod-machine-made double espresso, and a brief pep talk to myself in the bathroom mirror later, we were ready to leave. I checked my phone quickly, but there were no new messages from Julia or my mother. I noticed that Phoenix hadn't asked about his mum, which made me wince again. Maybe he knew better than to ask.

"Right," I said. "It's not a long walk, and it's a nice day, so this should be great!"

Phoenix gave me a look that asked why I was addressing him like he was an old and lazy dog who had to be cajoled into his daily walk, but he only nodded.

Fresh, salty air hit my face as soon as I opened the front door, giving me a much-needed boost in spirits. This, I thought, was why I loved living in Brekkie Beach. The smell of salt and sand always made me feel like things would turn out for the best, like life really would be okay. I just hoped that it might have the same effect on Phoenix.

As Phoenix and I made our way towards the footpath, the front door of the cottage-dump next door suddenly creaked open, and the last person I could possibly have expected came out, yawning into the late morning sun and stretching out her arms.

I stopped, my mouth hanging open stupidly, as Michelle looked over, and her eyes met mine.

"Patrick?!"

Shit.

3 Michelle

A sock. That was the only possible comparison I had for how my mouth felt when I opened my eyes in the too-bright bedroom (the curtains could have been made of tissue paper, for all they did against the morning sun). A well-used, sweated-in, and now dried-out sock.

"Eurgh," I sputtered, sitting up and reaching for the water bottle that someone – probably Tessa – had left by the bed. I took long gulps, swallowing it like the antidote to a life-threatening poison. Which, technically speaking, alcohol was.

As I shoved my glasses haphazardly onto my face, the night before came crashing back to me. Landing in Sydney to the delight of my sisters. The pub, with its glorious beach views. Meeting Patrick, dancing with him, kissing him, and then him abruptly ghosting me. Bastard! Then there was...alcohol. A lot of alcohol. And I was pretty sure my sisters and I had convinced the DJ to play the Macarena. My arms definitely felt like I had Macarena'd.

So much for going home with a handsome Aussie for a holiday fling. Instead, I was alone, extremely hungover, and my lower back wanted to speak to a manager about the poor quality of the mattress.

I fumbled for my phone, wondering if my sisters felt better than I did.

Abby: i just woke up, i feel ROUGH. are you two as hungover as me?

Tessa: yes. but dylan brought me coffee and painkillers in bed <heart emoji>

Abby: show off

Tessa: you were the one who wanted me to be happy!

Abby: i do. just not right now. i want everyone to feel as horrible as me

Michelle: well, i definitely feel horrible. is australian alcohol stronger? it definitely feels stronger

Tessa: it probably hit you harder after your long flight. altitude or something <sad face emoji>

Abby: or it was the tequila shots

Michelle: we did tequila shots?

Abby: we did

Tessa: tequila is never a good idea

Abby: but it always seems like a good idea. especially after the first one

Michelle: well, i did have to drown out the embarrassment of getting ghosted <clenched teeth emoji>

Tessa: that patrick was a dickhead!

Abby: total prick. on behalf of brekkie beach, i apologise

Michelle: much appreciated

Abby: so, who wants to get coffee and croissants and then go for a swim to wash the dust off?

Michelle: that sounds amazing. if i can manage to get out of this shitty bed

Tessa: bad mattress?

Michelle: pretty sure it's got actual rocks in it. and the curtains let in all the light

Abby: you should definitely make a complaint to air bnb

Michelle: which they will ignore

Tessa: you're probably right. meet down at the coffee shop at ten thirty?

Michelle: i think i can drag myself down there

Abby: i might have to crawl

Just before ten thirty, I managed to get out the front door. My bikini had somehow become horribly tangled, and it had taken three uses of the 'F' word, one broken nail, and contortions worthy of a circus performer to get it onto my body. Then I had slipped on a kaftan and sandals and decided that pilfering one of the threadbare towels to take to the beach was acceptable.

As I opened the door and bright sunlight hit me, I realised that I should have made more effort to find my sunglasses. My eyes still felt gritty, and it had been a stinging, pain-ridden struggle to get my contact lenses in. Blinking against the assault, I made my way down the steps. My scraped knees told me I may have crawled up them the night before.

When my eyes adjusted to the bright Australian sun, I saw two figures emerging from the much nicer house next door, a man and a boy. There was something oddly familiar about the man's sun-streaked blonde hair and the line of his shoulders. And then he turned.

"Patrick?!" The word was out of my mouth before I could stop it.

Patrick stopped dead, staring at me with an expression I could only describe as somewhere between surprise and abject horror.

"Michelle!" His voice sounded oddly strangled, and the boy beside him looked up from his phone in curiosity. "What are you doing here?"

Well, that was a fair question. It probably wasn't every day that the woman he had snogged and ghosted at the pub turned up next door. Just when I had thought the crappy cottage didn't have any more horrible surprises for me.

"I'm staying here," I said, inclining my head at the cottage. "I booked it on Air BnB."

"They rent that place out on Air BnB? Seriously?" Patrick looked almost as shocked to hear that as he had been to see me.

"Apparently, they do," I said, hovering by the creaking metal gate and wondering how long we'd have to interact. And who was the dark-haired boy with him? He looked around thirteen or fourteen, so if he was Patrick's son, Patrick would have to have been a very young dad. Either that, or Patrick had access to an anti-aging serum that I'd commit medium to severe acts of violence to get my hands on.

"Uh, right," Patrick said, looking away from me and down at the boy as though he had only just remembered he was there. "Uh, this is Phoenix. My nephew."

And that made me want to laugh. Patrick had been rude enough to ghost me at the pub, but now he remembered his manners? I wanted to scoff at him and walk off without another word, but that wouldn't exactly be fair to the kid. I remembered all too well how sensitive teenagers could be.

"Hi, Phoenix," I said with a brightness I didn't quite feel. "I'm Michelle."

Phoenix looked up at me with big black eyes. "Hi Michelle," he said quietly and looked back down at the ground.

"Anyway, I'm just on my way to the coffee shop, so I'd better get going," I said, banging the creaking gate behind me and raising my hand in an awkward half-wave.

"Oh. So are we," Patrick said, his tone making it sound like he was confessing to something embarrassing.

"Right," I said, trying to think of a way to avoid walking with him that wouldn't seem rude to his shy, polite nephew. "I see."

We fell into an uneasy step together, and I wracked my brains for something cutting to say to him that wouldn't arouse suspicion from Phoenix. Nope, my brain was still too tequila-soaked to come up with anything. The best I could do was ignore Patrick in favour of conversation with Phoenix.

"Do you like living near the beach, Phoenix?" I asked. "I'm from England. Our beaches are nothing like this."

Phoenix looked up and gave me a very small smile. "I don't live here," he told me. "I'm just staying with Uncle Patrick for a bit."

"Oh," I said, hating myself for being insanely curious about why that was. "I guess you're on holiday too, then."

"I guess." Phoenix looked down at his feet, and I noticed he was wearing expensive sneakers that seemed too small for him; his toe was almost emerging from the tip of the left shoe.

"I haven't been swimming in ages," I went on. "Do you swim a lot?"

Phoenix shrugged. "Sometimes," he said. There was a pause. "I like watching the surfers."

I latched onto that with the enthusiasm of a struggling rock climber to a firm handhold. "Yeah? Surfing would be pretty cool. I've never done it, but my sister Abby likes to paddleboard. Have you ever tried that?"

"I was supposed to go paddleboarding with my mum last year, but..." Phoenix looked down at his too-small shoes again as we headed down the hill and towards Brekkie Beach's main street. "We didn't."

"If you want to go paddleboarding, I'll take you," Patrick suddenly cut in. "We could rent some boards. Or if you want to try surfing, I think they do lessons down at Dee Why. It's not far to drive. What do you think?"

Phoenix looked up at his uncle. "It's okay," he said after a moment.

"Well, if you want to try it..." Patrick began, and he looked a little helpless. Seeing such a tall man, with obnoxiously broad shoulders and irritatingly muscular arms, look helpless made me want to laugh. Whatever Patrick did for a living, I was sure it didn't involve talking to teenagers.

"There's the coffee shop!" I said with far more excitement than sighting Nick and Nikki's warranted, even in my hungover and caffeine-deprived state. "And there's my sisters!" I could see Tessa and Abby standing outside the café, both wearing enormous sunglasses and bemused expressions.

"Uh, right," Patrick said. "We might go straight to the bakery." He let out a half-laugh that was very clearly forced. "I'm desperate for a croissant. Bet you are, too, huh?" He nudged Phoenix, who just looked up at him with a blank face.

"I don't mind," Phoenix said softly. Something about his expression, or maybe the way he was trying so hard to be undemanding, made my heart ache. Poor kid, I thought. I knew what it was like to keep quiet about what you wanted and what you needed because you had learned not to be a burden.

"It was really nice to meet you, Phoenix," I said. "Hope you get to go paddleboarding soon, huh?"

"It was nice to meet you too," he said, clearly having been taught it was polite to say so.

I didn't even look at Patrick as I went to join my sisters, but somehow, I knew – just knew – that he was looking at me. Well, I'd let him look. He had his chance, and he chose to piss off like a total coward. Tessa was right. He was a dickhead. Even if he did have spectacular arms and an annoyingly appealing hopeless expression when he tried to talk to his nephew.

"Um, was that Patrick?" Tessa asked me in a low whisper when I joined my sisters. "How did he find you?"

"Did he apologise?" Abby demanded, her voice far louder. She sent a scowl at Patrick's retreating back. "And he has a kid?!"

"His nephew," I clarified, massaging my temples. "And no, he didn't apologise. It turns out that he's my neighbour."

Abby groaned as we made our way into the coffee shop. The smell of freshly ground beans made me perk up just a little, as though my body was pre-empting how much better it would feel with at least one coffee inside me. "I knew that bloody cottage was cursed!"

"You said it was a dump, not cursed," Tessa pointed out. She bent down to examine a glass case full of not-very-tempting treats. Honestly, what could be in a sugar-free paleo brownie?

"Hello, ladies!" The barista waved at us enthusiastically, his greying hair pushed back from his forehead with a broad black band. "What can I get you? Just coffee, or are you in the mood for a treat? Nikki's made some amazing matcha and spirulina protein balls!"

The balls in question were displayed on a glass serving platter and looked like the mess sometimes left in the lobby by my neighbour's Labradoodle back in Glasgow.

"Just coffee for me," I said hurriedly. "A large latte, extra strong."

"You should have a flat white!" Abby nudged me. "Because you're in Australia now."

"We do a mean flat white." The barista, who must be Nick, grinned. "Greatest Aussie invention since the ride-on Esky."

I was slightly annoyed with Abby's pushiness, but I wasn't in the mood to argue. "A large flat white, then."

"Make it two." Abby was clearly satisfied.

"Three, actually," Tessa added. "We'll sit just here." She motioned to where three milk crates adorned with cushions were clustered around an industrial spool that served as a table.

"I'll bring those right out."

I sat down with a groan, trying to get comfortable on my milk crate. "Why do trendy places refuse to use actual chairs?" I asked in a low whisper. "I like chairs. Chairs are kind to bottoms. These aren't!"

"Amen to that." Tessa sighed. "I guess we're all a slave to our aesthetic, huh?"

"Enough about the chairs." Abby waved a hand. "Let's rewind here. Patrick is your neighbour? As in, you'll be seeing him every day?"

"Only if I'm very unlucky," I said, reaching into my pocket for my phone and wondering if Abby would tell me off if I checked my work emails.

"What are the chances?" Tessa wrinkled up her nose. "Was it super awkward?"

"Oh yeah," I said, nodding. "I wanted to blank him, but I couldn't be rude in front of his nephew. I had to walk down here with them."

"What did you do?" Tessa was wide-eyed. "I would have run away."

"I just talked to Phoenix," I said. "And ignored Patrick. Phoenix seems like a nice kid, though. Very polite and kind of reserved. Like he doesn't want to ask for much."

"I thought teenagers were supposed to be sullen and demanding," Tessa said.

"Not this one."

"So, why is his nephew with him?" Abby asked. "Did he mention anything about that last night?"

"We didn't talk much last night," I said, a treacherous rush of heat surging through me at the memory of Patrick's strong hands on my body, pressing me against him, and then his lips on mine, confident like he was claiming me as his own. That was an utterly ridiculous thought. I sent a furious memo to my body to stop getting hot and bothered at the memory. Patrick was a *jerk*. I was not attracted to him. My body totally ignored me, possibly in retaliation for the amount of tequila I had forced into it the night before.

"It just doesn't make sense." Tessa frowned. "Why he'd run off like that. I mean, you're so gorgeous! Any man should be lining up for a chance to spend time with you."

"Maybe he had a better offer."

Abby snorted. "I doubt it," she said. "No one's better than you, Michelle." She put a hand on my arm and squeezed. And that was why I would always forgive Abby for being an overbearing big sister. She was so freaking supportive; it was impossible to stay mad at your own personal cheerleader.

"Three large flat whites!" Nick appeared, setting the steaming mugs in front of us. If a noise of acute need escaped me, it was nothing my sisters hadn't heard before when it came to me and coffee. "Enjoy!"

"We will!" Abby told him. "Thanks."

"No worries!" Nick flashed us a bright smile once more.

"No worries," Tessa repeated. "Australians say that a lot, but not even the combined power of Zoloft and my psychologist can get me there."

"But it's better now, isn't it?" I frowned because I knew how hard Tessa had worked to manage her anxiety.

"Much better," Tessa confirmed, nodding. "But still, 'no worries' sounds pretty awesome."

MICHELLE FINCH STICKS TO THE PLAN 57

"Pretty impossible," I said, taking a sip of my very hot coffee. And okay, Abby was right. Flat whites *were* superior to lattes. I was a convert. Not that I'd tell her that.

"It's a shame Patrick turned out to be a jerk," Abby said thoughtfully, her fingers wrapped around her own mug. "He would have been super convenient for holiday booty calls right next door."

"Maybe something could still happen," Tessa suggested.

"Not a chance in hell!" I said indignantly. "What, you think I'd sleep with him after he ghosted me like that!? Anyway, he clearly doesn't want to. Hence the ghosting!"

"Maybe he had a good reason."

Abby scoffed. "You always see the best in people," she told Tessa. "I still think he's a jerk. But a hot jerk. And totally your type, Michelle."

"My type," I informed her, "is not men who ghost me. My type is men who actually want me. A lot. And show it."

"Cheers to that!" Abby raised her coffee mug. "I'm glad you're here, Michelle. Even if you are in that dump with a dickhead next door."

I smiled. "Me too."

・♥・♥・♥・♥・♥・

"Are you wearing sunscreen?"

"No," I admitted. "My brain was too full of tequila to attempt that this morning."

"Well, you're going to put some on now." Tessa pulled a giant bottle from her bag. "I'm not going to let you turn into a giant lobster like I did. Even if you and Abby don't have my pasty skin." Abby and I had inherited our father's olive complexion, while Tessa was the authentic English rose of the family.

"You have beautiful skin. Like a porcelain doll."

"It's the worst in Australia," Tessa complained. "You two are lucky."

"Hey, I still need sunscreen!" Abby said. "Just because I don't burn doesn't mean I can't wrinkle!"

"Or get skin cancer," I pointed out.

"I guess that's important too. Give me a squirt, Tess."

Tessa dutifully squeezed a very generous amount into Abby's hand and then into mine, and I began rubbing the thick white liquid into my shoulders.

"Only squirt I'll be getting for a while, huh?" I joked, looking down at the mess of white on my chest.

Tessa let out a giggle while Abby laughed loudly enough to attract looks from the family sitting nearby. "Not with that attitude," she said. "I think we should go out to the city tonight. We can find you a proper holiday fling and get you well and truly shagged. That should get your mind off your bloody job."

I grimaced. I thought I had been subtle, checking my emails while Abby had gone to the bathroom, but apparently not. "It would take more than a one-night stand to do that," I said, rubbing the rest of the lotion in.

"What would it take?" Tessa asked, slicking a coat of bright yellow zinc on her nose.

"A lobotomy."

My sisters laughed again, and I stood up, trying to rub sunscreen into my upper thighs and the parts of my bottom that my bikini didn't adequately cover.

"Don't look now," Tessa said in a low voice. "But you've got an audience."

I looked. Of course, I looked. With temptation like that, who wouldn't? I turned, expecting to see a few middle-aged men staring, but instead, I saw...

I whirled back around. "Shit!"

Sitting on a bench on the grassy area behind the beach was Patrick and Phoenix. They were munching on croissants and looking out at the waves. Or at least Phoenix was looking at the waves. Patrick was definitely looking at me. I was more than a little tempted to turn once more to give him the finger, but that would have been inappropriate with his nephew beside him.

"Who does he think he is, checking you out after he ghosted you like that?" Abby was indignant.

"Well, he's only human," Tessa said. "And Michelle's a hottie."

"True," Abby said, but she was frowning. "Still, it's bloody cheeky of him. Want me to go up there and tell him off?" Abby half-rose from her towel, and I knew she would have loved to do it.

"No," I told her. "I mean, in any other circumstances, yes. But he's got his nephew with him."

"I could tell him off in child-appropriate language," Abby protested, but she sat back down.

"I've got a better idea," I said with a wicked smile. "You know, I'm feeling a bit sore after a night on that mattress. I might just stretch out a bit." With that, I sank into an interpretation of downward facing dog, my bikini-clad bottom very much on display to any handsome but sadly dickhead-ed Australians who happened to be looking.

Abby chuckled. "Nice one."

"He's definitely still looking," Tessa reported. "Can't take his eyes off you."

And if that sent a rush of heat between my thighs, there was no reason my sisters – or anyone else – had to know.

"Good," I said, and then spread my legs wide, resting my forearms on the hot, slippery sand. "Is he still looking?"

"Yep," Abby said. "Seeing exactly what he missed out on."

"Bastard," I said again. "He could have had all this." I jiggled my bottom a little, just for good measure.

"Pretty sure he's regretting it now," Abby said. "Men are so stupid."

"Except Dylan," Tessa cut in. "Well, I guess he was a bit stupid when we were getting together."

"Very stupid," I agreed, and then, a little reluctantly, I stood up. "But enough about men. Who wants a swim?"

· ♥ · ♥ · ♥ · ♥ · ♥ ·

"Sorry about the noise," Tessa apologised. "The kitchen's almost finished. Actually, they said it was almost finished two weeks ago. It was meant to be done before you got here."

"Don't apologise!" I waved a hand. "I'm just happy to be here. This house is amazing." And it was. It was an older property, but it had, as real estate agents loved to put it, 'great bones'. Sunlight filtered in through huge windows, and the deck was big enough for a large table and chairs, a barbecue, and what looked like a hot tub. I really hoped it was a hot tub.

"Thanks," Dylan said, grinning at me. "A worthy home for your sister, then?"

"Absolutely," I said, returning his smile. I had been eager to meet the man who, after a whole lot of trouble, was making my sister so happy. So far, I was impressed. "And I can see how good that kitchen will look when it's done. Not that I'm complaining about the food now."

"Tessa's been teaching me to cook." Dylan beamed. "Not that steak and salad takes a whole lot of cooking."

"Hey, getting steak right is an accomplishment!" Abby brandished a piece of perfectly seared steak on her fork. "And your dressing-to-salad ratio is spot on."

"Abby, was that a compliment?" Dylan pretended to be shocked.

"I can be nice!" Abby insisted. "I just have to keep you on your toes. Make sure you don't break my sister's heart. Again."

"Abby," Tessa warned.

"I'd want to murder anyone who hurt Tessa too. Abby and I have that in common." The look that Dylan gave Tessa was enough to make me wish that I could fast forward myself into the future when I made Partner, and I could find a man who'd look at me like that. If I was ever so lucky.

"I'm so glad you stopped being stupid," Abby said to Dylan. "And got over your whole 'I can't do this right now' thing."

Dylan coughed slightly. "Yes, well," he said, looking at Tessa again. "Circumstances weren't really in our favour, but when it's right, it doesn't matter."

"Wrong place, wrong time, right guy." Tessa squeezed his hand.

"You two are goals," I said warmly. "One day, I hope I can—"

MICHELLE FINCH STICKS TO THE PLAN 63

But I was saved from having to say what I hoped might happen by my phone's insistent buzz. Frowning, I looked down. Crap. This was definitely a call I had to answer.

"I'll just be a minute," I said, pushing up from the table.

"You're on holiday!" Abby began, but I ignored her and went inside, pulling the door closed behind me.

"What's up, Ash?" Ash, a financial analyst like myself, was somewhere between colleague and enemy. We could have been friends if we hadn't been competing against each other for every juicy project and minor increase in responsibility.

"I thought you'd want to know the forecasting meeting for Wind Corp has been moved up to today," Ash told me. "I've got your presentation here, but I just wanted to be sure about some of the figures—"

"It's not supposed to be until next week when I'm back!" I interrupted. "Why did it get moved up?"

"One of the Partners came up from London; he wanted to jump on it while he was local." Ash sounded very pleased about this. "Anyway, your estimates seem a bit high, based on that potential change to the legislation on carbon credits—"

"Why do you have my presentation?" I felt anger bubble up inside me, ready to spill out. "That's my work!"

"And you're not here to present it," Ash said smoothly, and I could tell he was enjoying this. "Martin sent it to me; he asked me to present it."

Martin was my direct supervisor and a genuinely gifted financial analyst. He was not, however, a skilled people manager. Under his watch, this happened all the time. Analysts stealing work from one another, taking credit for each other's ideas, backstabbing just to get ahead. Martin was one of the many reasons I was hoping – I'd even considered praying, to any god who'd help me – to get a transfer out of the Glasgow office.

"I'm sure he did," I said through gritted teeth, knowing that Ash would have badgered Martin into sending the presentation and probably told him I had said it was okay. "And there's nothing wrong with my figures. That legislation will have a big impact." I hated it when anyone questioned my work; I knew I was overly sensitive about it. But Ash questioning my figures made me feel like he was calling me stupid, and that brought up feelings and memories I didn't want to deal with right now.

"Well, if there are any problems, I'll be sure to let them know to discuss it further with you," Ash finished. "When you're back in the office. After your holiday."

I suppressed a groan. That sounded right. Ash was ready to take credit for my work if it was well received and throw me under the bus if not.

"Thanks for calling," I said, my voice heavy with sarcasm. "Do call again if anything urgent comes up."

"Oh, only if it's very urgent," Ash said. "I'd hate to disturb you."

"Bye." I finished the call and let out a sound of frustration that earned a startled look from the two carpenters who were busily slotting what I assumed must be the new kitchen cabinets into place. I let myself take a few deep breaths, closed my eyes, briefly contemplated flying back to Glasgow to disembowel Ash in person, and returned to the sunlit deck where my sisters and Dylan were finishing their steak and salad.

"What was all that about?" Tessa asked. "Trouble at work?"

"Not really." I sighed again as I sat down. "Just a colleague calling to tell me a meeting got moved up, and he's going to present my report without me. He was just calling to gloat, really."

"This is why you shouldn't be answering work calls!" Abby told me. "It's just upset you for no reason."

"I'm not upset. And I'd rather know now than be blindsided when I get back. Besides, it's not like you ignore your phone."

"That's different," Abby objected. "I'm a sole proprietor. I don't have colleagues to cover for me!"

"I know how it can be," Dylan interrupted, looking sympathetic. "When I was building my start-up, I was working every hour I was awake. I never had time for anything else. Not much of a life."

"It's not that bad," I said, but I was grateful for his understanding.

"It's definitely that bad," Abby said. She had her glass raised in one hand and was gesturing with the other. Always a bad sign. It usually meant she was about to tell you something you didn't want to hear. "You know, it's probably a good thing you're not looking to meet anyone right now. If you walk out on dates for work calls, I don't reckon most dudes would stick around."

There was silence. I watched as Tessa and Dylan exchanged an uncomfortable look.

"Thanks for that, Abby," I said drily. "Good to know you've decided I'm not worth sticking around for. I needed another reminder, after last night."

"I didn't mean it like that!" Abby said quickly, setting down her glass. "I just meant—"

"You know, I'm actually really tired." I stood up from the table once more. "And if we're going out tonight, I need a nap. I'm supposed to be on holiday, after all."

"Don't be like that, Michelle," Abby started to say. "I'm sorry, really."

"I'm not going to argue with you," I said wearily. "I just want a nap. Dylan, Tessa, thank you for a lovely lunch and your hospitality."

"Do you want me to walk you back?" Tessa's brows were furrowed. "Make sure you're okay?"

"I'm fine." I shook my head. "I just need a nap. And some space. See you tonight."

· ♥ · ♥ · ♥ · ♥ · ♥ ·

When I got back to my absolute dump of a holiday residence, I saw, to my relief, that the shiny blue SUV was missing from Patrick's driveway.

Why, I wondered, had he decided I was no longer worthy of his attention after dancing with me and kissing me like that at the pub? I knew it was stupid to keep thinking about it, but I just couldn't work it out. It wasn't like a man had never rejected me before, but Patrick had seemed so keen. After all, he had been the one to approach me, to ask if he could kiss me, and then...

"Am I totally shit at kissing?" I forced the rusty key into the door, eventually opening it with a shove of my shoulder. "Do I have bad breath? An overly enthusiastic tongue?"

No one had ever complained before. In my university days, men had still tried to kiss me after seeing me throw up in a pub toilet on more than one occasion. I could hardly be repulsive, could I?

"Why does he have to live next door to this dump anyway?" I asked out loud, peeling off my kaftan and seeing that I was not burnt, thanks to Tessa being so forceful with the sunscreen. I tried to untie my bikini top, but when the knot was resistant, I settled for wrenching it off and throwing it to the ground, my breasts happy to be free of their neoprene prison.

And they were *nice* breasts, I thought, looking in the bathroom mirror. Okay, maybe if I was designing myself from scratch, I would have treated myself to an extra cup size or two. "But they're good boobs! Stupid Patrick could have had these boobs if he wasn't so—"

And what was he, exactly? I didn't know. That was the whole problem. I didn't understand *why* he had ghosted me like that. Was it me, or was it him?

"It doesn't matter," I told myself firmly, turning on the creaking ceiling fan that sounded like it might fall and decapitate me at any moment. I flopped face-first onto the bed. "It doesn't matter," I repeated into the lumpy pillow.

But it didn't stop me from wondering.

4 Patrick

"Is Michelle your ex-girlfriend?"

"What?" I looked at my nephew, startled by the question.

"Michelle. That lady we met. Is she your ex-girlfriend?" Phoenix said it more slowly, like he thought I might be having comprehension problems. I noticed he was twisting his hands together, almost like he was trying to pull off his own fingers.

"No," I said firmly, shaking my head. "We only just met, actually. Last night at the pub."

Phoenix frowned. "Oh," he said and looked down at the brown paper bag that had held his croissant. He folded it once and then again until it was a small, neat square.

"What makes you ask that?"

"Just..." Phoenix shrugged. "She was nice to me but seemed really surprised to see you. Like she was kind of mad at you or something. So, I thought maybe..."

I bit my lip and considered. I had never thought I'd need to explain how I met women – or the limited amount of time I spent with them – to a kid. I could either come up with a convincing lie, or—

"You're fourteen," I said, looking at Phoenix. "I think you're old enough to know the story."

At that, Phoenix sat up a little straighter, like he was pleased to be let in on an adult's secret.

"I was at the pub with Khalid last night. Just having a few drinks, and I saw Michelle with her sisters. And, uh, I thought she was pretty," I began, unsure how much detail was appropriate.

Phoenix nodded, and though he was still twisting his hands, he was maintaining eye contact with me instead of staring at the ground. Encouraged, I went on.

"Anyway, Khalid noticed me looking at her and insisted we go over, and I asked Michelle to dance. So, we did, and, uh—" Why was this so awkward? "Well, I kissed her."

If I had been expecting Phoenix to be shocked, I was sorely disappointed. "Is that all?"

"Not quite," I said. "I was enjoying spending time with her, and we were going to keep chatting, but when I went to the bar, Khalid told me he had all these phone calls about—" I stopped, horrified. Shit. Shit on a stick. I had forgotten that Julia's breakdown was why I had left the pub.

"From Mum?" Phoenix filled in.

"Uh, yeah," I said. "Well, from your grandma, actually. Sorry, I didn't mean to upset you."

"I'm not upset," Phoenix said quickly. "I didn't mean to ask personal questions."

"You can ask me personal questions," I said. "I'm your uncle, after all."

Phoenix shifted and then looked up. "So, Michelle is angry with you because you had to leave after you kissed her?"

"Actually, I sort of left without saying anything," I admitted. "Michelle was waiting for me to come back, and I... Well, I was worried about your mum, so I just left."

There was a pause, and then, without warning, Phoenix let out a tiny laugh, seeming to surprise even himself. It was the first time he had laughed since I had picked him up. For a moment, he looked younger, happier, and less worn down from cares too old for him. "You just left?"

"I did," I confirmed. "Which wasn't a very nice thing to do. So, that's why Michelle was surprised to see me and why she might be a bit angry with me. She's got a right to be."

Phoenix made a slight noise in his throat that sounded like quiet agreement.

"She looked like she wanted to slap me," I went on. "Good thing I had you there to protect me."

Phoenix looked up at me then and smiled faintly. "She must be a nice person."

"Yeah?" I didn't doubt it, but I wondered why Phoenix thought so.

"She was really nice to me, even though she was mad at you."

"She was," I agreed. I had noticed that Michelle seemed far more able to engage Phoenix in conversation than I was. "I guess she is nice, then."

"Is that why you were looking at her butt?"

I made a sound somewhere between a gasp and a choke. "Uh, I wasn't—"

"I saw you," Phoenix said. "You did."

"Maybe a little," I admitted. "I shouldn't have done that. It's generally considered rude to look at people's butts."

Phoenix appeared to accept this with a faint nod of his head.

The truth was, I hadn't been able to take my eyes off Michelle as she rubbed sunscreen into her thighs, that little bikini barely covering the curves I could have been touching if my life hadn't become so complicated all of a sudden. And when she had realised I was looking, I could have sworn she put on a little show just to flaunt what I had missed out on.

As if I needed reminding.

"We should get going," I said, glancing out to where I could see the top of Michelle's head bouncing in the waves with her sisters. I doubted she was thinking of me at all.

"Okay," Phoenix said, pushing himself up from the bench. "I thought maybe you wanted to keep looking at Michelle."

"I don't think that's a very good idea." I'd have to be careful, I thought. My nephew, it seemed, had grown uncomfortably perceptive in the last three years.

· ♥ · ♥ · ♥ · ♥ · ♥ ·

"I've got a bit of work to do this afternoon," I said to Phoenix as we returned to the house (thankfully without bumping into Michelle). "Woodwork stuff, I mean. Do you want to watch?"

Phoenix puckered his mouth as though he was thinking about it. "Okay," he said finally. "If I won't be in your way."

"Not at all," I told him, surprised that he'd think that. "It'd be good to have some company. I'm chucking an oil on, though, so it might smell a bit. I'll keep the door open."

"I don't mind," Phoenix said, and I was starting to wonder if that was his catchphrase. He was very polite, my nephew. Even when he had asked me awkward questions about Michelle. But he was so hesitant. Three years ago, he had been full of questions and laughter. Just what had the last few years with Julia been like for him?

I tried to put it out of my head as Phoenix followed me to the garage I had converted into a workshop. My car was exposed to the inclement weather and possibility of spray paint wielding youths, but it was more than worth it to have this set up. French cleats lined one wall, allowing me to hang my hand tools right where I could see them, while my heavy tools sat on neat shelves underneath. In the middle was a huge workbench, the very first project I had completed after buying the house.

"If you press that button." I pointed. "The garage door will open. Keep the air flowing."

Phoenix nodded and dutifully pressed the button. Then he looked around as though unsure of what to do with himself.

"Grab one of those stools." I pointed again. "This shouldn't take too long. I'm putting the second coat of linseed oil on."

"What is it?"

"It's a window seat with custom storage," I explained. "It's Tasmanian Oak, and the buyer was keen to keep it all-natural, so that's why I'm using linseed oil rather than a varnish. Takes a few more coats, but it looks pretty good by the end."

Phoenix didn't look all that engrossed, but this particular project had some features I hoped would interest him.

"And check this out," I said, pressing the bottom panel of the window seat. A drawer popped out, and I was pleased to see the castors rolled smoothly. "Secret drawer."

"That's cool," Phoenix said quietly, and it was hard to tell whether he meant it or not.

"It's got this, too," I said, pressing another panel. From there, a tray table pushed out, just large enough to hold a laptop or, better still, snacks. "It's kind of my signature thing, furniture with hidden features. I don't know if you remember the last time you were here, but you helped me test that bookcase with the—"

"Gun safe hidden in the bottom?" Phoenix finished. "I remember."

"That was cool," I said, nodding. "I mean, I'm not the biggest fan of guns, but it was a cool project."

"Why did you decide to do it? Like, making furniture as your job." Phoenix looked at me as I liberally poured linseed oil onto a soft cloth and began rubbing it into the wood in neat, firm circles. "Mum said you always used to ask the prop guys about their tools and stuff when you were on set, and she never knew why."

"I don't know." It wasn't like I had a good answer. Not a neat, clean answer for a fourteen-year-old. "I never really liked acting that much. Your grandma didn't believe me when I told her that, but I didn't. It was your mum who was the actress; I was just along for the ride. But I always liked making stuff with my hands."

Phoenix nodded, and I felt compelled to continue. How could I explain that woodwork was something I could do entirely on my own terms, with no boss – or bossy mother – to answer to? It was enough like a real job to stop me from feeling totally useless while still giving me the freedom to set my own schedule.

"When I was at school – before we got cast in *Outback Adventures* – I did a woodwork class. I made this key holder for mum; I burned our family name into it and everything. I thought she'd love it, but she was really mad at me. Didn't want me to do stuff that might be dangerous, mess up my face or something so I wouldn't get cast in commercials anymore," I said, suddenly wondering if that was too traumatic a memory to share with my nephew.

But Phoenix just made a soft sound. "That sounds like something my mum would say."

There was an uncomfortable silence. "Well, acting was always Julia's big dream," I said. "And your Mum was really successful too, got cast in way more stuff than I ever did, until *Outback Adventures*. I never would have got that part if it wasn't for her." Julia had told me that enough times.

"Until she had me," Phoenix said, running the tip of his sneaker over the concrete floor in slow circles. "And she didn't get any more jobs."

I swallowed, setting down my rag. "Mate, that wasn't because she had you. I mean, heaps of child actors really struggle to get adult roles. It's like the directors reckon the audience will only ever see them as kids."

"That's what Mum says, too. But sometimes, I know she thinks it's because of me."

"It was never because of you," I said softly, my heart swelling with grief for how guilty the poor kid felt for something he had no control over. "It just didn't work out for her. Acting's a tough business. Heaps of amazing, talented people don't get very far. She did better than most. A lot better."

My nephew made another noise, and then he looked away. I looked around, helpless, for inspiration. "Hey, do you want to try out the table saw?" I asked, thinking of how exhilarating I had found it the first time I had used one. A rush of endorphins might be just the thing to get a proper smile on Phoenix's face. "It's pretty safe; I'll help—"

"No, thank you." Phoenix shook his head. "Mum doesn't like me doing dangerous stuff. Like you said."

"Ah," I said. "Yeah, nah, you're probably right. Stupid idea."

"I'll just watch. If that's okay."

"Of course, that's okay," I said, letting out a breath. "That's just fine."

· ♥ · ♥ · ♥ · ♥ · ♥ ·

"Hey, dudes!" Khalid came into the kitchen brandishing a large paper bag that smelled amazing. "You should lock your door, mate. Anyone could come in."

"Anyone did. What's all this?" I tapped the paper bag.

"I brought food," Khalid said, as though that was obvious. "So poor Phoenix here doesn't have to deal with your sad, bland cooking."

"I don't mind."

"I can cook!" I retaliated. "I can do...chicken and vegetables. Steak and vegetables. Lamb and vegetables!"

"So long as the lamb comes pre-marinated and the vegetables come in a microwave bag," Khalid chided. "Phoenix is a growing boy; he needs actual flavour!"

I stuck my head in the bag. "Thai!" I said, delighted. "Do you like Thai food, Phoenix?" I doubted he'd admit it if he didn't.

"Yeah." Well, that was no help.

"Go and get some plates, Patrick," Khalid said, unpacking the plastic containers full of food that was admittedly far better than anything I could cook. "And Phoenix, reckon you could rustle up some knives and forks?"

A few minutes later, my mouth was pleasantly full of chilli basil chicken (no rice for me, despite Khalid's cajoling), and I was pleased to see Phoenix munching Pad Thai with a decent amount of enthusiasm. I still didn't know if he *liked* Thai food, but it seemed safe to say he didn't hate it.

"Thanks for this, Khalid," I said, standing and opening the fridge. "I've got some beers in here for you, or are you still doing Dry January?"

"Sadly, I am," Khalid grimaced. "I could use a beer, though. It's been a massive day. I had this client insist on changing all the fonts on a brochure when it was supposed to be at final approval." He swallowed a piece of chicken. "I'm a graphic designer," he told Phoenix. "If you like photoshop and dealing with irritating people all day, I can highly recommend it as a future career option."

Phoenix gave him a faint smile around his mouthful of noodles.

"Sounds rough," I said. "We had an interesting day. Well, interesting morning. You know the place next door? Apparently, it's an Air BnB now."

"Really?" Khalid looked incredulous. "Who would actually pay to stay there? It should have been demolished years ago."

"Michelle's staying there," Phoenix spoke up unexpectedly. "She wasn't very happy to see Uncle Patrick."

"Michelle?" Khalid looked confused. "Michelle who?"

"Michelle from the pub," I said, inclining my head. "You know, the woman I, uh..."

Khalid's eyes widened, and then he began to laugh. "Wait, that Michelle?! She's living next door! Oh man, what are the chances?"

"She's not living there," I said quickly. "Just staying there. For her holiday."

"I feel sorry for her, then," Khalid said. "It's a complete dump. Not to mention," he said, "she probably wasn't pleased to see you after..." He trailed off with a glance at Phoenix.

"I know all about what happened," Phoenix said with an air of great maturity. "They kissed, and then Uncle Patrick left without saying goodbye. Michelle seemed kind of mad at him this morning. But she was nice to me."

Khalid laughed again, even louder this time. "Mate, that is some seriously bad luck," he chuckled. "Talk about awkward."

"It's no big deal," I said. "Like I said, she's just here for a week."

"Plenty more chances to run into her, then," Khalid sounded pleased. "And apologise."

"Do you think I should?"

"Yes," Phoenix and Khalid said at precisely the same moment, making Khalid laugh once more and Phoenix smile his faint, tired smile.

"I do feel bad for ditching her. It wasn't like that was my plan."

"You should definitely apologise," Khalid said. "Or the poor woman will think she did something wrong."

"Actually, I think she just thinks I'm an arsehole—" I paused. "Sorry, Phoenix, a jerk."

"I'm fourteen." Phoenix frowned. "Even PG movies have 'arsehole' in them."

"Indeed, they do," Khalid agreed. "And arsehole's not really swearing, anyway. It's just a useful noun to describe a certain kind of person. Like most of my clients, for example."

Before I could enter into that debate, there was a burst of noise from next door, somewhere between cheering and shrieking.

"What's going on over there?" Khalid asked, rising from the table. "Michelle must be having a party." He pushed apart the Venetian blinds, looking out.

"Don't spy on her!" I said, though I was deeply curious myself.

"Oh, it's not a party," Khalid reported. "Just her and her two sisters; looks like they're leaving for a night out. And wow, that's quite a tiny dress."

And maybe I was doing a terrible job of being a mature role model for Phoenix, but I jumped out of my seat and looked out through the blinds beside Khalid. Yep, that was indeed a tiny dress. Michelle's lithe curves were wrapped in what I thought was called a bandage dress, and it covered only slightly more than her bikini. I watched as she laughed at something Abby said and got into the back of an Uber.

"Girls' night out," Khalid said, nodding like he knew all about it, and took his seat once more. I let the blinds fall back into place and returned to the table, embarrassed. "Probably going clubbing in the city. Drinking, dancing, meeting people."

I made a noise of disapproval in the back of my throat. "Clubs are crap. Too crowded, too noisy."

"You sound so middle-aged!" Khalid snorted. "Clubs are a great place to meet people. As you well know."

And I knew he was referencing the various women I had met – and known for a very short time – in clubs over the years, but I could only think of Michelle. Michelle, in her tight black dress, surrounded by a sea of men, all staring at her, *wanting* her. There was an unpleasant tightness in my stomach, squeezing the vast quantity of spicy chicken I had consumed. I didn't like the thought of Michelle meeting men, dancing with them, and maybe bringing one back to that dump of a cottage with her. Which was ridiculous because I barely knew her, and I had absolutely zero right to be jealous.

"Mum says she met my dad in a club," Phoenix said, putting down his fork. "But that didn't work out very well."

"Well, it meant you were born," I told him. "So, I'd say that worked out pretty well. Maybe clubs aren't so bad after all."

And that earned a small smile from Phoenix.

"Right," Khalid said, nodding. "I'm so full I might burst. It's time for..." He pulled a pack of cards from his pocket. "Poker!"

"Are you suggesting we teach my nephew to gamble?"

But Phoenix brightened up at the sight of the cards. "I know how to play poker. Texas Hold 'Em, or Five Card Draw?"

"Oh man, this kid's a professional." Khalid grinned. "We're in trouble, mate!"

And Khalid was probably right, though not about the cards. I was in trouble when it came to Michelle. I'd go over to apologise tomorrow morning, I decided. After all, she was my neighbour.

5 Michelle

Michelle: we cannot drink like this the whole time i'm here. my liver can't handle it

Abby: maybe we should do wheatgrass shots this morning

Michelle: let's not be hasty. i want to be less hungover, not spend all day on the toilet

Tessa: how about smoothies and a swim?

Michelle: now there's an idea

Michelle: do either of you know why I have a bruise on my thigh?

Tessa: this one guy kept trying to dance with you, and you hurdled over a table to get away from him

Abby: you're not much of a hurdler

Michelle: i hate men

Abby: you sure did last night. none of the guys we met was good enough

Tessa: still thinking about patrick?

Michelle: absolutely not. see you in half an hour for smoothies

·♥·♥·♥·♥·♥·

As I battled to lock the front door, my phone began to buzz. I considered ignoring it, but that was hardly realistic. I let out a groan as the screen showed it was Martin. I had to answer.

"Hello?" I said, making my way down the steps. When I looked up, I saw a face I didn't expect. Patrick was pushing open the creaking gate. Shit. I could hardly tell him to go away while I was on the phone. Stupidly, I found myself wishing I was wearing something more attractive than my loose black tank dress and a ponytail so messy it looked like I had done it while wearing oven mitts. Not that I cared what Patrick thought of my hair, but it would have been more satisfying to look devastatingly gorgeous whenever he happened to see me.

"Michelle, sorry to call you on holiday," Martin began, and I tried to focus on what he was saying. I pointed to the phone, hoping Patrick would get the message and leave. But instead, he just stood there. Waiting.

"It's fine," I said. "Um, what's the problem?" Patrick was looking at me with his head slightly tilted, the bright morning sun bouncing off his tousled hair and making me wonder if he paid a lot for those white-blond streaks or if he was just a lucky dickhead as well as being a regular dickhead.

"It's about your forecast presentation for Wind Corp," Martin said. "Ash presented it the other day, and it went down a treat, but now they want more detail. I can't find your follow-up report."

I mouthed a swear word, and Patrick took a step back, holding up his hands. Automatically, I shook my head at him, even though he probably deserved that word too. He nodded and then gave me that smile that might have made my knees weak at the pub but absolutely was not doing anything for me now. Definitely not.

"Well, the meeting was supposed to be a week after I got back," I said cautiously. "So, I haven't finished it yet. If Ash was so confident to give my presentation, why can't he write the follow-up report?"

"It's just that he's so busy." Martin sounded like he was chewing the end of his pen, a nervous habit of his which annoyed me. I had wanted to yank it out of his mouth and shove it up his nose – or other orifices – on more than one occasion. "I was hoping maybe you had something. Just some notes to get us started. Wind Corp is such an important client, you know. And your reports are always excellent."

I let out a breath. I did have notes; I always had notes. But they were in no fit state to be shared with anyone. I never let anyone see my work until I was sure it was completely free from errors; another hang up from my childhood trauma (if I wanted to be dramatic and call it that). I'd have to organise my points, add more details, and some citations before sending them over, and I'd be late to meet my sisters. I knew what Abby would say, but—

"Sure," I said. "I'll just tidy those up and send them to you. It won't take more than an hour, tops."

"Oh, you will?" Martin sounded deeply relieved. "Thank you, Michelle. I always know I can count on you. You're a team player."

"I sure am," I said through gritted teeth. Team player seemed to mean 'willing to get walked all over'. But what could I do? If I refused, I knew Ash would make sure the Senior Partners knew I was the reason the report was delayed. The call ended, and I looked up at Patrick.

"Hi," he said, his hands in his pockets. "Sorry to drop by while you were on the phone. I didn't know if I should come back or—"

"What do you want?" I asked, not very politely. But I was hungover, annoyed about my job, and my smoothie consumption had been delayed.

"To apologise," Patrick said abruptly, and my mouth fell open in shock. "And explain why I left you in the pub like that."

"It's no big deal," I said because I didn't want him to think I had been wondering why he had done that for days. Especially since I absolutely had.

"It was rude of me," Patrick insisted, taking another step towards me. "And if I made you feel bad, I'm really sorry. You didn't deserve that."

"Like I said, it doesn't matter."

"The thing is, when I went up to the bar, Khalid caught up with me," Patrick began. "My mum had been calling and calling. I didn't know because I left my phone in the car. But it was about my sister, she's..." He paused as though searching for a word. "She's fragile, I guess. She was having a really bad time, so I had to go and pick up Phoenix."

"Oh," I said softly, sudden realisation dawning on me. That was why Patrick didn't seem entirely comfortable with his nephew. Phoenix living with him in Brekkie Beach was brand new.

"I wanted to come and at least explain, but it was an emergency, and I didn't even know if everyone was okay, so I..." He shook his head. "That's why I took off. It wasn't because I changed my mind or you did anything wrong. Things just got really complicated."

"I had no idea it was like that," I said, feeling like I was being smothered by an enormous blanket. The weighted kind, heavy on my chest. Patrick wasn't a dickhead. He was actually a very decent guy. The type of guy who'd leave a potential hook-up to look after his nephew.

"You couldn't have known," Patrick said. "I know I must have just seemed like an arsehole, so..." He paused. "Well, I guess I wanted you to know I wasn't. Especially since we're neighbours for the week."

"Thanks for telling me," I said. That seemed inadequate. I had the strangest urge to hug him but quickly suppressed it. I might have kissed him at the pub, but a hug? That was way too intimate. "It's really good of you to look after Phoenix. That's a very kind thing to do."

"It's no big deal." Patrick looked uncomfortable with the compliment. "I mean, I'm not exactly the fatherly type, but he's my nephew."

"I still think it's very kind of you."

Patrick just shrugged.

"Um, I'd better go back inside. I don't know how much you heard, but apparently, my boss needs some notes to write a report for a presentation I was meant to give when I was back at work."

"Bummer," Patrick winced. "It's such a nice day; you should be enjoying it."

"I will later," I said, moving back towards the treacherous steps. "I guess I'll see you around."

"I'd like that a lot," Patrick said. "Well, I'll be busy with Phoenix, so it's not like I—" He paused. "I'll let you get back to work."

I watched as he made his way down the overgrown path and out through the creaking fence, and when he turned to give me a half-wave, my stomach flip-flopped in a way that told me I was still very much interested in Patrick.

As if I didn't already know that. But now, it was even more complicated. He was every bit as handsome and charming as the first time we had met. But now? Now I knew he was a *good* guy. A genuinely good guy.

I'd have to be careful not to catch feelings for my new neighbour.

· ♥ · ♥ · ♥ · ♥ · ♥ ·

"Finally!" Abby said as I sat down next to her on a picnic rug patterned with maniacally grinning starfish and strangely aloof flamingos.

"I'm sorry!" I apologised. "Look, I know what you're going to say about my job and me being on holiday, so just say it so we can move on."

"No, I'm not going to say it." Abby sighed, and she handed me a cup. "I got you a smoothie."

"Thanks," I said, taking a grateful sip.

"It's called Strawberry So Strong. It's got protein powder, but it still tastes pretty decent."

I took another sip, but then a groan caught my attention. "What's going on there?" I could see a group of five women, all visibly pregnant, bent over on the sand and reaching for their toes. In front of them, a tanned and perky woman in flowing linen fisherman pants and a crocheted excuse for a crop top clutched her own (flat and toned) stomach with both hands.

"Prenatal yoga class," Tessa told me. "They don't look very at one with the universe."

"Reach into yourselves, sisters!" The perky woman urged the group. "Connect with the power of your sacred womb and let your womanly spirit flow!"

"If she makes us do that one more time, I'm going to pee myself," I heard one woman whisper to her friend. "I thought this was meant to be relaxing."

"You know what I'd find relaxing? A big cold glass of Sav Blanc."

"I'd strangle someone for a glass of wine!"

I laughed and saw that Tessa and Abby found it just as funny as I did.

"Being pregnant doesn't look like much fun," Tessa observed.

"Not at all," Abby agreed. "So, you aren't going to be popping out mini Dylans any time soon?"

"Definitely not soon." Tessa looked thoughtful. "But one day, I think I'd like to. Dylan would be a great dad."

"And we know you have your whole thing about never having kids," Abby said, looking at me. "Which is totally your choice, and I support you one hundred per cent."

"I don't want biological kids," I corrected. "One day, when I've got more time, I'd like to foster or adopt older kids. There aren't many people willing to deal with teenagers, which is completely unfair."

"That's very sweet," Tessa said approvingly. "Kind of like Patrick looking after his nephew."

"Oh, that reminds me!" I said, suddenly remembering. "He came over this morning. To apologise for ghosting me."

"He apologised?" Abby looked flabbergasted. "Did he give you a reason?"

"He did, actually." I wrinkled my nose. "And it's a really good one, so I can't be mad at him anymore. His sister was having some kind of crisis, and he had to go and pick up Phoenix right then, late at night."

"Wow." Tessa looked impressed. "He just dropped everything to look after his nephew?"

"Yep," I said. "Which actually makes a lot of sense because he doesn't seem that comfortable talking to the kid. It's all brand new to him."

"What's wrong with his sister?" Abby looked curious.

"I didn't ask. Seemed rude."

"You're probably right," Abby said. "But I'm nosy. I want to know."

"So do I," I confessed. "I totally want to know the whole story."

"Maybe you will," Tessa said. "I mean, you're not mad at him anymore, and he's still, like, really handsome. You could still have your holiday fling, and I bet he'd tell you during the pillow talk."

"That is not going to happen," I said flatly.

"And why not?" Abby prodded me. "He's right next door! Conveniently located casual sex partner!"

"Because he's busy looking after his potentially traumatised nephew!" I said, exasperated. And okay, I didn't know if Phoenix was traumatised, but he might be. "He can't be swanning off to seduce random tourists."

"You're not a tourist; you're a visitor," Abby said. "The kid looked like a teenager; no reason Patrick couldn't leave him alone for a few hours. He'd only be next door."

"No," I said again, even though I had already entertained that possibility, especially after Patrick had told me he'd like to see more of me.

"You weren't interested in any of the guys we met last night," Tessa pointed out. "And some of them were cute."

"They were gross."

"They were cute," Abby said. "You're just hung up on Patrick."

"I'm really not," I said, but even as the words left my mouth, they felt just a little bit like a lie.

· ♥ · ♥ · ♥ · ♥ · ♥ ·

I couldn't resist admiring myself in the bathroom mirror, even though said mirror was cloudy and ominously cracked down one side. I was wearing a red and white polka dot dress, with a full skirt and a halter neck. I had owned the dress for three years but had never been able to wear it in Glasgow. It was nothing like the tailored dresses and crisp suits I wore daily for work. The dress was from someone else's life. The kind of woman who baked, had a colourful sleeve tattoo, and went to rockabilly gigs every weekend. The type of woman I absolutely wasn't.

"But I'm on holiday," I told my cloudy reflection. "And I can dress up for one night, can't I?"

I gave myself a nod and then let out a snort of amusement at my own ridiculousness. Checking my phone, I saw that it was time to step outside and wait for Abby and her van to pick me up. Tonight, we were driving down to Manly to enjoy a quiet dinner and zero tequila.

That was the plan, anyway. But when I slammed the creaking door behind me, my phone began to buzz.

"Bloody hell," I swore, pulling it from my bag. Maybe, if I was quick, I could finish the call before Abby arrived and told me off for answering it.

"Hi, Martin. What's up?"

"Michelle," Martin sounded frantic. "Have you seen the news?"

"The news?" I repeated. "Um, not really." The truth was, I had avoided my usual morning news binge in an effort to put myself in holiday mode, even if I couldn't resist answering work calls.

"Ah," Martin said. "So, you don't know about the baggage handlers' strike in Europe?"

"Uh, no," I said, trying to digest that information. "Wait, wouldn't that screw up flights?"

"Yes!" Martin was clearly frazzled. "It's absolute chaos. Mass flight cancellations, airports closed everywhere. And there's talk that the flight attendants might join them."

"Are you serious?" That was a stupid thing to say. Martin wasn't a joker, Batman-esque or otherwise. "So, is my flight home going to be cancelled?"

"All flights are cancelled! And there's no way of knowing how long this will go on for, but even when the airports re-open, there's going to be a backlog, and—"

"How am I supposed to get back?" I felt sick panic rising in my stomach, my chest tightening beneath my obnoxiously cheerful dress. Suddenly, I hated the stupid dress and wished I could rip it off and stomp on it, grinding it into the overgrown path for good measure.

"I don't think you'll be able to get back here for at least another two weeks," Martin said. "It could be longer, but we just don't know."

"But I've got so much to do." Crap, I could feel tears springing up, hot and angry. "I mean, I can work remotely, but—"

"We'll just have to manage," Martin sighed. "I don't know what we'll do without you; the past three days have been bad enough."

I swallowed hard because there was no way I was going to let my boss know I was on the verge of crying. "Well, thank you for letting me know," I said, fighting to keep my voice steady. "I'll check for updates. Our admin pool will be working on getting flights when they can, right?"

"When they can." He paused. "I do hope this doesn't spoil your holiday."

I let out a laugh that had the distinct possibility of turning hysterical. "I'd better go," I said quickly. "Bye." I ended the call and sank down onto the uneven front steps, even though that would likely give me splinters in my bottom. Arse splinters were the least of my problems right now.

"Fuck!" My voice was loud enough to startle a seagull perched on the telephone wire. It flapped its wings and gave me a beady glare. "And fuck you too!" The seagull squawked loudly and flew off, probably to find a resting place with fewer crazy women shouting at him.

"What am I going to do?" I whispered. That was when the tears came. Hot, urgent tears of frustration. And I knew it was silly to cry over my job. To cry over being forced to stay in Australia with my beloved sisters for longer. But I knew – knew all too well – just what being away from the office would do to my career. In a few weeks, Ash and the other analysts would cut me out of every project, every client, and I'd have to start all over again when I returned. My reputation, my hard-won respect? All of it would be destroyed.

"Michelle?"

I knew that voice. I looked up, my face hidden between my fingers, to see Patrick. Patrick, who was pushing a lawnmower out of the garage and wearing a threadbare singlet and shorts that were only just on the decent side of being hotpants. For a brief moment, I was distracted from the utter destruction of my career at the sight of Patrick's bare arms, tanned and muscular. And damn, his thighs weren't exactly hard to look at, either.

"Are you okay?" Patrick had abandoned the lawnmower and cleared the fence between his very nice house and my dump of a cottage in a deft hurdle. Exactly like I had failed to do last night at the club.

"I'm fine," I said, trying to wipe my eyes even as more tears fell. "I just got a call from work. Did you know there's a baggage handler strike in Europe? It means my flight home's been cancelled, and I have no idea when I'll be able to get back."

"Shit." Patrick's face crinkled up, his very green eyes concerned. "That sounds bad."

"It's nothing to cry about," I said firmly, still wiping furiously at my treacherous tear ducts, which disagreed. "But I just... I've been working so hard for my next promotion and being away from the office will put me behind, and I don't even know how long it's for and—" I was sobbing now. Actually sobbing; heaving cries that rattled my whole body. I was well past ugly crying and into scary crying.

A big hand rested cautiously on my back as though unsure of how it would be received. It felt warm, solid, and far more comforting than said hand had any right to, especially given I had only stopped thinking its owner was a dickhead that very morning. Instead of a tentative pat, Patrick rubbed my back in small, firm circles, right between my shoulder blades.

"It sounds totally shit," he said. "And completely unfair."

I took a long shuddering breath. "It is." I sniffed. "All the guys in the office will be saying, 'Oh, Michelle. She's still on holiday. She's not very committed, not like us.' I've had to work so hard to be taken seriously and get to where I am. And it'll all be for nothing."

Patrick stopped rubbing my back then and wrapped his arm around my shoulders in a tight hug. "Hey," he said

MICHELLE FINCH STICKS TO THE PLAN

softly. "Look, I don't know much about all this, but I don't reckon all your work will be for nothing. There's no way they'll forget how good you are just because you're away a few weeks."

I let my head drop to his shoulder, breathing in the smell of him. Soap, laundry, sun, and salt. *I want to lick him.* I started at that sudden thought, trying to drive it from my head. I was having a crying breakdown on the steps of my horrible cottage, and my not-a-dickhead neighbour was being very kind about it. I should *not* be thinking about licking him.

"Thanks for being so nice to me," I managed to say, unwilling to move from the comforting warmth of his embrace. "I didn't mean to emote all over you like that. Especially about work. It's just...my job is important to me. And I feel so *stupid.*" Stupid was, in my opinion, the worst possible thing you could feel.

"Hey, I was the one who came over here," Patrick said, his mouth quirking into a half smile. "I'd say I invited the emoting. I wish I could get Phoenix to talk to me like this. I'd give anything for him to emote on me a bit, but he's so..."

"Reserved?" I suggested.

"Something like that," Patrick said. "You're better at talking to him than I am, and that makes me feel like a failure. Reckon that's toxic masculinity?"

I smiled at that. "Nope," I said. "You're his uncle; it's natural you'd want him to open up to you. And you obviously care about him a lot."

"I love that kid," Patrick said quietly. "But I haven't seen him since he was ten. He's fourteen now. My sister... Well, after the last time I saw him, she cut contact. I used to be pretty close to him, but now it's like we're strangers. I knew how to talk to kid Phoenix, but teenage Phoenix is..." He shook his head. "I need to take him shopping; he's barely got any clothes. But he's just going to say it's okay or that he doesn't mind. That's what he says about everything."

"Maybe I could help," I said because something about Phoenix's anxious, drawn face and obvious desire not to be too demanding pulled at my heartstrings and reminded me of a younger Michelle. A Michelle who had learned to hide her feelings and not expect too much from her parents. "Taking him shopping and talking to him, I mean. He seemed to like me."

"He does like you," Patrick agreed. "But you don't have to get involved. I mean, it's not your problem, all this."

"Well, it looks like I'll be your neighbour for longer than I thought. And I've got a soft spot for sad kids. A big one."

"You're a kind person, Michelle," Patrick said it like it was a statement of fact, not his opinion.

"You don't know that," I objected. "I could be a total bitch."

"Nope. I don't think so."

I wiped at my eyes again to hide how his words had made me feel and saw just how much mascara was now on the back of my hand. "Oh crap, I must look like a total mess," I grimaced. "I'm supposed to be going for dinner with my sisters; Abby will be here to pick me up soon."

I rifled in my bag for my make-up pouch, and Patrick pulled his arm back. I felt strangely bereft, like an essential item of clothing had suddenly disappeared, and I was exposed and naked on the crumbling steps.

Flicking open the mirror, I scowled at my face. "I look like a raccoon. A raccoon in a My Chemical Romance tribute band."

"I'd definitely go to that show," Patrick offered me a grin, and then he took the mirror from me, his fingers brushing against mine. "I'll hold this. You do whatever you need to do."

"You don't mind?"

"Nope," Patrick assured me. "Beats mowing the lawn, anyway. Do you reckon it's child labour if I get Phoenix to do it?"

"Only if you don't pay him," I said, wiping under my eyes with a cotton pad and then carefully reapplying mascara. I should invest in the waterproof kind, given that my life – or at least my career – seemed in danger of spiralling into chaos.

"Oh, I'd definitely pay him."

"Then he'd probably jump at the chance," I said, painting on a fresh, bright pink pout. My skin was still a little blotchy, but that would have to do. I was just smoothing concealer under my eyes when a horn honk made me – and Patrick holding the mirror – jump.

"That's Abby," I said, standing up. "Um, thank you for this. I really..." I took a quick breath. "I really appreciate it."

'Appreciate it' wasn't enough. That's what I would have said to a particularly efficient administration officer who had managed to score me the best conference room at short notice. But what did you say to your handsome neighbour who had hugged you while you cried about your shitty job? I had never read a professional etiquette guide that covered that one. Did the rules change, I wondered, if you had previously kissed said handsome neighbour in a pub?

"No worries," Patrick said, and then he gave me that smile that I was sure must give all the women – and some of the men – of Brekkie Beach permanently weak knees. Everyone must be stumbling around like Bambi with that smile in their proximity.

"Um, I'll see you later," I said, making my way down the overgrown path and towards Abby's van. The door slid open, and Tessa stuck her head out and waved.

"See you later, Michelle," Patrick said, pushing up from the steps.

I watched him go and winced as I headed into the van, knowing I'd have to explain to my sisters why Patrick's arms had been around me.

Not to mention having to explain how it had made me feel to myself.

6 Patrick

Letting out a grunt, I pushed the barbell up and racked it. Rolling my shoulders, I could feel the pleasant burn of my muscles working. I swung my arms back and forth, trying to decide whether I should squeeze in one more set. The house seemed quiet, and while that was no guarantee that Phoenix was still asleep, he hardly needed me hovering over him when he woke up like the creepy kind of uncle.

I took a long swig of water and let the rest run over my flushed face, rubbing it into my sweaty hair. Every time I worked out, I was glad I had gone to the effort of building a home gym. It wasn't because I was cheap – whatever Khalid might say. What I liked was the privacy. I had tried out the gym in Brekkie Beach when I had first moved here, but I could barely get through a workout without someone coming up and asking me if I was that guy from *Outback Adventures*. And yeah, that had led to a few flings with former fans that had been both fun and distracting, but it wasn't worth the constant interruptions and requests for selfies.

Besides, a home gym meant I could get a few sets in whenever the mood took me, and no one complained if I sweated all over the equipment and blasted my choice of music (Megadeth was *life*) at top volume.

And now, my home gym had one more advantage. There was the possibility that Michelle might wander out to the tiny yard behind the cottage and see me looking sweaty, buff, and all things appealingly masculine.

"I probably shouldn't be thinking about that," I muttered.

But not thinking about Michelle was proving difficult. Especially now that I knew she'd be staying in Brekkie Beach for at least another two weeks, or maybe even longer. Perhaps I could have ignored how she made me feel if she was leaving in a few days, but now? Now I wasn't so sure.

"I should be thinking about Phoenix," I said out loud as I unstacked plates from the bar. "Not about my neighbour. Even if I would have taken her home if things hadn't gotten so complicated that night at the pub."

There was a rush of heat that had nothing to do with my sweaty workout, and I felt distinct tension in an area my weights routine definitely didn't target. What would it have been like to take Michelle home with me? We were complete strangers then, drawn together by chemistry alone. And yes, I had been down that road with a lot of women before. But somehow, I knew that with Michelle, it would have been—

"Stop thinking about it," I told myself, towelling off my sweat-drenched hair. "Life got complicated. And now it's never going to happen."

Right?

· ♥ · ♥ · ♥ · ♥ · ♥ ·

"Hey, you're up," I said, wincing at how redundantly cheesy that sounded as Phoenix came into the kitchen and silently poured himself a glass of water.

"Hello," he said quietly, sitting down at the table.

"What do you fancy for brekkie?" I asked, sounding like an alarmingly enthusiastic children's YouTuber in my effort to be cheerful. "Toast? Cereal? I could do some bacon and eggs if you'd like."

"Just toast is fine," Phoenix said, and he abruptly stood up. "I'll make it. I don't mind."

"I'll do it!" I insisted. "You're my guest."

Phoenix sat back down, but he had a tiny frown between his brows, just visible under that thick fringe. I selected two pieces of bread from the loaf I bought for Phoenix –

and was trying not to be tempted by myself – and put them into the toaster. "I've got Vegemite. How do you like it?"

"It's okay. I can do it."

"Sure," I shrugged. "Far be it from me to spread someone else's Vegemite. We all like it a different way, huh?"

Phoenix looked like he was thinking very hard about that but didn't say anything as I took the vegemite and butter from the fridge and set both on the table.

"So, it looks like you'll be staying with me a while," I said, trying to choose my words carefully. "At least until school starts."

"Did you speak to Mum?" Phoenix's head popped up at that, and I saw his hands twist together, fingers writhing like a nest of eels.

"Not exactly," I said, hating the disappointment that flashed over his young face. "Your grandma texted to let me know."

"Oh," Phoenix said, staring at the black and yellow jar of Vegemite as though he had never seen the stuff before. "That's okay."

"I thought she might be keeping in touch with you," I ventured. "Your mum, I mean."

"Not yet," Phoenix shook his head. "But if she's not feeling well, I understand. It's okay."

It wasn't okay, not at all. A fourteen-year-old shouldn't have to deal with his mum sending him away in the middle of the night and then cutting off contact with him. I knew

Julia had her demons; of course, I did. And I knew she tried – in her own way – to be a good mum. But I couldn't help judging her right at that moment. Was she really incapable of sending her kid a bloody text?

"Anyway, because you're staying on a bit, I thought we could go shopping. Get you some more clothes," I said. "Because you don't have much with you. Which is totally fine; how could you have known how much to pack?" I added the last part quickly, not wanting it to sound like I was criticising him.

"It's fine," Phoenix said, now turning the Vegemite in slow circles. "You don't need to buy me stuff. Mum wouldn't—" he cut himself off. "It's fine."

I knew exactly what he had been going to say. His mum wouldn't like me buying him things. She'd take it as a criticism, like me buying a few t-shirts and some sneakers was the same as me telling her she was an inadequate parent. I had been through it before, when I had turned up with a Lego set one Christmas, which happened to be larger and more expensive than the set she had given him. My sister was very sensitive about things like that.

"Well, Michelle needs to go shopping too," I said, deciding now was the time to play my trump card. "I told you about how all the flights got cancelled, that baggage handlers' strike? She's staying for longer than she planned too, so she needs..." I wracked my brain for something other than 'underwear' and tried valiantly to stop imagining

Michelle in said underwear. "T-shirts and stuff," I finished lamely. "The plan is that we'll hit the shops together."

"Michelle wants to go shopping?" Phoenix brightened up ever so slightly at that.

"Yeah." I nodded. "She's never been shopping in Australia. We can show her all the sights. I mean, she's probably never seen a Kmart!"

Phoenix let out a soft chuckle at that. "Are you happy she's staying longer?"

And wow, that was a hell of a question for this time of the morning. "Um," I began, chewing my lip. "Yeah, I guess so. I mean, it's nice having a neighbour."

Phoenix let out a faint breath. Before he could say anything else, the toaster popped, and I ran over with way more excitement than double cooked bread warranted. "Toast!" I said, putting the two pieces on a plate and serving them to my nephew with all the pomp of a butler to the royal family. "Enjoy!"

"Thanks." Phoenix busied himself with the butter and vegemite.

As I watched him while trying not to look like I was watching him, I thought again about what he had asked me. Was I glad Michelle was staying longer?

It shouldn't matter. It shouldn't matter to me how long Michelle was spending in Brekkie Beach.

But I was happy she was staying on. Happier than I had any right to be.

· ♥ · ♥ · ♥ · ♥ · ♥ ·

"I wonder if Abby would like these." Michelle scrunched up her face as she examined a set of navy pinstriped bedsheets. She was wearing glasses today, which she had seemed oddly embarrassed about, muttering something about her eyes needing a day off from contact lenses. I didn't know why she was embarrassed about them because Michelle looked *good* in glasses. Like a sexy, stern librarian.

"I thought they were for you?" I asked, confused.

"Oh, they are," Michelle agreed. "But I'll give them to Abby when I leave, so it makes sense to pick something she'll like. She'll be using them longer than me."

"That's very thoughtful," I said, not wanting to think about Michelle leaving Brekkie Beach while being annoyed with myself for caring. "We should get you some new sheets, too," I said to Phoenix. "The ones in the guest bedroom are a bit boring. We can get something you like."

"I don't mind," Phoenix said, looking down at his feet, which were still clad in those too-small Supergas. Sneakers were definitely on my list for him today. "The ones in there are fine."

"Nah, we could do with an extra set," I said. "And I want you to pick something you like. It's your room."

Phoenix looked startled, as though he had never been asked to pick something he liked. Knowing my sister, that was entirely possible. Damn.

"My mum always chose everything for my room when I was younger," Michelle said, the pinstriped sheets under one arm. "She liked the shabby chic look; lots of white and floral, stuff made to look antique when it wasn't. It was gross."

Phoenix managed a small smile at that. "Yeah?"

"Yeah," Michelle said. "But we stayed with my Nana a lot, and she'd always let us choose duvet covers for our beds at her place. Abby always liked ones like this." She held up the pinstriped sheets. "Tessa chose plain white. She never spilled stuff like I did."

"What did you like?" Phoenix looked genuinely interested, and I silently thanked Michelle for her uncanny ability to get the kid to talk.

"Tons of different stuff," Michelle told him with a grin. "My favourite set had all the planets on them. I've always loved watching documentaries about space exploration and stuff. But I had One Direction sheets for a while, which was creepy now that I think about it. Fifteen-year-old me sleeping under all four of them."

Phoenix laughed louder than I had ever heard before, the corners of his eyes crinkling.

"Anyway, my point is," Michelle went on. "It's fun to choose stuff you really like, even if you go off it later."

"Yes," I nodded vigorously. "I want you to choose something you like, Phoenix. Even if it is One Direction."

Phoenix wrinkled his nose. "One Direction are, like, really old."

"Oh, ouch!" Michelle laughed. "Nothing like Gen Z to make me feel ancient."

I was about to jump in and assure Michelle that she was far from ancient when I felt a tap on my shoulder.

"Hey, are you that kid from *Outback Adventures*?" Two women were looking at me eagerly.

"Yeah, I was that kid," I said, giving them a practised smile. "Not wrestling many crocs these days, though."

The two women laughed indulgently, but they were looking at me like I was a particularly juicy bit of meat in a butcher's window, and they were hungry stray dogs. "I told you it was him!" I heard one whisper loudly to her friend.

"Can we get a selfie?" The bolder of the two women was already pulling out her phone.

"Sure." I had long since learned it was easier to give people what they wanted, and I didn't want any unpleasant stories about me being rude popping up on social media.

The two women wrapped their arms around my waist in a more intimate way than I would have liked and pouted at the camera. If my smile was rather fixed, I'm sure they didn't notice.

Without another word, they moved away, still whispering to each other and looking at the photo. "He's still really hot!" I heard one of them exclaim, and while I supposed that was a compliment, I would have preferred a 'thank you'.

"Um, am I missing something here?" Michelle looked bemused. "Are you famous or something?"

"Not really," I said, realising that with Michelle being English, she wouldn't know about *Outback Adventures*. "I was in a TV show when I was a kid; it's not a big deal."

"A TV show?" Michelle's eyes went wide. "No way! I had no idea. What was it called?"

"*Outback Adventures*," Phoenix said, coming out from behind a rack of pillowcases where he had disappeared at the approach of the women. "Him and Mum were in it together. They were this brother and sister who lived in the outback and solved mysteries and stuff. It was on for five years. There was even a movie."

"It was a made-for-TV movie," I said quickly. "Not a real movie."

"That's so cool!" Michelle enthused. "I can't believe you didn't tell me."

"I don't think about it much anymore," I said, perfectly honestly, although ever since Phoenix had moved in, I had thought about *Outback Adventures* more than I had in years. "It would have been a weird boast, telling you something I did as a teenager."

"Mum still talks about it a lot," Phoenix said, and when we both looked at him, he looked away. "Um, I'm going to look over there." He pointed and disappeared.

"So, do you still do acting?" Michelle asked. "I just realised I've never asked what you do for a living, which is pretty rude of me."

"Well, we've always had other stuff to talk about," I said, trying not to think about how we hadn't talked much at all that night at the pub. "But, no. No acting these days. I was never really into it, but my sister was, and I went along to her castings, and it just kind of happened." I shook my head. "Now, I do woodwork. Custom furniture pieces, mostly."

"Oh, that makes sense," Michelle said. "Because you're so—" She cut herself off as her cheeks turned pink. "I mean, you're in great shape, so it makes sense you've got a physically demanding job."

"Everyone's in great shape around Brekkie Beach. Even accountants," I quipped, though I was pleased to know Michelle seemed to approve of my body. A life without carbs was definitely worth it.

"I've noticed," Michelle said. "So, the acting was your sister's big thing? Is she still doing that?"

"Ah..." I lowered my voice. "Her career never took off the way she wanted it to. She had Phoenix pretty young, and she thinks that's why. I don't know, honestly. It's kind of a sensitive subject."

"Sorry," Michelle said, looking around for Phoenix's dark head as though hoping he hadn't overheard. "I didn't mean to—"

"No, it's fine," I said. "I just didn't want Phoenix to hear us talking about her. It upsets him. Well, I think it does, anyway. He doesn't talk much about how he's feeling."

"He will," Michelle said, her face reassuring. "This is all still really new for him. It can take teenagers a while to open up. You get some who'll tell you their whole life story at the bus stop, but others need more time. You're doing a good job, Patrick."

The look she gave me was so warm, so reassuring that for a moment, I felt like it was true, that I really was doing a good job. Perhaps I could do enough for my nephew to make up for how much crap he had endured in his life so far.

"Thanks," I said. "I'm just glad you're around to help me."

"These are on sale." Phoenix reappeared, clutching a set of sheets with a dark green and black galaxy print. "But if you don't like them, it's okay."

"Those are awesome!" Michelle took the sheets and examined them before handing them back to Phoenix. "Good choice!"

"I like space too," he ventured. "I saw this cool documentary about black holes last week."

"*The Edge of All We Know*?" Michelle asked. "That one was awesome!"

"Yeah." Phoenix raised his chin slightly. "It was."

"Well, I think the sheets are cool," I said. "Even if I don't know anything about black holes."

"And they're on sale," Phoenix repeated like he wanted to convince me.

"Is that why you picked them?" I asked. "I really do want you to choose something you like."

Phoenix squirmed slightly. "No," he said finally. "That whole table is on sale, but these were the coolest ones."

"You did good," Michelle said. "Come on, let's go buy these, and then I need a coffee before we hit the next shop."

Phoenix nodded, still holding the sheets. "Are you sure they're okay?"

"Definitely," I said. "Green and black are good colours."

"And they won't show any stains if you eat in bed like I do," Michelle said. "Very practical."

"I don't think Mum would like them."

"That's okay," Michelle said. "These will live at your Uncle Patrick's house, so your mum never has to see them." She paused. "Why don't you find a black fitted sheet to go with them?"

"Is that okay?"

"It's a great idea," I said, nodding at him until he darted back between the shelves like he was on a secret mission.

MICHELLE FINCH STICKS TO THE PLAN   117

"Thank you," I said again, looking at Michelle. "You're good with him."

"Well, I do really like space documentaries," Michelle said. "And I remember what it was like, being his age and feeling..." She bit her lip. And I couldn't help it. I reached out to squeeze her hand for just a moment, wanting to express my gratitude. More than gratitude. She looked shocked, but then, her small, warm hand squeezed mine.

"I..." I shook my head. "Thanks."

"You got this, Uncle Patrick," Michelle said warmly and let go of my hand.

I wished she hadn't.

· ♥ · ♥ · ♥ · ♥ · ♥ ·

"You know, I think your new sneakers are cooler than mine," Michelle said to Phoenix, taking them out of the box and examining them. "If we were the same size, I might have tried to steal them."

Phoenix gave a little laugh, and then he looked at me. "Thank you, Uncle Patrick," he said for about the millionth time. "For all of this stuff." He gestured to the kitchen table, which was laden with shopping bags.

"No worries," I said, giving him a grin. "We should put your new sheets on. Then you can sleep in the galaxy tonight." I rifled through one of the bags, pulling them out. "Maybe Neil DeGrasse Tyson will narrate your dreams."

That earned a small smile from Phoenix. "I can do it myself."

"You sure you don't want some help?"

"I can do it," Phoenix said again, and he slipped up the stairs, sheets in hand.

"Sometimes you just want to do that stuff yourself," Michelle said with a shrug. "Personally, I hate changing the duvet cover. I'm very spoilt; my apartment in Glasgow comes with a weekly maid service who does it for me. I'll have to wrestle with my bed all by myself here."

"I could help you," I said and realised that might be too intimate an offer. "I mean, I wrestled animatronic crocodiles on *Outback Adventures*, I reckon I could take on a duvet."

Michelle laughed. "That's very kind, but I'll rope my sisters into helping me. I bet Abby has some clever technique on how to do it easily. I told you she's a professional organiser, right?"

"Can she come over here? My pantry isn't looking too good."

"Do not say that to Abby if you ever see her again," Michelle warned. "Because she'll absolutely take you at your word and turn up here with fifty plastic tray containers and her label maker."

"Now that's a terrifying image. Uh, can I make you tea or coffee?" I asked, moving to the kitchen. "My pantry might be messy, but I can make a decent cuppa."

"Tea would be great," Michelle said with an appreciative sigh. "That's the one thing I miss about the UK. People offer you tea every fifteen minutes, minimum."

"That's the only thing you miss?" I flicked on the kettle and got out the box of teabags.

"Honestly, yes," Michelle said. "I mean, I don't have any family left there. Tessa and Abby live here, and my parents have mostly lived in their villa in Spain since I was a kid, anyway. And what am I going to miss? The weather?"

"I didn't know you spent a lot of time in Spain," I said, selecting the only two matching mugs I owned because, apparently, I wanted to impress Michelle with my fine crockery. "Do you speak Spanish?"

"Oh, I didn't live there," Michelle clarified. "Mum and dad did. Like I said, my sisters and I stayed with my Nana a lot."

"That must have been tough," I said cautiously, not wanting to delve into potential childhood trauma.

"It didn't make me feel great," Michelle admitted. "But I had my sisters, and that's all in the past now." She waved a hand. "So, can I say something that might be way out of line?"

"Go for it," I said. "You just spent the afternoon helping me for no reason at all; you can say whatever you want."

"It wasn't no reason," Michelle frowned. "Phoenix is a good kid, and you're doing a kind thing, looking after him. I wanted to help. But that's the thing." She took a breath. "Phoenix is a good kid, but he's..."

"Quiet?" I offered. "Withdrawn? Cautious?"

"Anxious," Michelle said finally. "He spends way too much time thinking about whether what he says and does will upset people. Teenagers are supposed to be kind of selfish, but he's not because he's so focused on making sure he doesn't get a negative reaction."

"That's true," I said. "My sister is... Well, it's been hard for Phoenix."

Michelle made a soft sound. "I'm not going to ask about your sister because it's not my business. But you said it only just happened, him coming to live with you. So, I wondered, have you considered arranging for him to talk to someone? Like a psychologist or something?"

And wow, that wasn't what I had expected her to say. I looked down at the two mugs, where steam was slowly rising from the hot water. "I hadn't thought of it," I admitted. "But it might be a good idea."

"Please don't think that me suggesting this means you're not doing a good job," Michelle said, and she looked like she really wanted me to believe her. "You are. Seriously. But sometimes, it's easier to talk to a stranger rather than to people you know and care about. Especially when you've got difficult feelings. Things you think people don't want to hear."

I nodded, leaning against the kitchen bench. "I was hoping he'd open up to me, but if you think he needs to talk to someone professional, then—"

"I think he needs both," Michelle corrected. "I was always close to my sisters and my Nana growing up. It wasn't like I couldn't talk to them, and they helped me a lot when I—" She cut herself off, and I wondered what she had been about to say. "Sometimes you need family who care, and professional help too."

"I get that," I said, feeling a surge of anger at Michelle's parents for abandoning her, when she must have needed them.

"I think it's harder for Phoenix, though," Michelle said. "He doesn't have siblings, does he? He needs to feel like it's safe to open up to you; maybe a psychologist could help with that. With your sister, do you think maybe he's been taught it's not okay to talk about how he really feels?"

I closed my eyes, a wave of sadness passing over me. "Yes," I answered, opening my eyes. "My sister, she's...troubled. She does her best, but—" I couldn't say more. Not yet, anyway. "I think you're right."

"Thank you for taking that so well," Michelle said. "I'm used to men being super defensive when I make suggestions they hadn't thought of. At work, I mean."

"Sounds like you work with some men who aren't very secure in themselves, then."

"That's an understatement."

I brought the two mugs of tea over to the table, setting one down in front of her. "Does that look okay?" I asked. "Not too much milk?"

Michelle picked up the mug and took a small sip. "That's perfect," she said, looking right at me, her blue eyes warm and bright. "You sure know how to please an English lady."

I let out a loud laugh at that, but inside, all I could think about was how much I regretted missing my chance to please this English lady in a way that had nothing to do with tea.

· ♥ · ♥ · ♥ · ♥ · ♥ ·

"Sheets look awesome, dude," I said as I poked my head into Phoenix's room, a basket of freshly washed laundry on my hip like I was an overburdened 1950s housewife.

"Thanks." Phoenix ran a hand over the green and black pattern.

"Is it okay if I come in for a chat?" I asked tentatively.

"Um, yeah?" Phoenix sounded like he was surprised I had asked. "Did I do something wrong?"

"No!" I said hastily. "You've been great, honestly. Michelle said so, too." And I knew that was manipulative, mentioning Michelle, but I wanted Phoenix to understand that what I said next wasn't a criticism, that he hadn't done anything wrong.

Phoenix looked down at the sheets, tracing a nebula with one finger.

"I was just thinking," I cleared my throat, leaning against the dresser. "That maybe, with everything that's happened with your mum, and now moving in with me, you might like to talk to someone."

He looked up, frowning under his long fringe. "Talk to someone?" he repeated. "Do you mean like a counsellor?"

"Well, yeah," I said. "A psychologist, maybe. Just to...talk about things." And wow, I was doing a great job of explaining, wasn't I?

"I thought you said I hadn't done anything wrong," Phoenix said, speaking to the nebula and not to me. I didn't blame him for not wanting to look at me. This was a bloody awkward conversation.

"You haven't!" I said quickly. "Seriously, you've been great. But with everything that's happened, it's a lot for anyone. And I want to make sure you get the support you need."

Phoenix chewed his lip. "It's no big deal."

"Maybe," I said. "But what do you think about just trying it out? Michelle told me she wished she had seen a psychologist or something when she was your age. Her parents moved away and left her and her sisters with her

Nana. So, she thought maybe it could be good for you." That wasn't exactly what she had said, but it was close enough.

"It's Michelle's idea?"

"Yeah," I admitted. "She's really smart. Smarter than me, that's for sure."

Phoenix huffed out a tiny breath of laughter. "You like her."

"She's a nice person," I ventured, unwilling to admit to too much. "You like her too, right?"

"She's cool." Phoenix gave a faint nod, his bangs falling from his eyes for a moment. "But you really like her. Like, in a girlfriend way."

"I don't know about that." And wow, that was a giant lie. I wondered what Phoenix's future psychologist would say about uncles who told enormous fibs to their teenage nephews. "She's not going to stay here forever, you know, so it's not like we can..."

"You still like her," Phoenix said it as though he was stating a fact, and it was me who was being obtuse.

"I guess I do," I said, ducking my head.

And that was true. I was starting to like Michelle way more than I should.

7 Michelle

"Like I said, this is just a quick catch-up to talk about how we'll manage until you're back at work," Martin said, scraping a hand through his thinning hair.

"I've got my laptop and reliable internet," I said, praying that the internet I had claimed was reliable didn't disappear at some point during this meeting. Australia's internet infrastructure appeared to have been constructed from old coat hangers and installed by a team of malevolent emus. "So, there's no real reason I can't work as usual. I can run all my regular meetings; do everything I'd do in the office—"

"But you won't actually be here," Martin interrupted. "It's not the same. Ash was just saying how different it will be not having you in the office."

"I bet he was," I muttered darkly but then forced a professional smile onto my face. "I've made a plan of how I'll cover my existing projects," I said smoothly. "Including that regression analysis for Solar Grid, and—"

"Actually, I'm going to put Ash onto Solar Grid," Martin interrupted me again. "We had a chat the other day, and he made some excellent points about how they'd prefer a local analyst. Someone they can meet with."

"I'm not going to be away very long," I said through gritted teeth. "I'd only be doing one meeting by video, maybe two at the most."

"Ah, but we don't know how long this strike will last." Martin shook his head as though it personally saddened him. "There's talk that the flight attendants might join in, and things will get even worse."

"I've heard it's going to be resolved in the next few days," I said, not mentioning that I had gleaned that piece of information from internet message boards and not any reliable news sources.

"But until you're back here, it makes sense to shift your bigger projects to the team," Martin said. "You just focus on looking after our smaller clients who don't expect as many face-to-face meetings. And besides," he said, puffing up his chest, "there are no small clients, only small analysts." He laughed, and it took considerable self-control not to flip him off.

But if I had flipped off a colleague every time I had wanted to, my career wouldn't have lasted ten minutes.

"I really feel I can continue to do my job as usual," I said, even though I knew it was useless. "With my current project load. I've always shown myself to be capable of—"

"Oh, it's not a question of capability." Martin waved a hand. "More of optics, you know? Ensuring our clients get what they're paying for. And that means someone here to meet with them whenever they need it."

"But everyone knows about the strike!" I let a little of my frustration into my voice. "This isn't normal!"

"All the more reason to give them a sense of normality," Martin said. "It's nothing personal, Michelle. When you're back, I'm sure we'll get you up to full speed again eventually."

Eventually. The word I had been fearing. This was going to be a setback, and I knew it. When it came time for my annual review and discussion of promotion opportunities, my record would show that I had been taken off my biggest projects. And no one would care about the circumstances; the strike would be long forgotten. What mattered was results, and I'd have nothing. And then I wouldn't get my next promotion, and my plan would be at least a year behind and—

"Thanks," I said, very ungraciously.

"Well, I'll leave you to it," Martin said. "I bet it's a nice day there in Sydney. Enjoy yourself, won't you?"

"I sure will," I lied and ended the video call.

"Dickhead!" I pounded my fist on the rickety kitchen table, making it wobble. It was a terrible temporary desk and deserved to bear the brunt of my anger. I couldn't help but feel like this was an insult to my abilities, and there I went again, taking it personally. Feeling like Martin thought I was stupid took me back to being that sad, bullied kid, sniffling behind a book I didn't understand. I knew that this was just shitty office politics, but it *hurt*. Hurt a lot more than it should.

For an hour, I tried to review my current projects and come up with compelling reasons why I shouldn't be chucked off them simply because the baggage handlers' union had gone on strike. In my anger at Martin, I was increasingly on the side of the baggage handlers. If their bosses were anything like him, I understood why they'd want to strike.

"To hell with this!" I said out loud, slamming my laptop shut. I couldn't concentrate due to my seething resentment. My brain kept coming up with revenge scenarios involving glitter bombs, three blow-up sheep, and a mariachi band for my so-called team back in Glasgow. And I knew, no matter how unfair it was, that even if I could come up with ten excellent reasons why I shouldn't have my projects redistributed, it wouldn't make a difference. I wasn't there to get in Martin's ear or run interference when the rest of the team had a go.

If I wasn't in the office, I might as well be invisible. Or dead.

Before the crisis in the aviation industry, I had planned to spend today on a tour of historic Sydney, ending in an afternoon pub crawl. But after my phone call with Martin, the last thing I felt like doing was making small talk with strangers. My sisters, having careers of their own, weren't free until the evening. I was all alone in Brekkie Beach, and I wasn't feeling quite desperate or brave enough to knock on Patrick's door and demand he cheer me up.

Even if my sisters had made excited shrieking noises when I had told them how he had taken my hand, just for a moment, in the middle of the linen department on our shopping trip.

What I needed was a distraction. Letting out a sigh, I made my way into the stuffy bedroom and rifled in my suitcase for the rom-com I had brought. Reading romance – especially the kind with naughty bits – was one of my guilty pleasures. Scratch that. It wasn't a guilty pleasure; it was just a pleasure. Being able to read for leisure was a privilege; I knew that better than most people.

In Glasgow, I usually read on my tablet while cycling on my stationary bike or when I was stuck on public transport. But for my holiday, I ordered an actual paperback. I had imagined myself sprawled on a beach towel, a pina colada in hand, blissfully whiling away the hours and lost in the story of people with more promising love lives than mine.

"I don't have a pina colada," I said aloud. "But I am going to read my book in the glorious sunshine, and I will enjoy it, damn it!"

Stuffing my newly purchased beach towel and a can of my favourite premixed vodka raspberry into my bag, I made my way out the door and towards the little park at the end of the street. Sitting at the top of the hill, it boasted glimpses of the ocean and far less foot traffic than Brekkie Beach itself.

And if I glanced towards Patrick's house and was pleased to see his car was in the driveway, well, sue me. I'd take my sparks of joy where I could get them on this crappy and infuriating day.

An hour later, I was settled on my towel and just starting to get into the story of a newly divorced woman getting the attention of a mysterious (and irresistibly sexy) local surfer. My vodka raspberry was empty and, although another one sounded like paradise in a can, I couldn't bring myself to walk back to the cottage and break the pleasant spell I was in.

Gently waving palm trees shaded me from the sun's fierce rays, and I had managed, with some difficulty, to finally get comfortable by wedging my bag into a kind of pillow shape. I wasn't going to move. Not for anyone or anything.

MICHELLE FINCH STICKS TO THE PLAN   131

"Michelle?"

I sat up abruptly. "Patrick!"

"Sorry, I didn't mean to scare you," he said, his smile bright as ever. I could see why the producers of *Outback Adventures* had chosen him. He was the iconic Aussie guy; sun-streaked blonde hair, a beach tan, sparkling green eyes, and a lazy grin that seemed to say 'no worries' without words.

"You didn't." I shook my head, even though he totally had. "I was just caught up with my book."

"What are you reading?" Patrick sat down on the grass beside me and tried to look at the cover. Immediately, I tucked it under the towel.

"Uh, something for work," I said, unsure why I had lied. Somehow, the idea of Patrick knowing I devoured romance novels was entirely too much like vulnerability. And besides, wouldn't it make me look kind of desperate? Damn it, I was feeling guilty over my pleasure again.

"I didn't know finance analysts needed to keep up to date on shirtless dudes." Patrick pretended to look surprised. "You learn something new every day."

"You saw." I scrunched up my face and retrieved the book. "It's a rom-com. A sexy rom-com."

"Why did you hide it from me?" Patrick looked genuinely confused. "You thought I'd judge you for reading a fun book on your holiday? I'm insulted you'd think that of me, Michelle."

"I didn't mean it like that," I said, feeling remorseful. "Dudes tend to give women a lot of shit for reading romance. I had an ex who used to tell me off for not reading something improving, like Proust. Dickhead. He never read Proust! But I like what I like, and it's nice just to...read." I couldn't tell him why enjoying reading was so important to me. Not yet, anyway.

"He does sound like a dickhead. But I'm not that kind of dude." Patrick shrugged. "Who doesn't love a good rom-com, anyway?"

"No one sensible," I said with a smile. "So, where's your smaller half?"

"Well, he found my old Xbox and told me he'd always wanted to try retro gaming. Do you have any idea how old that made me feel? Retro!"

"Kids these days, huh?"

"Good news is, he's on board with the idea of a psychologist," Patrick said. "Especially when he heard it was your idea."

"That's great!" I said, genuinely meaning it.

"Anyway, I decided to take a walk down to the beach, grab some coffee, and then head back to get to work on my next piece. It's just a coffee table, but the guy who ordered it supplied the timber. It's from his wife's grandad's farm; he arranged to save the tree before the place was sold."

"Now that's romantic," I said, rising to my feet. "Total romance novel stuff right there."

"I thought so," Patrick agreed. "You want to join me?"

I hadn't even realised I was packing my bag because my brain had decided, without making me aware, that I would join him. "If you don't mind. I had a horrible morning, so I kind of want to get out of my own head."

"Work stuff again?" Patrick asked as we made our way down the avenue that would take us to the main drag of Brekkie Beach.

"How did you know?"

"Just a guess." He gave me another flash of that smile that might have literally made him a million dollars. I didn't know how much five years of TV and a movie paid. But he deserved at least a million for that smile.

"The thing you have to know about my job is that it's super competitive. Everyone on my team is out for themselves, and they'd absolutely stoop to stealing someone's project out from under them if they could," I said, trailing my fingers along a picket fence.

"Sounds rough." Patrick raised his eyebrows.

"I'm used to it. Technically, my boss is supposed to stop that from happening, but he's..." I rolled my shoulders. "Not great. Anyway, he told me today that he's giving all my biggest projects away to my colleagues because, apparently, the clients won't be happy without someone on the ground. As if it matters! But they must have got in his ear, and now I'm screwed."

"That sounds...deeply unfair," Patrick offered. "All because you'll be away from the office for a few weeks? Haven't they heard of the remote work revolution?"

"Nope," I said with a sigh. "And frankly, I don't know how much work I'll even be able to do here. My kitchen table wobbles whenever I type, and my 5G connection drops out every five minutes."

"Well, I can fix one of those problems. I'll give you our Wi-Fi password; I've got NBN. Which is slightly less crap than 5G."

"Are you sure?" I asked, even though I was quivering at the thought of decent internet. "I'll only use it for work. No streaming movies or anything."

"I'm sure it can take a bit of streaming. So long as you're not using it to mine Bitcoin."

"If I was mining Bitcoin, I wouldn't be in this mess at work. I'd be...well, I actually was just lying around reading with a drink in my hand, but you get my point."

"So, if you had heaps of money, you wouldn't work?"

I paused. "Actually, I definitely still would. I've got this plan to make Partner at my firm by the time I'm thirty-three. And I've been working so hard to get there, and it's...it's really important to me that I achieve that." I looked away. "So, no, I wouldn't quit, even if I had a ton of money."

"Partner by thirty-three, huh?" Patrick chewed it over in his mouth. "That sounds impressive. But why thirty-three?"

"That's the earliest I can reasonably expect to do it. I've got it all mapped out; if I stick to the plan, I'll make Partner by thirty-three. And then I can actually have a life," I said, my hands waving of their own accord to emphasise my point. "You know, meeting someone, getting married. Having hobbies. A family."

"You can't do that stuff now?" Patrick was giving me a strange look.

"Not really," I said. "My hours are crazy, and it wouldn't be right to bring someone else into my life when I couldn't give them the attention they deserve. Like I said, it's important to me that I make Partner. I guess I'll feel like I've proven myself when I've done that. That I'm worthy or something." I couldn't explain the whole story to him; that was definitely too much vulnerability. Far more so than admitting I read romance. "This is the fourth time I've booked a holiday to see my sisters and the first time I've made it. And after how that's turned out, I don't know if I'd risk it again."

"Wow." Patrick let out a breath as we turned the corner and came up on the row of shops and cafés parallel to the soft waves and sun-bleached sand of Brekkie Beach. "That's a hell of a sacrifice."

"It's worth it," I said with a little nod. "I can wait. One day I'll get to do all that stuff. I hope."

"I think you deserve it now, Michelle," Patrick said quietly, and he was looking at me with an unexpected intensity. "Makes me kind of sad to think how much you're missing out on. I think you're worthy right now, Partner or not."

"I—" I didn't know exactly what I was going to say, and luckily, I didn't have to. At that moment, a man with a baby strapped to his chest approached us.

"You've gotta be Patrick Dalton!" he said, looking at Patrick with something bordering on awe. "Dude, I frigging loved *Outback Adventures*. Awesome show!"

"Thanks," Patrick said, smiling the smile I was starting to recognise he could switch on for fans. "Did you want a selfie?"

"Mate, I'd be stoked!"

· ♥ · ♥ · ♥ · ♥ · ♥ ·

"Yo, Michelle, let us in!" I snapped to attention, coming out of my computer-induced daze. I looked at my wrist. Was it really that late already?

Apparently, it was, judging by the fact that my sisters were banging on the rickety door and sounded like they might break it down if I didn't let them in.

"Pizza delivery!" Tessa said, hefting the boxes.

"She'd prefer a big sausage special from Patrick," Abby quipped. The two of them laughed like this was both witty and clever.

"I hope you brought wine. It's been a day."

"Seriously?" Abby frowned, following me into the house, where she caught sight of my laptop on the rickety table. "Why? You're meant to be on holiday!"

"I am on holiday," I said. "But things are complicated, with me being stuck here indefinitely. And I have to stay caught up with work, or—"

"Or what?" Abby demanded, putting the pizza boxes down on the table and producing a bottle of wine from her bag and then another.

"Or I'll be even further behind when I do get back," I said, shutting my laptop and putting it aside.

"You know, these plates are so old they might actually be collectable," Tessa said, examining the brown and orange crockery as she set out places for each of us. "We could steal them."

"I don't think my life circumstances necessitate pilfering crockery from an Air BnB. My day wasn't that bad." And it hadn't been, especially after Patrick had found me in the park. That had made my day a whole lot brighter. Not that I had any intention of telling my sisters that.

Abby flipped open a box to reveal super supreme with double pineapple, and my stomach growled in recognition. "Look!" she said proudly. "They made your special horrible pizza!"

"It's not horrible," I objected, helping myself to a slice. "Pineapple is the lord's work."

"No comment." Tessa held up her hands. "If you like it, that's what matters."

"I bet you'd say the same thing about heroin."

"Ooh, the slippery slope argument," Tessa raised her eyebrows and selected some chunky tumblers with scratches and chips for our wine. "Although, research has shown that the decriminalisation of drugs, even heroin, results in better community health outcomes."

"The same can't be said for pineapple on pizza," Abby said darkly, flipping the second lid to reveal a margarita with thick, oozing cheese and a few scattered basil leaves.

"Let me have my one source of joy," I said around a mouthful of rather greasy but still delicious pineapple-covered goodness. "I deserve it."

"Is it really that bad at work?" Tessa looked sympathetic, and she filled my tumbler to the very top as though that might make me feel better. It probably would. "I thought you loved your job."

"I do!" I said, choking down my mouthful and banging my chest as my oesophagus resisted the quantity of pizza I was shoving down, like a goose being force-fed to make Fois Graz. "Well, I love some parts of it. The research, the analysis, my beloved data. You know how much I love data."

"There is a distinct possibility that your one true love is a spreadsheet. The right pivot table could sweep you off your feet," Abby chuckled, her pizza folded into a sandwich in one hand.

"It's the people that suck." I took a greedy gulp of wine as though I could drown my vile colleagues and even worse boss with it. "Martin is useless as a manager; he just lets Ash and the others walk all over him. Never stands up for me, even though he and I both know I'm the best analyst on the team. Well, sometimes I feel like that. Sometimes I really don't."

"You need a different job." Abby nodded as though it was decided. "I've said it before, And—"

"You'll say it again," Tessa finished. "I know you've told us about how changing jobs will put you behind on the whole Partner track thing," she said, chewing thoughtfully. "But you've been unhappy with your team for a while now. Is it really worth it?"

"Of course it is," I said, nodding as firmly as Abby had, just to show I was no less adamant than she was. "It's what I've always wanted. You know why this is important to me. Both of you do. After everything when I was a kid, I just want to prove myself."

"I get that," Tessa said with a little sigh. "And it's not like I don't think it's a good goal, but I hate to see my sister unhappy because she feels like she needs to prove something."

"It's not just about that," I said, even though it really kind of was. "I mean, the money will be nice when I'm a Partner. Very nice."

"Money is nice," Tessa conceded. "When I got the advance for my second children's book, I bought a handbag I'd been eyeing off in Vogue for a year. Dylan offered to get it for me for Christmas, but it felt so good to buy something like that myself."

"But money's not worth your happiness," Abby said. "And neither is proving yourself when you're already so successful. Not when these arseholes don't appreciate you. I feel like every other day, you're telling us how some dickhead has spoken over you at a meeting or cut you out of a team-building event. It's a shitty culture."

"I'm sure all Big Four firms are the same. I just have to stick it out until I'm a Partner."

"But you don't know they're all the same." Abby was clearly feeling pushy tonight. "And who says you have to work for one of the Big Four anyway? I bet somewhere smaller might be more—"

"Because it's my goal!" I shot back at her, banging my tumbler down. "Partner at a Big Four firm by the time I'm thirty-three. And I'm on track! Or, at least, I was before the baggage handlers' union ruined my career. I'll stop talking about it if it bothers you so much."

There was a silence, broken only by the sounds of chewing and swallowing.

"I'm sorry," Abby said, reaching out to squeeze my hand. "I was pushing too hard, wasn't I?"

"I know it comes from a place of love," I said, giving my sister a wry grin. "But yes."

"I hate seeing you mistreated when you deserve so much better. You deserve to be happy. Right now, not after you make Partner."

"That's what Patrick said." The words slipped out before I thought about whether I wanted to share that particular nugget of information with my sisters.

"He did?" Tessa looked at me wide-eyed. "When?! Since when are you two having those kinds of conversations?"

"We weren't really," I said hastily. "We just bumped into each other at the park and grabbed coffee. No big deal." I decided to leave out the part about the romance novel.

"Yeah, sure it wasn't," Abby said. "So, when are you going to invite him over to make your holiday truly satisfying?"

"Never!" I said indignantly. "He's, like, a friend."

"A friend," Tessa repeated. "Oh yes, I know all about friends. Dylan and I were going to be friends. Look how well that worked out."

"You're into him!" Abby insisted. "You can't be friends with someone you're into. And besides, you were ready to go home with him that night at the pub! What changed?"

"I got to know him," I said. "A little, anyway. I can't have a one-night stand with him because he lives next door, and I don't know how long I'll be stuck here! And I know his nephew, and we've talked about stuff and... It's too complicated now."

"You mean you've got feelings, and so you can't sleep with him because you won't let yourself have relationships that involve actual feelings until you're a Partner," Tessa said. "I do listen; it just seems so..."

"Unrealistic?" Abby guessed.

"Sad," Tessa corrected. "I mean, what if you meet someone you really like? You're just going to ignore it because of bad timing? My timing was awful with Dylan! His dad was my boss, I was working on my anxiety, and he was having a quarter-life crisis. It might never have happened if we had waited until the timing was right."

"Even if I was going to date someone before I'm a Partner," I said, taking off my glasses and cleaning them on my dress. "It wouldn't be him. He lives in Australia, in case you haven't noticed. And I don't."

"You could," Abby said, but Tessa nudged her.

"So, you like him too much for a one-night stand?" Tessa asked. "Is that it?"

"It would be complicated," I said, refusing to say more. "Anyway, enough talking about men. Let me enjoy having my sisters around to my dump of a cottage to enjoy our pizza and wine. Let me pretend this is my real life for a night."

"It could be, you know," Abby said, and then she held up her hands. "Okay, I'll shut up about it! I'm just saying this could be your life. If you wanted it to be."

I just shook my head and helped myself to another slice. Abby had no idea how much I *wanted* this to be my life. But I wanted to make Partner by thirty-three more.

Didn't I?

8 Patrick

"April?" I repeated. "Nothing until *April*?"

"I could put you on the cancellation list," the receptionist said in a tone that implied she'd be doing me a huge personal favour and that I might owe her my firstborn in return. "But there's no guarantee anything will come up. Do you want me to schedule Phoenix Dalton for the first available appointment on the sixteenth of April?"

"I don't know if he'll still be with me then," I said, running my hand over my stubbly chin. I needed to shave; I had gone right past five o'clock shadow and into scruffy. And if I had a particular reason to avoid looking scruffy, I saw no reason to share it.

"Do you want me to put you on the list or not?" The receptionist sounded like she wanted to get rid of me.

"No," I said with a sigh. "I'll leave it." I paused. "Thanks." But she had already hung up.

"Is everything okay?" Phoenix entered the kitchen, helping himself to his usual glass of water. But today, he retrieved two slices of bread and stuck them into my temperamental toaster. Feeling comfortable enough to help himself to toast was progress, right?

"Uh," I stalled, wondering if I should lie but eventually deciding not to. "I was calling some psychologists. The waiting lists are insane! This woman just told me they've got nothing until April. April!"

"It's okay."

"It's not okay! I said I'd get this sorted for you. You need to talk to someone now, not in bloody April!"

"I don't mind," Phoenix said, looking into the toaster as though his constant monitoring would stop it from burning the edges while leaving the middles untoasted.

"But I do," I said, standing up. "I know you always say you don't mind, but you don't have to. I know that sometimes—" I let out a breath, running a hand through my hair. "Sometimes you feel like you have to say things are okay because you don't want to upset anyone. At least, I know I did when I was your age."

Phoenix was silent for so long that I wondered if I had rendered him mute. But finally, he spoke. "Because of Mum?"

"Sometimes," I admitted. "Your mum, she's—" I paused. "She's great. I mean, she can be so amazing. But she's sensitive. And my mum – your grandma – was the same. Didn't take much to upset her, so I learned to always be okay. It was easier."

Phoenix nodded at the toaster and was silent again. "I just don't want to make Mum feel bad."

"And that's very kind of you," I said. "But it's okay to speak up for yourself, too, you know? I mean, you're a teenager. You're supposed to talk back and rebel and stuff."

"Did you?"

"Well, not really," I confessed. "Not until later. After *Outback Adventures*. That was when I moved out, started my apprenticeship, and did a lot of stuff my mum wouldn't have approved of. I was making up for lost time, I guess."

Phoenix nodded.

"The thing is, I don't want you feeling like you can't say what you want or how you feel because you're worried about how it might make someone else react."

"And that's why you want me to talk to a psychologist?"

"Well, yeah," I said, putting the butter and vegemite on the table. "And there's other stuff. Like what it's been like living with your mum and why you've come to live with me. Because that's not easy."

"I have to talk about Mum?" Phoenix looked like he was debating with himself in his head. "And say bad stuff about her?"

"You don't have to say anything you don't want to," I told him. "And when you're talking to a psychologist, it's not like talking to a friend or to me. It's just about helping you to... I don't know. Understand your feelings? Crap, I'm not an expert on this. I wish I was."

The toast popped up, and Phoenix placed the two pieces (not too blackened, I was glad to see) on his plate. He hovered in front of the bench for a moment and then looked up at me. "Can I get out the peanut butter?" he suddenly asked.

"Yeah, sure," I said, raising my eyebrows. "Not in the mood for Vegemite?"

"Actually." He paused. "I don't like it."

I let out a chuckle. "Glad you told me," I said. "See, it's okay to say what you really think."

But Phoenix didn't say anything else as he took the jar of peanut butter to the table and began to spread it thickly across his toast.

· ♥ · ♥ · ♥ · ♥ · ♥ ·

An hour later, I was ready to admit defeat. I had called seven child psychologists recommended by the internet, and the best I had been offered was the possibility of late February. But that was six weeks away, long after school would have started. And Phoenix would be home by then. Wouldn't he? This was such bullshit. I was trying to do the responsible thing here – though I had almost zero experience in being responsible – and was being thwarted by the system.

I had no idea how to tell the poor kid that the psychologist thing was a bust, so instead, I busied myself sketching out the plans for an elaborate custom-built bar with secret panels for the rarest and most expensive whiskey. The timber alone would cost a small fortune, but the customer had told me no expense was to be spared on this project.

Chewing my lip and scrunching up another piece of graph paper, I looked over at my phone. Yep, there was a text message. I swiped my thumb and saw that it was from Michelle. And if my stomach tightened, well, it wasn't like I could control what my stomach chose to do about getting a message from the woman that I absolutely was not pursuing.

How's it going finding a psychologist for Phoenix?

Shaking my head, I sent back a response.

Not great. The soonest I can get him in to see someone is in six weeks. I don't know if he'll still be here then.

I pressed send and picked up my mechanical pencil again, but my phone rang before I could put the pencil to paper. And what's more, it was a—

Video call? Quickly, I ran my hands through my hair and cursed myself for not shaving this morning. I didn't want Michelle to see me looking scruffy, even on video.

"Hi," I said in a voice that I hoped sounded smooth as I answered the call.

"Six weeks!" Michelle's face filled the screen. Her hair was in a tight ponytail, and her cheeks were red. Judging by the background noise and her heavy breathing, she was at the gym. "Six weeks is ridiculous!"

"I thought I'd be able to get him in to see someone next week, maybe. He really needs it, even if he doesn't think so."

"Send me the list of who you called," Michelle said, panting slightly. The sight of her, sweaty and out of breath, was doing all sorts of things to my lower half that I was very glad weren't visible on the video chat. She looked *good*. Like, 'I want to lick the sweat from your collarbone' good. "I'll see what I can do."

"You don't need to do anything," I said. "Especially not now. Are you at the gym?"

"Yep," Michelle confirmed, tilting the phone to show me she was on an exercise bike. I was treated to a brief glimpse of her thighs, glistening with exertion as she furiously pumped the pedals. "I don't know how long I'll be here, so I figured I'd get a temporary membership. Cycling is my stress relief, and you know I need it."

"Makes sense," I said, passionately wishing I was still a gym member and could come up with an excuse to be there right now. Wait, did that make me a creep? I decided not to ponder that too closely. "But seriously, there's nothing you can do about the waiting lists. It's the same everywhere. One of them told me nothing until April!"

"Like I said, send me those names," Michelle repeated. "Let me have a crack at it. I know how to work systems; it's my job."

"That's really nice of you," I said, still staring at the bead of sweat trickling down Michelle's neck and towards her crop top. Was it going to slide down between her breasts and— Inappropriate erection. *Highly* inappropriate erection. "I mean, to do that for Phoenix. Really nice of you to do that for Phoenix."

"He's a good kid," Michelle panted. "Leave it with me, okay? I'd better go. I'm about to start the hill climb, and I won't be able to talk. Or breathe, actually."

I chuckled, but I didn't think a hill climb would defeat Michelle. Nothing could. "Thanks again."

The call ended, and I sat for a long moment, still wishing I had shaved. As much as I believed in Michelle's determination, I didn't think she'd have better luck than me in securing an appointment. After all, I was very charming when I chose to be. Did Michelle think I was charming, I wondered?

"Stop it," I told my crotch. "We are designing a bar, not thinking about Michelle. Because she's not thinking about me." Gritting my teeth, I forced myself to get back to work.

I was ready to give up on my sketch pad and go into the house and try to convince Phoenix of the benefits of a Maccas run for lunch, or even a good kebab, when my phone buzzed again.

`Michelle: all sorted. phoenix has an appointment with evan jacobs on friday at 6pm <smiley face emoji>`

I stared at my phone in wonder. How the hell had she done that? Quickly, I texted my thanks, but I knew I'd need to do something better than that to really show her how grateful I was.

And no, I didn't mean with my penis. Unless she explicitly asked me to.

Going into the house, I didn't see Phoenix in the kitchen. Which was to be expected. Teenagers didn't hang out in common areas; it was against their very nature. I listened at the bottom of the stairs, and I could just make out the familiar sound of someone battering hoards of the ravenous undead on my retro Xbox.

"Phoenix?" I asked. "Good time to pause?"

Phoenix was perched on the end of the neatly made bed, controller in his hands, his face contorted in concentration, and his long fringe pushed back. Bangs must be a severe hazard when you were trying to save the world from zombies.

"Just a moment," he said, leaning forward as though that might make the character on the screen run just a little faster. I watched as the heavily armed character on the screen threw a grenade at a somewhat pixelated hoard and then moved to a loot box. "Got to the save point!" Phoenix informed me, and then he paused the game. "Yeah?"

"You asked me to wait," I said, sitting on the other side of the bed.

Phoenix looked down at the controller that was still in his hands. "Sorry." His mouth puckered up.

"No, it was good," I said, giving him a grin. "Asserting yourself and all. Nice one!"

Phoenix shifted uncomfortably at the compliment, then he set down the controller. "Everything okay?"

"Yeah, better than okay, actually," I said. "We've got you an appointment for Friday."

"Really?" Phoenix blinked. "But you said they were all booked up."

"They were." I shrugged. "But Michelle got on the phone with them, and..." I paused, still wondering how she had made it happen. "Well, you've got an appointment now."

"She really did that?" Phoenix looked wide-eyed.

"She did," I confirmed. "She's a nice person, huh?"

"I think she really likes you," Phoenix said, something like a teasing smile coming over his face.

"Nah," I said, even though the thought had crossed my mind. "Must be you she's after, huh?"

"Gross." Phoenix wrinkled his nose.

"Not into older women, then?"

"No way," Phoenix confirmed, still looking horrified at the idea.

"Well, I was thinking I should do something nice for Michelle to say thank you," I said. "What do you reckon?"

"Definitely." Phoenix nodded. "You mean like flowers?"

"I was thinking something a bit better than that. Do you think the world can spare you from the brain-eating hordes?"

"Yeah?"

"Well, come down to the garage." I motioned to him. "And help me do something nice for Michelle."

· ♥ · ♥ · ♥ · ♥ · ♥ ·

"This is heavy," Phoenix told me, struggling as we made our way up the overgrown garden path.

"It should be. It's solid Tasmanian Oak."

"Do you think she's in there?" he asked, looking at the house curiously.

"Her light's on," I said. "So I hope so. It might be weird if we just leave it on the veranda. Actually, it might fall through. Pretty sure the decking's rotten."

"Yuck," Phoenix said, looking dubiously at the porch.

Before I could set down our burden, wipe the sweat from my (newly shaven) face, or knock on the door, it flung open to reveal Michelle standing there in her adorable glasses and a black dress that I guessed was made from linen. It was creased, but somehow even the creases suited her.

"Hi," she said, looking at the two of us with a bemused expression. "What's all this?"

"It's us saying thank you," I said, motioning to Phoenix to set the desk down and stepping back. "For helping with the appointment."

"It's a desk," Phoenix added helpfully. "For you."

"You got me a desk?"

"Well, you said the kitchen table was rickety," I said, suddenly wondering if this was too much. "And you'll be here for a while, so I thought..." I trailed off. "I had it mostly finished anyway. The customer changed their mind last minute, so it was just sitting there, and I thought maybe you could get some use out of it."

"That," Michelle said quietly, "might be the nicest thing anyone has ever done for me." One hand flew to her mouth, and holy shit, were those tears in the corners of her eyes?

"It's no big deal," I said, squaring my shoulders. "Like I said, it was mostly finished anyway, and you really helped us out."

"It's a huge deal," Michelle said, still staring at me like I was an entirely new type of being, something she had never even seen before, like a roller-skating unicorn or an honest used car salesman.

"I did some of the varnishing," Phoenix said. "We used the quick-drying kind, but Uncle Patrick says it's still good."

"It's beautiful," Michelle carefully made her way down the steps (a good idea, as they looked like they might crumble with the slightest breeze). Slowly, she ran one hand over the desk. "Does it have any secrets?"

"Just one." Despite telling myself I wouldn't do anything that could be construed as flirting, I took her hand in mine and guided it to a seemingly decorative raised piece of wood. Gently, I pressed her fingers against the just-varnished timber. A small drawer popped out, with just enough room for...

"Is that for whiskey?" Michelle looked up at me, her fingers were still touching mine. I should move my hand away, and yet...

"Yeah," I admitted. "I think the guy who ordered it might have a problem with alcohol. That's probably why he cancelled, to be honest. But you don't have to keep whiskey in there. You could keep, um..."

"Chocolate?" Phoenix suggested. "Or headache tablets. My mum takes lots of those."

I chose to let that comment slide for now, but it was definitely fodder for the psychologist.

"With my job, I might need to keep whiskey in there." Michelle raised her eyebrows, and she drew her hand back. "I should let you guys in; sorry to keep you out here on the horrible lawn."

"You can help him move it in, right?" Phoenix said, looking up at Michelle. "I kind of wanted to go and finish my game. *Rise of the Dead* is awesome!"

"Of course. You show those zombies who's boss!"

Phoenix waved as he clambered over the sagging fence, leaving Michelle and me alone.

"Do you get the feeling he's trying to set us up?"

"That kid might have seen *The Parent Trap* a few too many times." I shook my head, feeling the awkward tension in the air. "Lindsay Lohan is my sister's idol."

"That's a terrifying thought," Michelle let out a slightly forced laugh. "So, uh, we should get this in."

"Yeah," I said. "I'll do the rear—" I cut myself off. "I mean, I'll take the back end. Of the desk."

"Right," Michelle nodded, and I could see her cheeks were flushed. Could she feel it too, the tightness in the air between us? It was somewhere between red-hot sexual chemistry and the reign of Yertle, King of the Awkward Turtles.

"On three?" I asked, and together, we hefted the desk into the house. I could see Michelle had no trouble lifting her end of the desk. That must be from all the time she spent working out. And I was going to stop imagining that right now and force my brain to delete the image of Michelle, sweat glistening over her collarbone and down into her crop top. At least until I was alone, anyway.

"This is going to be amazing," Michelle said, running her hands over the desk again like she wanted to hug it. "Thank you so much for lending it to me."

"Well, it's yours if you can find a way to get it back to Glasgow with you." I wanted the desk to be hers, to keep for always, even if I couldn't have explained why. "But that might be tricky."

"I don't want to have to leave it behind," Michelle said regretfully, one hand on the desk and her eyes fixed on me. "When I go back to my real life."

"Your real life, huh?" When did my voice get so husky? I sounded like I was auditioning to be a voice actor for audio erotica.

"My real life," Michelle repeated, a little sadly. "Being here is…amazing, really. But it's not my real life. My real life is just work, cycling, sleep, repeat. Grind for that next promotion until…"

"Until you make Partner," I finished. "I hope that happens for you soon. I mean, I'm sure it will. You're so smart and dedicated, and…" I trailed off.

"Thanks," Michelle said quietly. "At least I'll be able to stay caught up, now I've got this." She patted the desk. "Seriously, thank you."

"And thank you for helping Phoenix and me," I said. "You're a...very kind person." And that sounded stupid, didn't it? "Uh, I'm glad you moved in next door. Except that this place is a dump. That I'm not glad about."

Michelle laughed. "Well, even when I'm living my fantasy life here in Brekkie Beach, I can't have everything, can I? Got to have something to drag me back to earth."

"You deserve the fantasy," I told her, then averted my eyes. That was too much. Too damn much. I was not going to let myself say things I couldn't unsay. Not when there was no chance of this going anywhere. "Uh, I should get going. I found another controller for the Xbox, and I need to show Phoenix how multiplayer worked back in the olden days."

"Oh, of course," Michelle said, nodding vigorously. "Uh, I guess I'll see you around?"

"See you around," I said and left the crumbling cottage before I said something stupid or did something even stupider.

MICHELLE FINCH STICKS TO THE PLAN

· ♥ · ♥ · ♥ · ♥ · ♥ ·

"He's going to ask lots of questions, isn't he?" Phoenix looked up suddenly, having been previously absorbed by absurdist Gen Z memes that made zero sense to me. What was wrong with LOL Cat, anyway?

"Probably," I said. "Especially the first time you meet him. Psychologists have to ask heaps of questions to understand your background, and what's going on in your life. Are you feeling nervous about that?"

Phoenix shifted in his seat. "Kind of," he said. "But thank you anyway. For setting this up. I know you did it because you care about me or something."

"Or something?" I repeated. "Of course, I care about you! You're my nephew, and even if you weren't, you're pretty awesome."

Phoenix ducked his head at the compliment, but I could see a tiny smile on his face.

"Anyway," I went on. "It's Michelle you should be thanking."

"I thought we already did, with the desk."

"Yeah, I guess we did," I said. "I just hope it's useful for her, you know? While she's here, anyway. You'll have to help me move it back when she leaves."

Phoenix was silent again for a while. "You don't really want her to leave, do you?"

I let out something between a cough and a laugh. I had never really cared whether a woman I was seeing would stay or go. I had never been interested in a relationship that lasted longer than a few weeks. There was always someone else, and I didn't want to be tied down with commitments. But now—

"I hadn't really thought about it."

But we both knew that was a giant lie.

9 Michelle

"The kitchen looks...better?" I said, wanting to say something nice even though the kitchen still resembled an active demolition site.

"No, it doesn't," Tessa snorted. "But it will. Marble benchtops, all the cupboard space I could ever want..."

"And pull-out drawers in the pantry!" Abby looked smug. "At my suggestion."

"Insistence, you mean." Tessa poked her. "But they are space-saving. Besides, it might stop you from rearranging things whenever you come over."

"I wouldn't do that!" Abby pretended to look shocked at the idea, one hand over her heart.

"Yes, you would. And you did when you last came to visit me. I still don't know what you did to my socks to make them sit up like that."

"I could show you..." Abby said, pretending to consider. "Or, you could see what I dug up." She pointed at the TV, a look of glee on her face.

"Oh no," I groaned, a horrible thought surfacing. "It's not our audition tape for *Stars in Their Eyes*, is it?"

"No!" Tessa looked horrified. "Dylan might leave me if he sees that. Abby, that stays locked in your hard drive until fifty years after my death. A hundred, if I have kids."

"It's not that!" Abby waved a hand. "Although, that does give me an idea—"

"What is it, then?" I plopped down onto the very comfortable sofa, taking the bowl of popcorn from the table and shovelling in a mouthful. I noticed that the coffee table, while clearly a nice hardwood and perfectly serviceable, was kind of bland. Nothing like the desk that Patrick had made for me. No, not made for me. Loaned to me from his garage. I needed to remember that and stop thinking about those strong arms with their bulging muscles as he sanded the wood and—

"This!" Abby flicked the remote, and a cheesy-sounding theme song began to play.

"What in the—" I began and then covered my mouth. "Is this...?" I saw a very familiar but much younger face appear on the screen, sporting an Akubra hat and a tan that must have required industrial quantities of bronzer.

"*Outback Adventures!*" Abby crowed, sitting next to me and pulling the popcorn into her lap. "When you told us

Patrick was Australian film and television royalty, I had to see it for myself. I've only watched the first episode. I saved the rest for our viewing party."

"I thought we were going to watch eighties rom-coms and call them out for their lack of diversity, harmful stereotypes, and perpetuation of rape culture," Tessa said, amusement clear on her face. "You do love doing that."

"I do," Abby agreed genially. "But this is way better. I mean, Michelle made out with a real-life movie star!"

"One movie," I said. "And it was made for TV."

"Still counts," Tessa said, contentedly popping a piece of popcorn into her mouth. "He's so cute! Look at his little face."

"And that must be his sister." Abby pointed at the screen, where an older teenage girl with the same blonde hair, green eyes, and bright smile was stomping around the bush in a pair of Blundstones and shorts that were probably inappropriate for an underage actress. "She's pretty."

"Shhh, I want to hear what's going on!" Tessa nudged her, sending popcorn spilling out over my lap.

"Abby, staying quiet during a movie?" I raised my eyebrows. "Not likely."

"Rude! You two love my commentary."

"Shut up, or I'm going to turn on the subtitles," Tessa threatened, gesticulating with the remote. "I want to see this!"

"I feel kind of weird watching this," I said after a few minutes, in which Julia saved Patrick from treading on a brown snake that apparently had a 'really gnarly nip, mate!'

"Why?" Abby turned to me. "Because he's a kid in this, and you kissed him?"

"No, because..." I shook my head. "I don't know. It feels like I should have asked his permission or something."

"That's ridiculous," Abby scoffed. "It's freely available! I didn't have to download a VPN and visit some seedy Eastern European website to get it. It's on frigging Netflix!"

"And besides," Tessa added. "Everyone in Australia has seen it. Dylan said that he and Tad used to do impressions of it all the time." She paused. "What a ripper, mate!" she said in her very best Australian accent, which was somewhere between Welsh, South African, and a drunken pirate's slur.

I laughed, in spite of myself. "You're probably right."

"Tell him now!" Abby nudged me. "Send him a text or something. Then it won't be weird when you see him."

I opened my mouth to argue, but it was a decent idea. I pulled my phone from my pocket, ignored the urge to check my emails, and focused the camera on the TV screen until Patrick's face appeared. He was chewing his lip, just like he did now, and those big green eyes were focused on something in the distance. "Crikey!" the young Patrick said. "Looks like a dust storm! We'd better take cover!"

MICHELLE FINCH STICKS TO THE PLAN 165

Chuckling, I snapped the picture and then wondered what to text. Finally, I tapped out a message.

Michelle: my sisters had an interesting choice for our viewing party today...

Biting my own lip, I sent it.

Almost immediately, my phone buzzed to tell me that I had received a reply. And if my stomach flipped over a few times, I wouldn't tell my sisters.

```
Patrick: crikey, that's a ripper
choice...
Patrick: ...please don't judge me,
michelle. i was young and needed the
money <winky face emoji>
```

I laughed out loud at that, and Abby turned to me, frowning. "Are you ignoring this to text a guy?"

"It doesn't count if the guy I'm texting is in the show!" I protested. "You told me to text him, anyway."

"It was your idea, Abby," Tessa reminded her. "Now, will you two please shut up? How will they get those wallabies to safety before the dust storm hits?"

Still smiling, I bent my head back over the phone.

Michelle: it's a lot of fun! i can see why you ran for five seasons. but i have to ask, did you have a paid product placement deal with whoever makes plaid shirts? <winky face emoji>

I waited and realised I was actually holding my breath. Quickly, I let it out. I was not going to let myself asphyxiate for a guy.

Another buzz. Another exasperated sigh and exaggerated eye roll from Abby.

```
Patrick: i'm contractually obliged
to deny that <angel emoji>
Patrick: so, are you going to be
watching me all night, or do you have
some decent viewing planned?
```

"Are we still doing that beach photo thing?" I asked, looking up from my phone.

"Yes," Tessa said. "Now, shhh!"

I considered myself shushed.

Michelle: actually, we're doing a beach photo shoot at sunset. i know how that sounds, but tessa's boyfriend is a photographer, and it's been a while since we've all been together

I paused, clenched my teeth, and then sent a very risky text.

Michelle: you should come down and watch <winky face emoji>

Immediately after I sent it, my heart rate rose to levels I was sure my smart watch would record as vigorous activity. Target heart rate zone? No problem!

There were so many reasons why it was a terrible idea, but I couldn't resist flirting with Patrick. Apparently, my body thought we had some serious unfinished business from the night at the pub, even if my brain insisted that he was just a friendly neighbour.

A buzz. A glare.

`Patrick: i'll do that. see you later`

And if I finished the episode with a big fat smile on my face, well, I was just enjoying the show.

· ♥ · ♥ · ♥ · ♥ · ♥ ·

"It's cold!" Abby complained, wrapping her arms around herself. "And you just had to insist on summer dresses, didn't you?"

"It was supposed to be warm!" Tessa threw up her hands. "And it's summer; I thought this would be aesthetic."

"It's kind of a nice change, the breeze," I said neutrally. "I mean, Glasgow is freezing. This is just balmy."

"Ladies, can you try to look like you actually want to be here?" Dylan stood up from behind the tripod.

"Sorry!" Tessa scrunched up her face. "Abby is apparently freezing to death. Like a tiny kitten lost in a snowstorm, knowing that every moment could be her last. Tragic, really."

"Okay, okay." Abby nudged her. "You've made your point." She wrapped her arms around each of our waists. "Do I look happy yet?"

"Kind of frightening, actually," Dylan said from behind the camera. "Just talk; I want this to be natural."

"Natural," I repeated, digging my bare feet into the wet sand. "Because I'm always doing beachy photoshoots in Glasgow."

"Hey, think of me!" Tessa said. "I'm the pale one. I look like a ghost on the beach!"

"A beautiful ghost," Dylan said. "You know, like the ones that lure men to their deaths."

"A woman in white?" Abby wrinkled her nose. "I don't think that's a compliment, Dylan."

"Oh, it is." Tessa looked pleased. "To me, anyway."

"Damn, if I had realised I was crashing a modelling shoot, I would have dressed up," a familiar voice said from somewhere to my left. I looked around and saw Patrick and Phoenix walking down the beach towards us.

"You invited him?" Abby hissed in my ear. "I thought this was sister time!"

"I'm glad you did!" Tessa whispered. "Bold move; I like it!"

"Will you two please shut up?" I murmured, trying not to move my mouth.

Abby, however, ignored me entirely.

"What a ripper, mate!" she called out, waving.

"I probably deserved that," Patrick said, grinning at the three of us. "I take it you enjoyed *Outback Adventures*?"

MICHELLE FINCH STICKS TO THE PLAN 169

"Oh, they did," Dylan said. "If the giggles were anything to go by. I'm Dylan, by the way. Just the hired help. And Tessa's boyfriend."

"Patrick," I watched as Patrick held out a hand with easy confidence. "And this is Phoenix, my nephew."

"Hey dude," Dylan said, as though unsure how to address Phoenix.

"Phoenix is interested in photography." Patrick put a hand on his nephew's shoulder. "So, I thought we'd come down so he can see how the magic happens."

At his words, I felt like the wind had been let out of my sails. Patrick had only come because Phoenix was keen on photography. That was very nice of him as an uncle, but I had imagined that my presence was the drawcard. Apparently not.

"I won't touch anything," Phoenix promised, his hands behind his back. "Just watch."

"You'd be welcome to try it out," Dylan said, giving Phoenix an encouraging smile. "I'll show you the settings and all of my lenses and—"

"Can we please get on with this before I turn into an iceberg and kill Leonardo DiCaprio?" Abby interrupted, and she actually looked like she was shivering. "I can't hold a smile if I'm getting hypothermia!"

"Okay, okay!" Dylan held up his hands. "Just try to look natural. Like you're having a good time. Patrick, got any tricks to make them laugh?"

I looked over at Patrick, and he gave me the tiniest wink. A tiny wink that sent a red-hot thrill burning through me, so hot I was surprised it didn't heat my apparently freezing sister.

"Crikey! You sheilas look hot to trot this arvo!" Patrick called out, using the exaggerated twang of his teenage self in *Outback Adventures*. "But watch out for the dingos. Could get gnarly!"

I couldn't help but laugh, and when Patrick mimed cracking a whip and warned us to steer clear of the crocs, the three of us could barely stay upright as we clutched each other in stitches.

"Just as good as I remember," Dylan said, looking at Patrick admiringly as he stepped away from the camera. "Seriously, you have no idea how much my mate Tad and I loved that show."

"Glad to be of service."

"Can I see the photos?" Phoenix asked, looking down at the camera on the tripod as though he would very much like to touch it but was being respectful.

"Sure!" Dylan said, and I noticed that Patrick, too, was craning his neck to see the pictures. I just hoped Dylan had captured my good angles...

...as if it mattered, given I was standing right there.

"We're done?"

"All done." Dylan nodded.

MICHELLE FINCH STICKS TO THE PLAN 171

"Finally!" Abby made for her bag and pulled out a parker, wrapping herself up like a sad and puffy snowman.

"Did you bring that thing with you from England?" I asked, trying not to laugh again.

"Yes," Abby said, zipping it up to her chin. "They don't make decent coats here. The one downside of Australia."

"Do we get to see these photos?" Tessa asked, looking over at Dylan.

"Sure," Dylan said. "Let's go back up to the house, load them on a decent-sized screen. And maybe get some hot chocolate for Abby. And a heated blanket."

"I know you're teasing me, but if there's even the slightest possibility you have a heated blanket, I want it," Abby said, still shivering. "My feet! They're blue!"

"We'll head home," Patrick said, steering Phoenix with one hand. "Maybe catch you later, huh?"

"Definitely," I said, looking right at him.

He gave me a little wave and headed back up the beach, Phoenix in tow.

"I can't believe you met Patrick Dalton at the pub on your first night here." Dylan looked longingly at Patrick's retreating back. "You're a lucky girl, Michelle."

"He's definitely into you," Abby declared. "Came all the way down here just to say hi, and watch you get your photo taken."

"No way," I disagreed, even though I wished it were true. "Phoenix, is into photography. And it's like a five-minute walk! No big deal."

Dylan whispered something in Tessa's ear, and she let out a shriek of glee that startled the seagulls milling around an abandoned packet of chips nearby.

"What?" I demanded. "What happened?"

"I hope you weren't thinking I could keep that a secret." Tessa looked at Dylan, and he laughed, his eyes crinkling fondly as he looked at her.

"Nope." He shrugged. "You can tell them."

"What is it?" Abby's hands were on her puffy hips. "Can you just spit it out so we can get out of here, and I can defrost? Your hot tub better be ready; I'm going to boil myself like a Christmas Pudding."

"Patrick asked Dylan to send him the photo of Michelle on her own." Tessa's smile was so wide it was in danger of splitting her face in two.

"What?" I let out a breath, not wanting to believe it. "Why?"

"Why do you think?" Tessa was bouncing from one foot to the other in an ecstatic dance. "Because he really likes you, idiot!"

"That sounds like a major sign he's got feelings," Abby said between chattering teeth.

"Maybe the lighting was just really good," I said. "You know, for Phoenix to see as an example."

"Oh, Michelle!" Tessa was indignant. "You can't come up with a logical explanation for this. He likes you!"

"He's liked plenty of women." I shook my head, even as my whole body tingled at the thought that famous Patrick Dalton, who could – and had – have anyone he wanted, had asked for that photo of me. "It doesn't mean—" I coughed, trying to break the tingly excitement inside me. "Anyway, I'll be leaving soon. It doesn't matter."

"What it means is you should be enjoying him while you're still here," Abby told me. "When will you ever have the chance to bang Australian royalty again?"

"She makes a fair point." Dylan hefted his tripod over one shoulder. "If my sexual preferences were different, I'd definitely bang him."

"I don't know whether to be worried or kind of aroused," Tessa said, looking up at him fondly.

"The only thing we should be worrying about,' I said, "is defrosting Abby. Let's get going."

But as we made our way up the slippery sand, all I could think about was whether my sisters – and Dylan – were right. Should I let myself enjoy Patrick while I could…

…or was that simply too dangerous?

· ♥ · ♥ · ♥ · ♥ · ♥ ·

During dinner at Tessa and Dylan's house, I had been introduced to an Australian classic; a burger featuring both beetroot (revolting) and pineapple (sublime, obviously). But I couldn't give the burger anything like the attention it deserved.

I kept looking at my phone, wondering if I should text Patrick and hoping he would text me instead. When I returned to the crumbling cottage, I had a firm conversation with myself in the bathroom mirror.

"Text him," I said to myself, pointing a finger. "Text him but do NOT mention that he wanted that photo of you."

My reflection looked suitably pepped by the talk, and I grabbed my phone.

Michelle: thanks for coming down today. dylan definitely got a kick out of meeting his childhood hero <laughing emoji>

I pressed send and then stared at my phone as though expecting it to do something exciting.

And strangely enough, it did.

```
Patrick: it was a lot of fun. i got
to reprise my most famous role, what
more could a washed-up actor want?
<winky face emoji>
```

MICHELLE FINCH STICKS TO THE PLAN

A moment later, the phone buzzed again.

`Patrick: i'm having a drink on the deck. want to join me?`

Joining Patrick for a drink sounded dangerous. Very dangerous indeed. But my fingers seemed to totally ignore this fact as I sent back a reply.

Michelle: be right there

As I got ready to leave, I checked that my photo shoot makeup was still in place, brushed my hair, and grabbed a few cans of my preferred sugar-free vodka raspberry premix from the fridge. If Patrick didn't judge me for reading romance, I was sure he wouldn't care that I had terrible taste in alcohol.

When I hopped awkwardly over the back fence, my dress riding up higher than was appropriate, Patrick was waving at me from the deck. He was bathed in the soft light of an electric lantern, making his skin glow almost gold. It was like a tourism ad for Australia; Patrick, in his denim shorts and t-shirt, enjoying what looked like a whiskey on the rocks and looking down over the water.

"Hi," I said, smoothing my dress down and taking a seat opposite him. Sitting next to him would have been too much, right?

"Hey." Patrick shot me that famous smile, but his crinkled eyes proved it was genuine. "So, how did the rest of the photos turn out?"

"Good enough that Abby forgave us for making her recreate Disney's *Frozen* this afternoon," I said, pulling a can of my sickly-sweet premix from my bag. "Oh, and this is the part where I tell you I can't stand beer. I'll never be a true-blue Aussie, huh?"

"I don't think you can pass the citizenship test without sculling a schooner of VB," Patrick said sadly. "It's not looking good for you."

"Guess it's a good thing I'm just a visitor, then," I said, popping open my can and taking a long sip.

"Actually, I don't drink beer very often," Patrick ventured. "Carbs, you know."

"You don't eat carbs?" I frowned. "Ever?"

"Well, sometimes I do. But generally, I try not to. It helps me stay in shape and that stops the magazines from talking about how I've gone from outback adventurer to pie-eating champion."

I bit my lip, pausing before I asked the next question. "Has that ever happened to you? Magazines publishing photos, talking about your body?"

Patrick shifted uncomfortably. "Less than it used to," he said finally, with a grimace that told me he didn't want to talk about it. Instead, he sniffed the air. "Is that a vodka raspberry you've got? Man, that smell brings back memories."

"Good ones?"

"I'm not sure," Patrick said, rolling his shoulders. Those shoulders should definitely be listed as one of Australia's top ten tourist attractions. His biceps could take another spot. The Sydney Opera House could move down the list, as far as I was concerned. "Julia used to like them."

"Ah," I said softly. "I guess that could be...complicated."

"You've never asked me about her," Patrick said, shifting in his seat, so he was leaning both forearms on the table and looking right at me, an intensity in those green eyes. "And I bet you must be curious about why I'm looking after Phoenix."

"I didn't think it was my place to ask. I mean, families can be complicated. And I figured if you wanted to tell me, you would."

Patrick's face showed a small, rather sad smile. "I appreciate that," he said quietly. "She's...well, she's troubled, I guess. After *Outback Adventures*, she moved to Los Angeles, trying to make it big, you know?"

I nodded. I could imagine a starry-eyed Julia thinking she'd be sure to become a star in a matter of weeks. "It didn't go that way?"

"No," Patrick agreed. "When she came home, she was pregnant with Phoenix. I don't know much about the dad. He was older and, apparently, it wouldn't have been a good look for him to have an illegitimate child with a young actress. He pays a shit ton in child support so long as she doesn't go around shooting her mouth off."

"Shit," I said. "That sounds rough. Does Phoenix know?"

"Sort of," Patrick said. "She hasn't told him much. But he's a smart kid; I think he's probably figured it out. They live very comfortably, even though Julia doesn't do more than the occasional commercial these days. I think she's still waiting for her big break, honestly."

"That must be really hard on her," I said, thinking of a young woman whose dreams had turned into the mundane reality of single motherhood.

"It is," he said. "But she doesn't make it any easier on herself. Julia's always been so up and down. She'll go through these phases of working out three hours a day and drinking nothing but green juice. Then she'll meet a guy and be on top of the world. Then it ends, and she'll fall off the wagon, drinking and worse. When that happens, she's in bed for days, crying about her life being a failure and..." He shook his head. "I feel bad for her. Honestly I do, but it makes me so angry sometimes thinking about how it's been for Phoenix. Seeing all that."

"Bloody hell," I murmured. "I had no idea. I mean, I knew there must be something. I didn't think it would be like that, though."

"Phoenix doesn't like to talk about it," Patrick said, looking suddenly more tired than I had ever seen him. "I just hope he's been telling that psychologist you found him."

"You found the psychologist," I demurred. "I just helped with the scheduling."

"I'm not even going to ask how you did it." Patrick raised his eyebrows. "You know, until he came to stay with me, I hadn't even seen Phoenix in three years. Can you imagine that? Packed off in the middle of the night to someone who's practically a stranger?"

"I mean, you're not a stranger," I said. "I can see how much you love him. But yeah, that sounds traumatic as hell for the poor kid. Did your sister—" I stopped, unsure if I should ask.

"Cut me off from seeing him?" Patrick finished, and he took a sip of his drink. "Yep," he confirmed. "And you know why? Because the last time he was here, he asked if he could stay with me. Permanently."

I felt like my insides had deflated as a massive wave of sympathy went out to the teenage boy who was probably massacring zombies inside the house. "Oh, shit," I whispered. "I mean, I can see why he'd want to, but..."

"Julia was furious," Patrick told me. "Said that I was trying to steal her son, just like I'd taken everything else from her. I don't know exactly what that means, but I guess she's always been jealous that I didn't want an acting career and that I've been happy just doing my own thing after *Outback Adventures* was over. That's all I wanted, to live my own life without commitments or responsibilities. I think she's jealous of that, too."

"I don't want to say anything bad about your sister," I said, biting my lip. "So, I'm not going to. But wow, that's rough for Phoenix."

"And he's just had to put up with all of it." Patrick sighed. "I don't know if he would have been better off staying here, even if she had agreed. I mean, I'm..." He looked right at me then, his eyes dark in the soft light. "Well, I've been living pretty selfishly. Not exactly a family man."

Immediately, an image flashed into my head of a parade of women – each more gorgeous than the last – going through Patrick's front door and out again like they were on a conveyer belt. I had been under no illusions about how Patrick spent his free time. It wasn't like I was judging him. Of course not. But the thought of him with other women made me want to throw up my vodka raspberry all over the outdoor table that Patrick had probably handcrafted with those strong, calloused hands of his.

"I don't think that matters. I mean, it's not like you would have paraded your private life in front of him, right?"

"Of course not," Patrick said firmly. "But still, could I really be his full-time guardian? Like, be his *dad*?"

"Yes," I said the words without even thinking about it. "Because I've seen how much you care about him. How hard you try to connect with him. And you don't push him, you give him space." I took a breath. "You could definitely do it. And you'd do a good job."

"I don't know about that. But it's nice of you to say so," Patrick said, taking another sip of beer. "Anyway, it doesn't matter. Julia would never allow it, and I don't think he'd even want it now."

"But would you do it?" I had to know. "I mean, like you said, you like your freedom. And that would be one hell of a commitment."

"It would be. But yeah, I'd do it." Patrick was adamant, nodding slightly so that his tousled hair caught the light of the lantern and flickered white and gold. "Of course I would. Might put a dampener on my personal life, but what can you do?"

"I think the right woman—" I swallowed, feeling a lump in my throat. "The right woman wouldn't mind at all. She'd be proud to be with someone who'd step up like that for his nephew."

"I haven't been looking for the right woman," Patrick admitted. "Not for something long-term. I just never..." He paused. "My mate Khalid – you know, from the pub – always said one day I'd meet someone who'd change my mind. I didn't believe him, but—"

And just as I was waiting to find out what was coming after that all-important 'but', my phone rang. I let out a groan and pulled it out of my pocket.

"Work?"

"Yes," I admitted. "I don't want to take it, but..."

"But you have to," Patrick completed my sentence.

"I do," I admitted. "And it's a bloody video call! Do I look okay? Like a professional who hasn't been knocking back cans of vodka raspberry?"

"You look perfect," Patrick said, and then he turned his head away. "I'll leave you to it."

Before I could say anything, he went inside, and I was left alone on the deck with my still-buzzing phone.

And as I swiped over the screen to reveal Martin's flustered face, I was left with one thought.

I had *never* resented work so much as tonight.

10 Patrick

"So, I've got you booked for another session with the psychologist next week," I said to Phoenix as we made our now customary pilgrimage to Nick and Nikki's for a flat white, iced chocolate, and the chance to make fun of their experimental baked goods. "Is that okay? I mean, do you want to see him again?"

Phoenix looked down at his new Nikes, scuffing his feet along the path. "I guess so," he said. He was silent for another moment, and then he spoke. "Mum called me last night."

"She did?" I was careful to keep my tone neutral and not ask him why she hadn't bothered to even text me. "How's she going?"

A shrug. "She sounded...okay. But she said she's still not feeling good."

"I'm sorry to hear that," I said cautiously. "You must be worried about her."

"I guess." Phoenix was still studying his sneakers as we made our way down the pavement. "But she's with Nan, so it's not like there's no one to look after her." He paused again. "I didn't tell her about Evan."

"You think your mum wouldn't like it?"

"I don't know," Phoenix said in a voice that belonged to someone much older. "But I didn't want to upset her or something. So, I didn't tell her."

"I get that."

"She didn't say when I could come home." Phoenix looked up at me then, brushing his long fringe from his dark eyes. "I don't know how long you'll have to look after me."

"It's not that I have to," I said quickly. "I like having you here. You're welcome as long as you want, you know that. Or at least, I hope you do. However long you need to stay, I'm happy." I paused. "School starts in a few weeks, right?"

"Yeah," Phoenix said slowly. "Do you think I'll be home by then?"

"I don't know," I admitted. "But if not, the high school here's pretty good. Dylan, you remember, the photographer? He went there."

"You mean I could stay?" Phoenix stopped walking, and he was looking right at me. "For school and stuff?"

"Of course, you can, mate," I said. "Look, I get that everything's complicated with your mum and..." Damn it, I wanted him to know this. "But you've always got a home here with me. Even if you're twenty-five and sitting on my couch playing Xbox all day."

That made Phoenix smile slightly, and he started walking again. "Thanks, Uncle Patrick," he said, his eyes once again on his shoes. "But I don't think Mum would like that. When she gets better, she'll want me to come home and I..." He seemed to chew over his words. "I don't think it's good for her to be alone."

And that just about wrenched the heart right out of my chest. How could my fourteen-year-old nephew think it was his responsibility to look after his mum? He should be thinking about Xbox, boobs, and those weird memes he liked, not this stuff. He was just a kid! I was the one who should be taking on adult responsibilities, even if I had been avoiding doing that all of my adult life.

"She's got your grandma. It's not all on you."

"But she's my mum," Phoenix shot back, something defensive in his voice.

"I know, mate," I said, letting out a tiny and hopefully inaudible sigh. "And we don't know what's going to happen, do we? But you'll have a bedroom here, even if it's just for a weekend or something. You've even got your own sheets."

"Yeah." Phoenix nodded. "I guess so."

"Anyway," I said, forcing myself to sound cheerful. "Do you reckon I should try one of those charcoal and algae brownies they've got at Nick and Nikki's?"

Phoenix wrinkled his nose. "They look gross."

"They totally do. Maybe I'll just stick to coffee."

"Coffee's gross too," Phoenix told me, a faint smile returning to his face. "Adults are so weird."

"We are, dude," I agreed, clapping him on the shoulder. "We really are."

· ♥ · ♥ · ♥ · ♥ · ♥ ·

"I'm here, and I've got chicken for lunch!" Khalid called out as he came into the kitchen, hefting a bag that smelled heavenly. I was supposed to be fasting today, but I knew that chicken was going inside me.

"Do you think my cupboards are bare, like Old Mother Hubbard or something?" I gave him a one-armed hug. "I do have food, you know."

"Boring food." Khalid dumped the plastic bag on the table. "This is from that amazing Portuguese place down in Balgowlah, and yes, I got chips too. And flatbread."

"You know how I feel about that flatbread," I said, opening the bag and taking a deep sniff. "Why would you do this to me? I thought we were friends."

"It won't kill you to have one!" Khalid prodded my admittedly flat stomach with one finger. "Eat the carbs! You know you want to!"

"Why don't you eat carbs, anyway?" Phoenix appeared in the kitchen. "Are they bad for you? Is it okay for me to eat them?"

"Of course it's okay for you to eat them," I said, feeling like an arsehole. The last thing I wanted was to pass on my issues with bread and its delicious cousins to my nephew. "You're a growing teenager. But adults don't need them as much."

Phoenix wrinkled his nose. "Okay."

"You should definitely eat the bread," Khalid told him. "And chips, too. Your uncle is just being silly. It's not like one flatbread is going to ruin your chiselled physique, dude!"

"Fine, I'll eat the bread," I said, like it was no big deal. I pulled a flatbread from the bag and took a bite. Pure unadulterated carbohydrate goodness melted over my tongue, like god himself had wanted me to eat it. I'd get some extra cardio in later, but it was definitely worth it.

"Good man." Khalid nodded, and then turned his attention to Phoenix once more. "That's a cool t-shirt."

The t-shirt in question was one that I had bought him, with help from Michelle. It was black and featured an astronaut floating through the galaxy with the words 'I need my space' printed underneath. It was, undoubtedly, cool.

"Uncle Patrick got it for me," Phoenix said, going to the cupboard and taking out plates without being asked. I wondered how many times he had set the table and got his own dinner, all the while wondering if his mum was going to get out of bed. It made me want to shake my sister and tell her that I was very sorry that she was sad, but she needed to make a goddamn effort for her kid.

"Really?" Khalid scoffed. "Since when does he have any fashion sense?"

"Michelle helped," Phoenix said, returning to the cutlery drawer while I pulled glasses from the cupboard. "Do we need knives and forks?"

"Wait, hold up!" Khalid held up a hand. "Michelle helped you? Michelle as in pub Michelle? As in staying next-door Michelle? Why didn't I know you guys were going on little shopping adventures together?"

"Did I forget to mention that?" I said in an unconvincingly casual voice. The truth was, I hadn't told Khalid about 'hanging out' with Michelle – or how it had made me feel – because I knew he'd make a big deal about it. Because I didn't exactly hang out with women I had attempted to sleep with. Or had actually slept with. And I definitely did not do sickeningly domestic things like choose duvet covers and six-packs of socks with them.

MICHELLE FINCH STICKS TO THE PLAN 189

"You bloody well did!" Khalid looked aghast. "I can't believe you! I don't think you deserve any chicken." He held the Styrofoam container against his chest as though protecting it.

"Please," I begged, my face contrite. "I'll tell you everything. I swear. I need that chicken. I'd sell my soul for that chicken."

Khalid broke out into a grin. "Gees, mate, you don't have to break out the puppy dog eyes. Let me guess, fasting day?"

"Yep."

"Then we need to eat. I bet you're hungry too, Phoenix?" Khalid rubbed his hands together as he sat down.

"Yeah." Phoenix nodded. "I'm definitely hungry."

When every bit of chicken had been consumed, and only a few grains of rice salad remained, Phoenix disappeared upstairs, muttering something about a flame thrower. I really hoped it was part of the Xbox game.

"So," Khalid said, stretching out his long arms. "Michelle."

"Michelle," I repeated. I wasn't going to make this easy for him.

"I take it she's your next-door booty call until she heads home, right? Man, how lucky are you? You ghost some girl at the pub, she turns up next door, and she's still down to clown! Convenient, right?"

"No booty calls. We've just been...kind of hanging out."

"Kind of hanging out?" Khalid looked flabbergasted. "That's a straight-person euphemism for dirty nasty sex, right?"

"No!" I said. "Look, I apologised to her, and she was nice about it. And now she's stuck here, and we've been...hanging out. She's great with Phoenix; she helped me take him shopping and even arranged for him to get in to see a psychologist sooner than April. I told you about that!"

"You didn't tell me she was involved!" Khalid made it sound like I had betrayed him. I was Brutus, stabbing his poor Caesar in the crowded forum. "You've been talking to her about psychologists and Phoenix and stuff? That's wild."

"It's not wild," I objected. "We're neighbours. Friendly neighbours."

"Mate." Khalid was being patient now. "I've known you a long time. You meet a woman, sleep with her, and move on. Satisfaction guaranteed for all parties, no bullshit, no expectations. But you never," he pointed a finger at me, "hang out. Not like this. So, what's different about her? And why the hell aren't you sleeping with her?"

"I've been busy with Phoenix."

Khalid made a sound of utter disbelief. "He's not two, Patrick," he said. "You could have gone over after he was in bed, no trouble. Why didn't you?"

MICHELLE FINCH STICKS TO THE PLAN   191

"Because it's..." I sighed. "Complicated. I mean, she's living next door, right? If I slept with her, I'd need to see her again. And that'd be awkward."

"Not really." Khalid shrugged. "I mean, she's going home soon, so I don't get why you two aren't taking every possible opportunity to do the horizontal lambada. You had pretty great chemistry at the pub. I thought you'd be frothing at the chance to take care of unfinished business."

"Well, it didn't work out that way," I said. "I don't know what to tell you."

"Good, because I know what to ask you," Khalid said, still pointing his finger. "You like her, don't you? I mean, really like her. As in dinners and flowers. As in quiet nights in with wine and crime dramas. As in meet the parents. As in—"

"I get the picture," I interrupted, irritated. "And yeah, of course, I like her. She's a nice person."

Khalid rolled his eyes so hard I was surprised that his pupils returned to their original positions. "Don't bullshit me, Patrick Dalton. You *like* her. You want to sleep with her and see her again the next day."

"What if I do?" I threw up my hands. "Would that be such an awful thing? You always said I'd meet someone I really liked one day. You were right!"

"It's not awful at all." Khalid was beaming. "It's wonderful! So why the hell haven't you done anything about it? You realise that banging her doesn't prevent you from seeing her again, right? You've had so many one-night stands you might not know! But your dick doesn't actually banish women from the vicinity. Or, if it does, we've got a more serious problem on our hands."

"Did you forget the part where she's going back to Glasgow as soon as the baggage handler strike is over? So, if something were to happen between us, then...then it'd be over before it had even begun. And I think that—" I stabbed a finger onto the table. Khalid was clearly rubbing off on me. "Sounds pretty shit."

"Ah," Khalid said, and he steepled his fingers under his chin. "So, you think it's better not to start it because you won't be able to say goodbye?"

"Not like that," I grunted, even though it wasn't far from the truth. "Just, why start it when it's going to be over so soon?"

"Because it might be the most magical and fantastic time of your life and change everything?" Khalid said it like this was completely obvious. "Things don't have to last forever to be worthwhile, Patrick."

"It's a bad idea." I stood up and began to stack the plates. "I can't let myself get entangled with someone right now. I've got to think about Phoenix. And besides, Michelle might not even want—"

"Oh, I don't think you should worry about that," Khalid said smoothly. "I saw how she looked at you in the pub. She's on the hook; just reel her in." He mimed reeling in a fishing line with all the expertise of someone who had spent their youth in drama class and amateur theatre. "Look, why don't you see if she wants to 'hang out' tonight? I'll chill here with Phoenix; I love killing zombies!"

I paused. That was a very tempting suggestion. So far, my time with Michelle had been accidental, all very casual. The chance to spend time with her, take her out, and have her all to myself was...very tempting, actually.

"Maybe," I said. "I'll think about it. But can we just drop it for now? Why don't you tell me about that client you were having trouble with? The guy with the ruby earring and the tuna breath?"

"Fine," Khalid snorted. "But only because I've got a great story about the earring and the breath."

·♥ · ♥ · ♥ · ♥ · ♥ ·

After much prodding from Khalid, I sent Michelle a message that I hoped sounded casual.

Patrick: are you busy tonight? i thought i could show you some parts of sydney that visitors don't usually see. no worries if not

Khalid was convinced I should end the message with *i'd love to see you* and not *no worries if not*, but in the end, my fingers were stronger than his and my elbows much sharper, so I won the battle.

And Michelle had replied, too, almost immediately.

`Michelle: sounds great. what time?`

Khalid had been satisfied, Phoenix had seemed perfectly happy with the offer of a multi-player partner and a pizza, and now I was gripping the steering wheel more tightly than usual with Michelle by my side in the SUV.

"So, where are we going?" Michelle asked, looking out the window. "I don't know why I'm checking for signs; I have no idea what a Woy Woy is. Are we going there?"

I chuckled and relaxed my grip slightly. "Not quite," I said. "But it's near Woy Woy. It's a bit of a drive, but we should get there just at sunset. It will be nice."

Michelle made a sound of frustration that sounded a lot like a different sort of sound. The sort of sound that made my best jeans just a little too tight. I really hoped she wasn't looking. Or did I?

"Okay, okay!" I said, laughing a little too loudly. "We're going to the Hawkesbury River; it's up towards the Central Coast. Everyone in Sydney's all about the beaches and the harbour, but the Hawkesbury's pretty spectacular, with bushland and national parks on both sides.

"That sounds pretty." Michelle tilted her head.

I turned off the highway and towards a sign that read 'Mooney Mooney'. Michelle pointed and laughed out loud. " You Aussies have got to be having a joke with your place names. Mooney Mooney, seriously?"

"Come on, you're from England! You've got places like..." I searched my brain, and an internet listicle I had once read supplied examples. "Shitterton and Bitchfield."

"I hear Bitchfield is lovely in May. The bitches are in full flower."

"I'll take your word for it."

"So, what's so special about Mooney Mooney?"

"It's not Mooney Mooney we're going to," I said, recognising that the name sounded more ridiculous the more you said it out loud. "It's nearby. There's this big privately owned estate, and it's..."

"Yes?" Michelle was almost bouncing out of her seat.

"You don't like surprises, huh?"

"No." Michelle shook her head. "I like to have all the facts and all the information and make sensible plans based on those. You're lucky I came out tonight without a written itinerary."

I laughed, but my breath caught in my throat as I snuck a look at her in the passenger seat. No glasses tonight, but she looked perfect in her tight jeans and a little camisole that showed off the curves of her body, including that glorious path where I had wanted to follow a certain drop of sweat with my tongue. And I needed to stop thinking about that or I was going to crash the bloody car.

"Fine," I said. "It's where we filmed a lot of *Outback Adventures*, actually. Some of it was on location, way out west, but mostly, it was right here. I don't know, I thought it would be cool for you to see it. And it is beautiful."

Now that I was telling her, I had to wonder if this was a good idea. Did I seem like a conceited arsehole, taking her to see the location of my former fame? Or worse still, did she think I was pushing the whole 'I'm lowkey famous' thing as a ploy to get into her pants? As much as I would like to get into said pants, I knew that was a bad idea. So, what was I doing here? Taking out a friend? A neighbour?

"That's so cool!" Michelle interrupted my stream of thoughts. "It looks so beautiful in the show. Nothing like England, with our bloody green hills and picturesque cottages. I'm sick of cottages."

"I hope it's worth the trip. It's pretty spectacular at sunset. And there's a place not too far away where we can grab a bite to eat." The place in question was, in fact, an upmarket restaurant where I had booked a table, but Michelle didn't need to know that. That sounded too much like a date. Which this wasn't.

"I'm seriously a fan of this idea," Michelle said with a little nod. "I bet Abby and Tessa haven't been out here. Ha! I'll know Sydney better than them."

"A true local."

"I wish I could be," Michelle said, a little wistfully. "I've put in for a transfer to the Sydney office so many times to be closer to my sisters, but I keep getting knocked back. It's the curse of the Glasgow office. Once you're there, you're stuck."

"Like a corporate Hotel California? You can check out any time you like, but you can never leave?"

"Exactly like that." Michelle grimaced. "Of course, I didn't know that until I was already there. But I was a fresh-faced grad then, so excited to have a job with a Big Four firm that I wouldn't have cared if they had stationed me in the Hell office, with Satan as the Senior Partner."

"And you've never thought about getting a different job?" I asked, turning the car off the road and onto a dirt track.

"Lots of times," Michelle said. "Abby never shuts up about it. But changing firms, at this point in my career, would put me back at least two years on the plan. And then I'd be at least thirty-five by the time I make Partner, and... Well, it's really important to me that I stick to the plan."

"Ah," I said. "The plan."

I pulled the SUV to a stop at the side of a clearing. "We're here," I said. "And I know it doesn't look like much yet, but there's this track through the trees, and then—"

"I trust you," Michelle said, interrupting me. "Even if it does look like you've brought me to an ideal location to murder me and dispose of my body."

"You can trust me," I said, sitting up straighter. "Just scenery and food tonight. Absolutely no murder."

"Well, how can I say no to an offer like that?"

· ♥ · ♥ · ♥ · ♥ · ♥ ·

"It really is beautiful here." Michelle let out a contented sigh as she spooned another mouthful of fig and frangipane tart into her mouth. As her lips wrapped around the spoon, delicate tongue chasing the last fragments of pastry, I reminded my body to calm down for what felt like the six hundredth time. "It must have been so much fun making a TV show somewhere like this."

It *was* beautiful; she wasn't wrong. We had been lucky enough to score a table on the huge wooden deck of The Boathouse, right over the river. The sun had long since set, but we had been treated to the view of the last of the light disappearing into the trees and murky depths.

"It was fun," I said, licking salted caramel and dark chocolate mousse from my own spoon and wondering if my tongue caused Michelle to have any exciting reactions. "Well, kind of fun, anyway. Sometimes it was just long days of the director shouting at us to do it again and again, and my feet would be aching, and I'd wish I was at school like a normal kid."

"That part would have sucked. Especially since acting wasn't really your dream."

"It wasn't. But I only asked my mum if I could quit once. Julia went ballistic, and Mum couldn't stop crying about why I'd want to throw away such a huge opportunity. So, I didn't ask after that."

"Like how Phoenix has learned not to ask for things that might upset his mum," Michelle said quietly, folding her hands under her chin. "Poor kid."

"And Julia's trying to get him into acting, of course," I ventured. "But so far, he's only scored catalogue modelling gigs, and those have dried up now he's getting older."

"He's a cute kid. I can see why kid's clothing brands would snap him up."

"I don't think he likes it much," I said. "And it's awkward for him because he knows that he gets jobs because the mixed-race look is trendy. His agent told him as much. But he doesn't know much about his dad or why he looks like he does, and…" I paused. "It must be hard for him."

"Good thing he's got you in his corner. You could have done with an Uncle Patrick when you were growing up."

"No," I insisted. "I was fine. I didn't go through anything like what he has. I got a bit sick of acting sometimes, but I can't really complain without sounding like an arsehole. 'Oh, woe is me; I starred in a hit TV show and made a ton of money! No one has suffered like I have suffered!'"

Michelle huffed out a breath. "Still, it wasn't what you wanted."

"But now I can do whatever I want."

"Which is definitely a good thing," Michelle said, giving me a little smile. "Sometimes I wish I could just..." She paused. "But work is kind of my whole life."

"You're very committed. You know, with your whole plan to make Partner. I know it means a lot to you."

"It does," Michelle agreed, and she looked like she was thinking about something but not saying it.

"Look, if it's too personal, just tell me to piss off, but why is it so important? Your job and making Partner? I mean, most of us have to do something for a living, but why do you stick it out somewhere that treats you so badly?"

Michelle fiddled with her fork. "It's important to me to make Partner because..." She paused again. "Because I need to prove I'm not stupid."

"Stupid?" I repeated the word with a surprised breath of laughter. "Why would you need to prove that? You're obviously smart. Like, really smart."

"It wasn't always like that," Michelle said, looking down at her mostly finished dessert. "I don't like to talk about it, but..." She paused, and then looked up at me. "I didn't have the easiest time at school. I had a lot of trouble learning to read, so people called me stupid. And said I'd never amount to anything. Kids said it outright; teachers were more subtle, but I knew what it was."

"Shit," I said slowly. "I had no idea."

"I don't like to talk about it," Michelle said again. "But it was bad. I guess I had learning difficulties. I think they'd probably call it dyslexia or something now, but all I knew was that while every other kid in my class seemed to be able to just pick up a book and read, I couldn't. It was okay at first. I faked it for a while, memorising books when the teacher read them out loud. And I was good at maths, so that kind of made up for it. But when I was nine, it..." She seemed to draw in on herself, a haunted look sweeping over her face.

"What happened then?"

"The school sent my parents a letter, but they didn't care. Mum said I'd just work it out on my own, eventually. But then Abby found the letter."

"Wow," I said, trying to take it all in. "That's..."

"I was so ashamed at the time," Michelle admitted, her cheeks flushing. "I didn't want my sisters to know I was stupid. But it was the best thing that could have happened, honestly. Abby demanded to know who was calling me stupid and threatened to beat them up. She even wanted to take on the teachers, but she was only eleven. And Tessa..." She paused. "Tessa always loved to read; she was devouring chapter books by the time she was seven. But she had no idea about me. When she found out, she spent an hour with me every day, going back to basics, teaching me how to sound out words, put them together."

"It's awesome that your sisters were there for you," I said, feeling a tightness in my chest. "But shit, it shouldn't have been up to you kids to work it out. Your parents, or someone, should have—"

"Well, when my Nana found out what was up, she took me to have my eyes tested, and I got my first set of glasses," Michelle said. "They were pink. And glittery. That helped. But it was Tessa who actually taught me to read. By the time I went to secondary school, I had caught up. And I worked really hard, too, because I wasn't going to let anyone call me stupid again." Michelle raised her chin defiantly.

"And that's why you..."

"That's why it's so important to me to make Partner," Michelle finished. "If I can do that, get to that level of success, it's like I'm proving everyone wrong. Even myself, I guess. Because I definitely believed I was stupid. I never want to feel like that again."

"Michelle..." I breathed out her name. "I'm really sorry you had to go through that. And for what it's worth, I think you've already proven yourself. Not that you had to. But you've got to know, I think you're amazing."

Michelle shook her head as though awakening from a trance. "It's no big deal. I mean, we all have our childhood crap, right? You definitely do, with being forced to do all that acting when it wasn't what you wanted."

"It's not the same," I said, still trying to digest everything she had told me. I hated the thought of Michelle as a sad, bullied kid, believing there was something wrong with her.

"Anyway." Michelle tossed her hair, flicking it back over her shoulders. "Let's talk about something more cheerful. Like how ridiculously stunning this view is." She gestured to the river beneath us.

"It's nice coming back here on my own terms. With you. I haven't been back here in years, but tonight, I..." I trailed off, utterly unsure of how to end that sentence.

Michelle dropped her fork and bit her lip. "Patrick, what's going on here? I mean, with us?"

"What do you mean?" I knew perfectly well what she meant but didn't know how to answer.

"Are you just being neighbourly, or..." Michelle let out a breath. "Is this something else?"

"I..." I looked down at the remains of my dessert. "Well, I've never taken a neighbour out for dinner before."

Michelle let out a tiny sound of exasperation that absolutely couldn't be mistaken for a sex noise; my tight jeans were safe for now. "Right," she said. "So, when we get back to Brekkie Beach, what would you say if I asked you to come in for a drink?"

My jeans were no longer safe. Absolutely no longer safe.

"I'd say—" I closed my eyes for a moment. Be responsible. I had to be responsible and not let myself get caught up in whatever this was. "That I'd better not. I should get back to Phoenix."

"Of course." Michelle drew her chair back slightly, tossing her hair over her other shoulder. "Of course, that makes perfect sense."

And I was glad it made perfect sense to her. Because I was pretty sure it was the stupidest thing I had ever said. I was trying to do the right thing. The responsible thing.

So, why did it feel like a mistake?

11 Michelle

"Where's the maple syrup?" Tessa's head was inside Abby's fridge.

"In the Lazy Susan marked 'condiments', obviously," Abby said. "Second shelf."

"I should have known to check the labels."

"Your house kind of intimidates me," I said, opening a cupboard to find meticulously organised Tupperware, complete with gleaming rose gold labels. "It looks like Pinterest threw up."

"Thank you!" Abby set a plate of toaster waffles on the table. "But stop poking through my cupboards and come and eat. Sorry that these aren't homemade, but cooking is not my skill set."

"They smell great," I said, helping myself to one and covering it with cut strawberries, maple syrup, and ice cream because I was still technically on holiday, damn it.

"Making waffles is too much work," Tessa said, sitting beside me. "You need a waffle iron. And that takes up too much room in the cupboard."

"Hey, I'm just excited that someone made food for me," I said, enjoying a blissful mouthful. "Instead of getting delivery or sad supermarket salads."

Abby scrunched up her face. "I'd say you need to take better care of yourself," she said, patting my arm. "But that's what I eat ninety-nine per cent of the time too. Tessa got all the cooking genes in this family."

"I like cooking." Tessa shrugged. "It's kind of meditative. Good for my anxiety. Not as good as Zoloft, but pretty good."

"I'm so glad you finally got the help you needed."

"Me too," Tessa agreed. "Now, enough about my mental health. How did it go last night 'hanging out' with Patrick?"

"Can we just call it a date?" Abby interjected. "Because it was clearly a date."

"Look, it definitely had date-like qualities," I said, pausing to shovel more waffle onto my fork. "It was in serious date territory. I mean, he took me out to where they filmed *Outback Adventures*, and it's this beautiful bushland by a river—"

"That sounds romantic!"

"And date-like," Abby put in.

"Well, it kind of was." I frowned, helping myself to more syrup. "Especially when grabbing a bite to eat turned into this really nice restaurant by the water, and he had made a reservation and everything."

"On what planet is that not a date?" Abby banged the syrup bottle to make her point.

"You'd be proud of me, Abby. I actually asked him what was happening. Was he a good neighbour, a friend, or more?"

"And what did he say?" Tessa asked eagerly.

"He said he had never done something like this for a neighbour before."

"Well, that's a nothing answer." Abby rolled her eyes.

"Anyway, I asked him what he'd say if I invited him to come in for a drink when we got back," I said in what I hoped sounded like a casual manner, even though I had been battling a severe case of writhing stomach eels when I had actually asked. "Putting my cards on the table and all."

"And he turned you down?" Abby banged the syrup again. "What's wrong with him?"

"How do you know he turned me down? I mean, he did. He said he needed to get back to Phoenix."

"If he hadn't, I feel like you might not have made it to brunch." Tessa raised her eyebrows. "Because you'd still be rolling around that horrible bed with him."

"Exactly." Abby nodded. "So, he takes you on a date but doesn't want to go home with you? Did you even kiss?"

"No kissing." I sighed. "So maybe it wasn't a date after all?"

"That doesn't make sense." Tessa had her hands under her chin.

"I know! Especially since I get the impression that he's kind of...well, he gets around a bit."

"A man slut, you mean," Abby said. "And I'm not slut-shaming; you know I'm sex-positive!"

"But if he's happy to take home a different woman every week, why not me?" I didn't mean to sound so whiny. "I know I'm not entitled to sex, but it makes a girl feel kind of unattractive. He seemed keen at the pub, and we both knew where that was going. But now we're kind of friends, and I'm right next door, and he's all...nope."

"Maybe it really is about Phoenix," Tessa suggested. "If his mum's kind of unstable, maybe Patrick feels like he can't pursue anything right now. Even right next door."

"Or—" Abby held up her fork. "Maybe it's because you're not like all the women he usually takes home. The fact that you're kind of friends – as you put it – matters."

"Why would that matter?" I asked, even though I suspected I knew the answer.

"I think," Abby sat up straighter, "that Patrick actually *really* likes you. Like, properly. In a girlfriend kind of way. Not just a one-night stand. And I don't think he's got much practice with that. So, he can't let himself sleep with you because he's got *feelings*."

"Well, that's stupid," I said, even though the thought of Patrick having feelings for me made me feel like one of Australia's most terrifying inhabitants was squeezing my ribcage with its scaly body. "If he likes me so damn much, why doesn't he just make a move?"

"You are about to leave the country," Tessa said, scrunching her nose. "I get why he wouldn't want to start something when you've got one foot out the door."

"I think she's right," Abby decided, waving the spoon she was using to finish the last of the mango pieces. "He likes you too much to bang you."

"That's ridiculous," I scoffed. "I mean, we don't even know each other that well. I don't think he could possibly like me that much."

"Didn't he make you a desk?"

"And take you to somewhere important from his childhood?" Abby added. "But that doesn't matter. What matters is how much you like him."

I opened my mouth, but nothing came out. I closed it again and studied my syrup-smeared plate. "I know I'm attracted to him, and he's a great guy with a big heart. The way he's stepped up to care for Phoenix is..." I shook my head. "But you know I'm not looking for someone to have big feelings about right now. And definitely not someone in Australia!"

"Big feelings don't exactly wait to be asked. Remember how I kept telling you guys I wasn't that into Dylan?"

"We could tell you were lying, just for the record. Even to yourself."

"Exactly!" Tessa said. "But it's okay not to be sure how you're feeling."

I stared again at my plate. Was I unsure how I was feeling?

Or was I just unwilling to let myself admit it?

"He's probably right, anyway," I said. "Even if we did genuinely like each other – and I don't know if that's true – it's on a road headed to nowhere. He lives here. I live in bloody Glasgow. And even if I lived in Sydney, I told you, no serious boyfriends until—"

"Until you've made Partner. But you don't have to live in Glasgow, you know."

"Don't start that again." I gave Abby a warning look. "You'd be the last person to tell me to change my whole life, change jobs, change country, for a man."

"I would, you're right," Abby said. "It's just that you seem to hate your job. And you definitely hate Glasgow."

"I don't hate my job," I objected. "I hate the people I work with. That's a very different thing. I like the job."

"So, you could get a different job and—"

"You know why I can't!" I cut her off. "Please, Abby. Yes, my job sucks right now because my team sucks. But I like the work, and if I can just hold on for a few more years, I'll

MICHELLE FINCH STICKS TO THE PLAN

be a Partner. And you know how important that is to me. Just trust that I've thought about this and know what I'm doing."

"I know you have," Tessa said. "You think about everything, and you've always made detailed plans about what you want to do. I just hate seeing you stressed out and upset by the people at your job. They sound like a pack of feral psychopaths, but it's your choice. And I support you."

"And I do, too," Abby cut in. "Sorry, I just get all mother hen."

"Mother velociraptor, more like."

"I'll take that as a compliment," Abby said. "Fine, I'll stop talking about it, okay? Now, who wants more coffee?"

And that was a question that all three of us Finch sisters always answered in the extreme affirmative.

· ♥ · ♥ · ♥ · ♥ · ♥ ·

I was carefully setting up my phone, water bottle, and towel on a stationary cycle by the window when a male voice interrupted me.

"Hey there." A man with a beard that he clearly thought was impressive was smiling at me. "Are you new? I haven't seen you around."

"Just visiting," I said, tossing my ponytail like a horse shaking flies from its butt. "Temporary membership."

"Oh, right." Mr Beard looked a little disappointed. "Well, if you need any help with the machines or a tour—"

"I'm good," I said, making a big show of putting in my earbuds. He wasn't unattractive – if you liked beards – and he hadn't been impolite. But I wasn't interested in making small talk with random men. "Thanks!" I gave him a little wave that I hoped he'd take as dismissal.

Mr Beard slunk away with one last look over his shoulder. It was all I could do not to roll my eyes. I cued up my phone to start a brand-new audiobook from one of my favourite authors. My surfer romance was long finished, and I was starting a historical rom-com. The blurb had promised *Bridget Jones' Diary*, Edwardian style.

My book began to play, and I fiddled with the stationery cycle's touch screen until it promised a suitably punishing interval hill climb. I needed punishment. Or rather, I needed something to stop me from thinking about bloody Patrick and what he had meant by taking me out on a date, and then telling me he couldn't possibly sleep with me.

As my feet began to pedal, I felt the promise of a burn in my thighs. Did Patrick ever think about my thighs, I wondered? He had certainly seen them that day at the beach. And he had seemed to have trouble keeping his eyes off them. Had he ever considered the possibility of said thighs wrapped around his back or maybe around his neck?

...And I had completely missed the introduction of the heroine. I made a sound of frustration and restarted the chapter. I wanted the story of a feisty woman in fabulous dresses who had to choose between the rake, the scholar, and the millionaire, thank you very much. I did *not* want to think about my own life.

Because Patrick had definitely wanted to sleep with me that first time we had met in the pub. I felt a rush of wet heat between my thighs that absolutely wasn't sweat at the memory of his hot mouth claiming mine, big hands kneading my arse and holding me against him, our bodies throbbing to music with the promise of—

Shit, I had done it again. Apparently, my Patrick problem now meant I couldn't even enjoy my favourite distraction. I decided that Lady Elspeth and her trio of suitors would just have to wait, pulling up a suitably energetic playlist that promised to make me feel like a girl boss. I would have settled for 'vaguely competent adult woman', but they didn't make playlists for that.

As the music blasted, I focused on my breath, ready for my first hill climb. But the question that Abby had asked me was still burning in my mind. Forget if Patrick liked me or not. How did I feel about him? And that felt like a question I couldn't bear to let myself answer. Even though I knew – I *knew* – what it was.

I liked him. Of course, I liked him. And I enjoyed spending time with him even though there had been zero arse-grabbing or hot crushing lips after that night in the pub. I liked him, admired him, respected him, and couldn't stop lusting after him or thinking about what might have happened if he hadn't received that fateful phone call. Would we have had a blissful hook-up with no strings attached, few words exchanged, and zero feelings spilling out?

Or had it always been inevitable that if I had spent more than ten minutes with the guy, my emotions would get involved?

None of this, of course, solved the problem of what I was going to *do* about Patrick. Even if I really did like him, it didn't matter, did it? He wouldn't let anything more than a weirdly intense friendship happen, and then I'd be back on a plane to Glasgow and forget all about him. Right?

· ♥ · ♥ · ♥ · ♥ · ♥ ·

"Any news on the baggage handlers' union?" I asked after Martin had vomited his problems with a new client all over me. "I thought you might have some info, being on the ground."

"Not really." Martin sniffed. "I heard it could be resolved in a week, but it could be much longer before flights are running again."

"Right," I said. "So, until then, I'll keep working remotely. On the few remaining clients you've left me."

"Oh, don't be like that," Martin sounded pained. "It's just that we need to ensure that our clients have points of contact who are local, you understand. Once you're back, we can hand a few of them back to you. When you're ready."

I let out a sound between my teeth. When I was ready? They were my damn clients! "I see," I said. "Well, I'll talk to you later, I guess."

"And can you send those numbers through for that oil refinery?" Martin pressed. "Ash has been working on it. He's very good, but just to be sure."

I hated that I had to say yes. It would reflect poorly on me if I didn't just hand over my work to the person who had stolen one of my biggest projects. Besides, I needed the ego boost of my work being preferred to someone else's. When that happened, it made me feel like I could go back in time and tell the child version of myself that it would all be okay, that one day, no one would call her stupid ever again.

"Of course," I said. "And if it's too much for Ash, I'd be happy to take over again and—"

"Just the numbers, Michelle," Martin cut me off. "Until you're back in the office."

I muttered something under my breath that made an elderly couple scowl at me as I stalked out of the gym and towards Brekkie Beach's only supermarket. I had survived so far on eating out and things I could buy from the corner shop near my horrible cottage and handsome neighbour, but now, I needed to purchase some actual food.

"Michelle?" A soft touch on my arm made me whip around to see...

"Hi!" I said a little too loudly and with far too much enthusiasm. I hadn't seen Patrick since our date that wasn't a date. Which was kind of a good thing because I didn't have a clue what to say to him. Thankfully, he was accompanied by Phoenix, so there was zero possibility of our discussing sex, or indeed the lack thereof. "How are you guys going?"

"Just doing some grocery shopping," Patrick said, with that lazy smile I wanted to kiss off his stupidly handsome face. "I want to make sure we've got plenty of stuff that Phoenix likes, not just my low-carb crap."

Phoenix shrugged. "I don't mind."

"I need to get a few things, too," I admitted. "Since I'll be here for longer than I thought. And I can't go out to breakfast, lunch, and dinner every day. Not when I'm trying to actually work remotely."

"I thought you were already working remotely."

"No, no." I shook my head. "That's just my usual level of holiday work. I mean actually working. That starts tomorrow."

"Right." Patrick sounded like he didn't quite get it. "Well, you should come with us. I've got the car, so you won't have to lug everything back up there on your own."

I paused for a moment, but the thought of lugging my groceries in the hot sun after my hill climb workout was the opposite of appealing. Even if hanging out with Patrick was all kinds of confusing. Besides, it would be rude to refuse.

"That would be great," I said finally. "You two will have to help me out; Aussie supermarkets are a mystery to me."

Patrick laughed. "We'll show you where the Tim-Tams and Vegemite are."

"Not Vegemite." Phoenix wrinkled up his nose. "It's gross."

"It's just an acquired taste!"

"I know it's quintessentially Aussie," I said. "But the words 'fermented yeast spread' do absolutely nothing for me."

"She's right," Phoenix agreed with an unusually firm nod.

"You're both nuts," Patrick declared, giving me that megawatt grin that made me forget why spending time with him was awkward. I wanted to bask in that smile like other English tourists did under the punishing sun, and I was no less at risk of getting burnt.

"Well, it looks pretty normal," I said as we stepped through the sliding doors. Before me were aesthetically arranged rows of fruits and vegetables, fresh-baked bread and squashy-looking cakes, and then long aisles to the right. "So long as I can stock up on tea bags and salads, I'm happy."

"Oh, come on, you've gotta think bigger than that!" Patrick told me. "You too, Phoenix. It's mango season! Who doesn't love a mango?"

"Mum says they're messy," Phoenix said, examining a tray of sun-kissed yellow and orange mangoes, a slight frown wrinkling his young forehead. "But I think I like them."

"We'll get a case," Patrick decided, putting a cardboard box of twelve mangoes into the shopping trolley with a flourish. "What's next? Phoenix, you should choose some bread."

"Me?"

"You're the person who's going to be eating it."

"Okay." Phoenix made his way to the wall of bread, each bright wrapper proclaiming its superior vitamin content, mix of seeds, or ability to promote digestive health.

"How's he going?" I asked quietly. "You know, with making choices, telling you what he really thinks about stuff. It must be hard for him, with his anxiety."

"A little better, I think," Patrick told me, his lips dangerously close to my ear as he whispered. A shiver went through me, and I really hoped he didn't notice. "But he's still not exactly comfortable with it. It's not like I can expect one session with a psychologist to fix everything. He's happy to see Evan again, though, so that's good."

"Definitely good."

"Is this one okay?" Phoenix held up a loaf of plain white sliced bread.

"Looks good to me," Patrick said. "Bung it in. You should get some snacks, too."

"Snacks? Like what?"

"Chips, cookies, pizza rolls. Whatever you want. Your choice."

Phoenix didn't look very confident, so I decided to help the poor kid out. "Maybe get one pack of chips and one sweet snack. Just to start."

"Yeah." Phoenix nodded slightly. "Okay, I can do that." He darted off and Patrick turned to me with a grateful smile.

"Thanks," he said. "You're much better at this than me."

"Making choices can be hard when you're anxious about making the wrong one. Gotta start slow, I think."

"You're really good with him," Patrick said, his eyes fixed on me. "And I'm grateful."

And damn, I couldn't help but avert my eyes like some kind of virginal maiden under that gaze. "It's no big deal. I just think about what I wanted when I was his age. People showing me some basic empathy."

"It's more than that." Patrick's voice was low. "Did you ever think about doing psychology or something?"

"Me?" I let out a snort that I probably should have repressed, given I was still hoping that I might sleep with this man. "No way! People are too complicated. Numbers, research, analysis? That I can handle."

"You would have been good at it," Patrick said, adding a bag of plump white grapes, three heads of broccoli, and an extra-large bulk pack of chicken breasts to the cart. "I guess it helps anyway, in your job. Being good at managing people."

And that was true if I thought about it. I had always been able to handle Martin's indecisiveness and chronic inability to stick to a plan.

"I guess so," I said, not wanting to sound conceited. "But only when I'm actually in the office. Now that I'm not there, they're trampling all over me. But what can I do?"

"It's not right," Patrick said. "It's not your fault you got stuck here. And I think," he paused to look at a large pack of lean beef, "I think you're probably amazing at your job, and your boss is an idiot to give your projects to other people. And you deserve to be a Partner. Even if you don't need to do that to prove that you're awesome. And very smart."

"I'd like to think that was true." I sighed again and then checked myself. I couldn't go sighing all over the place like one of the Edwardian ladies in the audiobook I had utterly failed to get into. "But I'm not going to pretend it hasn't kind of destroyed my professional confidence, seeing how fast it can all get taken away from me."

"Sounds like a shitty place to work," Patrick said, taking a packet of chocolate biscuits from a shelf. "Hey, have you had these before?"

"Tim-Tams?" I recognised the packaging. "Oh yeah, whenever my sisters and I were here as kids, we binged hard on those."

"You've been to Australia before? I thought this was your first trip."

"Oh no," I said. "My dad's Australian, so we visited his parents a few times. Well, my sisters and I would stay with his parents; he and Mum usually went off to do something fun on their own."

"Seriously?" Patrick frowned. "That's...pretty shitty."

"It's just the way it was," I said. "We didn't have a bad time, really. It was kind of boring hanging around my grandparents' place in Adelaide. They didn't get out much, so mostly, we went to the park and hoped that handsome Aussie boys would approach us."

"Did that ever happen?" Patrick asked, eyebrows raised. "A teenage fling in Adelaide?"

"I was a bit young. But Abby snogged a guy with a skateboard once while me and Tessa watched from behind the slide. We thought it was the most romantic thing ever."

"He was a skater boy, huh?"

"Now that's going to be stuck in my head all day!"

"So, your dad's Aussie," Patrick repeated. "That means you could get citizenship, right? I mean, if you wanted to live here. If you got a transfer."

"I could," I agreed. "I thought that would be a point in my favour when I applied for a transfer. But apparently not. I think everyone in Britain wants to come out here. It's so competitive."

"But Glasgow's a fun city, isn't it? Great live music scene, pubs..."

"Maybe. But I don't get much of a chance to go out. Work is..."

"Busy?"

"I was going to say all-consuming. But busy sounds way less pathetic."

"I don't think anyone would ever describe you as pathetic, Michelle," Patrick said quietly, those green eyes fixed on me like there was more – a hell of a lot more – that he wanted to say.

"These are made of sweet potatoes." Phoenix suddenly reappeared, holding up an enormous bag of chips in one hand and a packet of Oreos in the other. "And I think these are mostly sugar, but I won't eat too many at once. I promise."

"I'm sure you won't, mate." Patrick gave him a broad grin. "Chuck them in."

"What are you getting?" Phoenix asked me, probably to be polite.

"Teabags." I held up the box. "Salad." I pointed. "And Tim-Tams. A perfectly balanced diet."

Phoenix laughed. "Those are the best ones," he said, nodding at the packet. "With the double coat."

"No way!" Patrick baulked. "If I'm going to let myself have a Tim-Tam, classic is the way to go. Why mess with perfection?"

"Double coat *is* perfection," I argued. "I mean, it's got double the coating!"

"It throws off the ratio completely!" Patrick protested. "Phoenix, grab a pack of the double coat too."

"But you don't like them."

"But you and Michelle do," he said. "And do you mind running over to the freezer and getting a box of Golden Gaytimes? I bet Michelle's never had one."

"Golden Gaytimes?" I asked, hoping my eyebrows arched attractively. "That's got to be made up."

"Nope." Patrick shook his head, clearly suppressing a smirk. "Golden Gaytimes are a national treasure. Ice cream covered with chocolate and little crunchy biscuit pieces.

And they say," his grin widened, "you can't have a Gaytime alone."

I couldn't help it; I giggled. "Is that so? Well, in that case, I'd be glad to share a Gaytime with you. If you think it's worth the carbs."

"Oh, it definitely is," Patrick said, and he winked in a way that gave me some very-much-not-gay feelings.

When we reached the check-out, Patrick, Phoenix, and their very full trolley went one way, and me, with my small basket, went the other. Self-checkouts, I knew. Even if my groceries scanning in dollars rather than pounds kept surprising me.

"Hi again," a voice said, and I looked up to see Mr Beard from the gym, scanning a large tin of protein powder. "Getting your groceries, huh?"

"Uh, yes."

"Tim-Tams," he observed, eyebrows waggling as I scanned the biscuits. "Well, I guess you can afford to treat yourself with a body like that."

"I guess," I said, keeping my eyes fixed on my shopping.

"You know, there's a place by the beach that does a great smoothie," Mr Beard said, his voice smooth and practised. "Perfect after a workout. We could head over there now. I'll carry your bags." He flexed one arm, and I couldn't help noticing his biceps were far less impressive than Patrick's.

"Actually, she's coming home with me." I looked up to see Patrick close behind me. He put his hand on my waist, and the feeling of his big hand, warm through the thin fabric of my tank top, was enough to make me wish we were somewhere private and not in the middle of a busy supermarket.

"Oh, right." Mr Beard shrugged as though it was no big deal. "Guess I'll see you around, then."

I didn't reply; I just watched Mr Beard make his way out of the store, still flexing those inferior biceps.

"Sorry." Patrick's voice was close to my ear once more. "You weren't interested in him, were you?"

"Definitely not," I said, my voice a little shaky. His hand was still very much on my waist, proprietorial. Like I belonged to him. "Thanks for...you know, seeing him off. He hit on me at the gym, too."

"Persistent." Patrick scowled at the automatic doors. "Look, I know you don't need a man to rescue you; you could have handled him. I just..." He removed his hand. "I didn't like the look of him."

"Me either," I said, feeling much warmer than I had even at the peak of my hill climb. "And maybe I shouldn't need a man to come in and warn off a guy like that, but..." I swallowed hard. "I'm glad you did."

I looked up into those green eyes, searching them as though they might tell me what on earth was going through his head. He wanted to protect me from other men, he took me to dinner, he bought the Tim-Tams I liked best, but he didn't want to sleep with me? It made no sense!

"Uncle Patrick, do we need any more reusable bags?" Phoenix's voice broke the moment, and I looked over to see him waiting in the queue, pointing at the nest of bags stuffed into the child seat.

"Uh, I'll come and check." Patrick stepped away from me, and I felt curiously bereft. "See you in a minute, okay?"

"Yeah." I nodded, wondering if I should buy a magazine to fan myself down.

I knew Sydney would be warmer than Glasgow, but nothing could have prepared me for getting this hot and bothered in a supermarket.

· ♥ · ♥ · ♥ · ♥ · ♥ ·

"Crikey, you're looking hot to trot," Patrick said, taking a step towards me. He was wearing a flannel shirt and Akubra, just like his character on Outback Adventures, but there was no doubt this was very much the grown-up Patrick. His character had never worn the flannel shirt open over his bare chest like that.

"Am I?" I said, stepping over the broken sticks and gum leaves that littered the floor of the clearing. On some level, I was vaguely aware this was a dream. On another level, I didn't care.

"You know you are," Patrick said, without the exaggerated Aussie twang. "You're beautiful, Michelle." Big hands gripped my waist, and I was in my workout gear again, just very short shorts and a crop top.

"What's happening, Patrick?" I asked, pressing my body into his. God, he was so firm, and he smelled like salt, sand, and clean laundry dried in the sun. I ran my hand over his back, feeling the muscles ripple beneath my skin.

"Whatever you want," Patrick said softly, deep green eyes fixed on mine. "I'm all yours. But we need to be quick. Before the crocs come and get us."

"I don't give a shit about crocodiles," I whispered and pressed my mouth to his. His lips claimed mine, just like in the pub, and it felt like I was floating through space and time, nothing real except his mouth, his hands on my body, and the heat of his skin. His hand pressed between my thighs, and I cried out, pressing into him and I—

Woke up in my bed, alone, sweaty, and very much hot and bothered.

"Why?" I asked the silent room. "Why wake me up when I'm getting to the good bit? That is rude and unfair!"

The silent room didn't answer. I considered rolling over and trying to recapture the dream, but now that I was awake, the wet heat between my thighs was more urgent than ever.

Turning on a light, I rifled in my suitcase for a certain device I had packed in the travel cube marked 'Personal

Care' (a gift from Abby, of course). I absolutely intended to care for myself.

Settling back into bed, I grimaced at the lumpy mattress, closed my eyes, and sank back into visions of Patrick in that Akubra and absolutely nothing else. It wasn't like there was any hope I'd ever get to experience the real thing.

Or was there?

12 Patrick

"So, this is a dovetail joint, right?" Phoenix pointed. "How do you know the pieces will match up?"

"Well, there are tools you can use to measure, but I usually just eyeball it. But you can only do that after getting it wrong a thousand times."

"And on the top, it's tongue and groove joints? That sounds gross."

"It does," I agreed, trying and failing not to think of my tongue and Michelle's grooves. "So, I've almost got these two pieces ready to go, just a little more work with the chisel and—"

My hand slipped, and the sharp edge of the chisel went directly into my palm. I saw the spurts of blood and quickly closed my fist. "Ow."

"Are you okay?" Phoenix looked alarmed. "Is it really deep? How much blood is there?"

"It's fine," I said, not wanting to look. "I'll wrap a tea towel around it, no worries."

"What should I do?" Phoenix was clearly panicking. "What do you want me to do?"

"You don't need to do anything. It's no big deal."

"I'm going to get Michelle," Phoenix said, and he was already halfway down the driveway, his face pale.

"No, don't—" I called after him, but it was too late. Phoenix was already clearing the fence like he had done it a hundred times.

I really didn't want Michelle to know I had managed to injure myself doing something so basic. Even if it had definitely happened because my stupid brain couldn't stop thinking about her. The way she had looked that day on the beach, bending over in her bikini so I could see those legs, the curve of her—

"That's what got me into this mess." Would Michelle think I had asked Phoenix to go and get her? That might be even more embarrassing than injuring myself. I let out a grunt and pushed myself to my feet so I could tell her it was a false alarm.

"I'm here!" Michelle entered the garage behind Phoenix, holding a small nylon first aid bag in her hand. "Phoenix said you've sliced your hand open! Do we need an ambulance?"

"It's barely a scratch," I said, scoffing to show just how ridiculous the idea of an ambulance was. "Seriously, I'll just get something wrapped around it, and I'll be fine."

"He doesn't even have band-aids," Phoenix reported scathingly.

"I meant to get some," I lied. "Look, it's no big deal, really."

"Come on, let me take a look," Michelle said, pointing to the stool beside the bar. "I've been lugging around this travel first aid kit since Abby sent it to me for Christmas; at least give me a chance to use it."

"Should've known it was Abby."

"She's got a whole Instagram series of aesthetically arranged medicine cabinets," Michelle said, unzipping the kit. "Now, show me your hand."

"There was a fair bit of blood," I warned her, sitting down on the stool. "You're not squeamish, are you?"

"Of course not. I don't get where the idea that women can't stand the sight of blood came from, anyway. Like we don't have a crime scene downstairs every month!"

Phoenix coughed awkwardly at the mention of periods and looked away pointedly. I'd have to have a chat with him about that. There was nothing worse than a grown man who was grossed out by periods, and I was sure my sister wasn't going to talk to him about them.

"Fair point," I said, and I unclenched my hand. It wasn't quite as bad as I had feared, but there was a deep, jagged cut and enough blood to turn a weaker stomach.

"I'm going to go and..." Phoenix still wasn't looking. "Make tea?"

"Tea sounds great." Michelle nodded at him. "Nice and strong, please." And then she knelt in front of me, taking my dusty, bleeding hand in her small, clean ones. "Yikes. How'd you do this to yourself?"

"Wood chisel." I shrugged and tried to focus on my blood loss and not the rush of blood to other areas that resulted from Michelle kneeling in front of me.

"I'm going to clean it up." Michelle dabbed at my hand with cotton wool soaked in saline. "And I'll chuck some antiseptic on it if you can stand it."

"Of course I can," I said, puffing out my chest a little. "But you don't need to go to all this trouble."

"Trust me, I was glad to get away from my computer." Michelle let out a little sigh. "There's only so many times I can answer an email about my own damn projects without wanting to introduce my laptop to the rolling blue waters of Brekkie Beach."

"I can imagine." I gritted my teeth as she swiped the antiseptic pad over the cut, determined not to flinch at the stinging pain.

"Very brave," Michelle said, looking up at me through her lashes. "You can admit it hurts, you know. I won't think any less of you; I promise."

"It's not that bad," I said, but I was glad when she pressed a piece of gauze over the cut and began to bandage it up. "How do you know how to do this, anyway?"

"I'm the designated first aid officer in my office," Michelle said, rolling her eyes. "When I was a fresh grad, I jumped at the chance to do the training. I thought it would make me look hungry for responsibility. Mostly, I just get requests for painkillers after one too many at the pub."

"You did a good job," I said, holding up my hand and admiring the neat bandage. "I would have just chucked a tea towel on it."

"That," Michelle informed me, "is disgusting. I guess I should be glad you weren't planning to wrap it in bark or something after *Outback Adventures*."

"Hey, the bush contains many healing plants! There was this one episode where an Indigenous man taught us about it."

"I bet," Michelle said. "Well, you're all set. Going to get back to making that bar?"

"But you haven't finished yet." I couldn't resist teasing her. "Aren't you going to kiss it better?"

"Are you five?" Michelle gave me a look, but she took my hand between hers once more and pressed her lips to my palm. I felt a rush of heat, and I wished I could just push her to the dusty, dirty floor of the garage and—

"Thanks," I said, pushing down those tempting but inappropriate thoughts. "I really appreciate you coming over to help me."

"Well, Phoenix did say it was an emergency," Michelle said. "And I wanted to help. I don't love the thought of you bleeding out, you know."

"I'm grateful," I said, and I had to force myself to look away from Michelle's face, from those blue eyes fixed on me, like she was trying to tell me something. Something I might be imagining or maybe just couldn't let myself hear. "And you deserve a thank you. We'll take you to lunch."

"You don't need to do that," Michelle insisted, zipping up her first aid kid and getting to her feet. "It was nothing."

"But you've got to eat, right?" Now that she was here, I didn't want her to leave. Not yet, anyway. "Come on, keep me and Phoenix company."

"Well, if you put it like that..." Michelle was still giving me that odd look. "I suppose I could take a break."

· ♥ · ♥ · ♥ · ♥ · ♥ ·

"Thanks again for lunch." Michelle followed me up the stairs and onto the veranda, looking out at the water.

Phoenix had already gone inside, probably to mow down hordes of zombies.

"You're welcome," I said. "I mean, you did bandage me up. And I think Phoenix needed a burger after this morning."

"Agreed." Michelle nodded. "You're doing a good job with him. Don't forget that, okay?"

"I'm just muddling along, really."

"You're being compassionate, caring, and not pushing him too hard," Michelle told me. "It's pretty awesome to see how you've stepped up to this kind of responsibility, honestly."

"And you didn't even know what a selfish arsehole I was before."

"I can't imagine you being a selfish arsehole," Michelle said. "Enjoying yourself when you're single isn't exactly a crime."

"I'm lucky I met you. Met you properly, that is. With you being next door, and..." I trailed off. "You've helped me a lot."

Michelle let out a tiny breath. "I'm glad I met you too," she said, looking up at me, one hand shading her eyes against the sun and stopping me from seeing into them. "Even if we didn't ever... I mean, if things didn't work out how I thought they would that first time we met."

"Well, it's not like I didn't want them to," I said, wondering if it was possible to have this conversation without it being horribly awkward. Probably not. "It's just, life got complicated and—"

"We don't have to talk about it," Michelle said quietly. "I'm okay with being friends. I mean, you're a great guy. How could I be disappointed to be friends with you?"

"Disappointed?"

"I didn't mean—" Michelle looked like she wanted to bolt away from me. "I mean, you're right. It's all so complicated, and I'll be leaving soon, so it's best that we never—" She shook her head like she was trying to force the idea out of it.

"Michelle, I don't want you to think I didn't want to—" She had to know. She had to know how much I wanted her. That the reason I hadn't pursued her was because I wanted more than she could possibly give me.

"I'd better get back to the cottage." Michelle went down the stairs, her speed increasing with every step. "I've got a conference call, and it's going to be brutal."

I sighed as I watched those cycling-toned legs walk away from me at considerable speed.

"I fucked that up again, didn't I?" I muttered to the tufts of grass growing over the edges of the garden path.

The tufts of grass didn't answer.

· ♥ · ♥ · ♥ · ♥ · ♥ ·

"My dudes!" Khalid entered the living room like he was making a grand entrance onto the stage. He always entered a room like that, to be fair. "What's cooking?"

"Me, apparently," I said, flicking off the TV I hadn't really been interested in, and Phoenix hadn't even been pretending to watch. Teenagers, it seemed, were allergic to any form of entertainment that couldn't be streamed. "You don't have any food for us today."

"That's where you're wrong," Khalid said, sitting on the sofa between us. "I've got a lamb tagine and couscous so soft, so fluffy, so fresh that you'd swear thousands of tiny angels were massaging your tongue."

"Your mum cooked, huh?" Khalid wasn't a better cook than me, but his mother certainly was.

"I told her you had Phoenix staying with you, and she was horrified that she hadn't sent food already. So, there's the tagine for tonight and approximately thirty-seven plastic containers for your freezer in my car."

"Wow," I said, pretending to be offended. "Your mum thinks I'm incapable of feeding my nephew?"

"Don't take it personally, I'm thirty-two and she thinks I'm incapable of feeding myself."

"There's a reason you always bring takeout."

"Oh, that's right!" Khalid rolled his eyes. "Bite the hand that feeds you! No tagine for you!"

Phoenix looked at him, clearly mystified.

"Like, no soup for you?" Khalid prompted. "The soup Nazi? From *Seinfeld*?"

"What's *Seinfeld*?" Phoenix frowned. "Is that an old TV show?"

"*Seinfeld* was the greatest achievement in comedy of the twentieth century." Khalid let out a sigh. "My dude, I can't believe you haven't seen it! It's a classic! The show about nothing!"

"About nothing?" Phoenix didn't look impressed. "But you said there were Nazis."

"No, just a soup Nazi," Khalid explained. "I'm not convincing you, am I?"

"Sorry." Phoenix shrugged. "We can watch it if you want, though."

"Not with that attitude." Khalid wagged a finger at him. "Come on, let's get this tagine out of my car and onto the table. You'll like it."

"I'm still kind of full from lunch," Phoenix admitted. "We went out with Michelle."

"You went out with Michelle?" Khalid looked immediately interested. "How very cosy!"

"I just wanted to thank her for helping me out this morning with my hand—" I held up the hand that was still bandaged.

"I'm getting Florence Nightingale vibes! Did she soothe your fevered brow? Give you a sponge bath?"

"There were no sponge baths," I said irritably. "I cut my hand, she bandaged it up, and I took her to a nice café for lunch. There's no story here."

"And when we got back, they were out on the veranda for a long time," Phoenix offered.

"Oh, were they?" Khalid was once again animated. "How long, exactly? Got a little snog in, finally? Or maybe—"

"Nope," I cut him off. "I'm going to get this tagine, anyway. Where are your keys?"

"I'll help you, given you're crippled."

"I'm not crippled! Tis but a scratch."

"I guess you haven't heard of Monty Python, either?" Khalid asked Phoenix.

"Sorry."

"One of these days, you and I are going to have a classic comedy night. It's going to blow your mind."

Phoenix just looked bemused.

When Khalid followed me out to the car, it was time for his attack. "So, what's really going on with you and Michelle?" he asked in a stage whisper.

"Nothing," I said. "Except..."

"Except what?" Khalid looked frustrated. "Do I need to torture it out of you? I'm totally willing to do that. I think there's a pair of pliers somewhere in my car."

"Pliers aren't necessary," I said. "It's just, with Michelle, it's complicated. She's going to leave any day now! As soon as the flight thing gets sorted out. I can't let anything happen because..."

"Because she's leaving?" Khalid snorted. "As if that's ever stopped you before. How many tourists have you banged in your time? You once hooked up with a chick in an airport bathroom!"

"That was you. And it was a man."

"Oh, yeah." Khalid grinned as though reminiscing. "Good times. But still, she's going to leave. Why is that a problem? Unless..."

"Unless I really do like her," I finished. "Fine, you were right. I do! I do like her!"

"But this is great!" Khalid looked delighted. "You're finally admitting you have real feelings about a woman!"

"And it just had to be one who'll go back to Glasgow the minute she can."

"So?"

"So what?"

"So why can't anything happen, just because she's leaving?" Khalid pressed. "You'd seriously rather never even know what it's like to be with her? And I don't just mean the sex; I mean being with her."

"But isn't it a bad idea? Starting something that can't lead anywhere?"

"What if she's here another month?" Khalid asked me. "No, don't answer yet. And you could spend that whole month with her. Having whatever passes for good sex among straight people, holding her hand, taking her to more nice little cafés. Being with her properly. Or you could spend that month doing this weird 'we're friends' thing until the sexual tension explodes and causes a medium to large earthquake and possibly a tsunami. Frankly, it's irresponsible of you."

Well, when he put it like that...

"You're being a coward," Khalid told me, handing me an enormous pot of tagine. "A huge coward. And missing out on what could be a wonderful time. Just because there's an end date doesn't mean it can't be good! Maybe it will be short. But it could be short and *amazing*. You think being with her wouldn't be amazing?"

"Of course it would," I said. "But I've got Phoenix to think about, and when she leaves—"

"Don't think about when she leaves." Khalid was cradling the couscous like it was a baby and shut the car door with his hip. "You'll cope. After all, it's not like you're in love, is it?"

"No," I said, even as my stomach squirmed uncomfortably at the word. "No, of course not."

"Well then I don't know what the hell you're waiting for. You want her. She, for some reason, still wants you even after she got to know you. Have your fabulous fling while you can. Because if you don't, you'll regret it forever. And you don't like to have regrets."

"I don't." That much was true, anyway. "I think maybe later, I'll go over and...see what happens."

"What will happen is you two bang," Khalid said. "And you'll be thanking me. You can send me flowers. Tulips are my favourite, but I'd accept an edible arrangement too."

"Fine," I said, following him up to the house. "Fine, I'll... Well, no regrets, right?"

"No regrets."

13 Michelle

Michelle: it's official. patrick isn't into me and never will be

Tessa: what makes you think that?

Abby: lies! i've seen the way he looks at you

Tessa: he asked dylan for that photo of you, remember?

Abby: he took you on a romantic date!

Michelle: we kind of talked today. he said he was glad he met me, and i said i was too, even if nothing ever happened between us. and he was like yeah, it just got too complicated. i got friend zoned, for sure.

Abby: the idea of the friend zone is toxic masculinity

Tessa: not the point, but agreed

Michelle: i know it's toxic masculinity! but given it seemed like he wanted to sleep with me the first time he met me, and now he clearly doesn't, i think it's valid to say i am in the friend zone. he got to know me, and decided i was a great friend, not a prospective sexual partner. that's fine and all but...

Abby: but you still really want him, huh?

Michelle: yes! i've been trying not to, because it's been becoming increasingly clear it's never going to happen, but yes

Tessa: <hug emoji> i still think he really does like you. maybe he doesn't want to make a move because you're leaving?

Michelle: men don't think like that

Abby: maybe he does

Michelle: look, we know he's kind of a player. i'm sure he wouldn't be thinking like that. if he wanted me, he'd be knocking on my door with a rose between his teeth or something

Tessa: do they remove the thorns first, when guys do that? otherwise it seems downright dangerous

Abby: and kind of unsanitary. do you know what kind of pesticides commercial flower growers use? you do not want that in your mouth, i'm telling you

Michelle: ...not the point. really not the point

Tessa: sorry. and i'm sorry it never worked out with him. i guess it's nice you made a friend?

Michelle: yes, it's great to have a friend i'm ridiculously attracted to who lives on the other side of the world. we all want a friend like that

```
Abby: well, on the bright side,
you'll be back in glasgow soon and
you'll forget all about him. you can
bang some highlander in a kilt, forget
the whole aussie thing. let hamish
mctavish show you his bagpipes!
```

Michelle: i get that you're trying to cheer me up, but there is nothing, and i mean nothing, sexy about the bagpipes

Tessa: gotta agree with you there, michelle

```
Abby: just me, then? that's a fetish
i didn't know i had
```

Michelle: i'm sure you can find someone willing to fulfil it. stick it in your tinder profile

```
Abby: i'm not on tinder!
```

Tessa: maybe you could try tinder, michelle

Michelle: i don't have time for this stuff anyway. it will be better when I'm back at work in glasgow and he's not parading around with his stupid smile and glistening golden muscles. i'll get over him

I had just been about to explain further why going back to Glasgow was an absolute necessity when it came to getting over Patrick Dalton when the knock came on my door.

Immediately, my stomach tightened, and my chest fluttered at the thought that it might be Patrick. Even as I sternly told myself, no, it couldn't be. He'd never come over late like this. It was probably an extraordinarily determined door-to-door salesperson or perhaps an insomniac missionary who thought I needed to hear the good news about Jesus.

Frowning, I got off the bed and went to the door. I didn't instantly fling it open, of course. I had seen enough true crime (for which I blamed Tessa) to know that answering your door when you were alone was not a wise move regarding murder prevention.

"Who is it?"

"Patrick," a familiar voice came. "I know it's late but—"

I flung open the door. And then regretted it because I was dressed in pink pyjamas with enormous yellow stars and smiley-face rainbows printed on them. Abby had thought they were an extremely amusing birthday present, as they were the exact opposite of everything I usually wore.

"Hi. Um, did you want to come in?"

"If you don't mind," Patrick said, stepping into the house and making the boards under the slippery vinyl creak.

We stood awkwardly in the cramped lounge room, staring at each other in the dim light. I was strangely aware of how loud my breathing was in the silent room.

"Um, so, is there something wrong?" I asked when Patrick didn't speak. "Is something wrong with Phoenix?"

"No!" Patrick said quickly, and he began pacing up and down. It didn't take very long, given how tiny the room was. "Michelle, I..." he began and cleared his throat. "I made a huge mistake. The other day, when we were at dinner, you asked me what I'd say if you asked me to come in for a drink..."

"You said you'd better not because you've got Phoenix," I said, my heart beating too fast and too hard in my chest like a rehearsal for the Edinburgh Military Tattoo.

"I've been regretting it," Patrick said. "Regretting it a lot. And not just the other night. I've regretted it every time I could have— I don't know how much longer you'll be here, Michelle. But I also know I'll regret it for the rest of my life if I let you leave without finishing what I started in the pub that night."

My mouth formed something like a perfect 'O' of surprise. Somewhere, in the back of my mind, I found it screamingly funny that I had been whining to my sisters about how Patrick didn't want me, right as he had walked up to the cottage to make this little speech. But that was in the back of my mind. Everything else was taken up with what he had said.

"I..." I swallowed hard. "I'd hate to make you live with that kind of regret." I took a step closer to him. "And I do believe in second chances. Even if I was kind of disappointed when you turned me down."

"Kind of disappointed?" Patrick quirked his mouth. "Just kind of?"

"Really disappointed," I said. "Because I—"

But I didn't have to say anything else at all. Strong hands caught me around the waist, and I could feel the heat, the strength of his body through my ridiculous pyjamas. And when those lips pressed against mine, confident, firm, and sure, I realised I had been wrong. That kiss in the pub had *not* been the best kiss of my life. Because this one, right now, was so much better.

Now, Patrick wasn't just a handsome stranger with a sexy accent; he was *Patrick*. The man I had come to know, to admire, and to care for so much. And he was kissing me like I was the most important thing in the world. Like he had spent the last few weeks just waiting to do this.

I moaned into him, pressing my body against his and revelling in the heat of him. He was all hard angles and firm muscle, except for the softness of his lips as he kissed me, devouring my mouth like he refused to let any part of me be unexplored.

"I'm so glad you did that," I whispered when we finally broke apart. "I might have actually exploded if you hadn't."

"You have no idea how many times I've thought about it." He mouthed over my neck. "About that night in the pub, that day at the beach when you were teasing me…"

"Oh, you noticed that?" I slipped my hands under his t-shirt, seeking out the warm, sun-kissed skin.

"You knew exactly what you were doing." Patrick's voice was almost a growl. "You liked me watching you."

"Well, I was still pretty mad at you then," I admitted. "But…yes. I liked knowing you were watching me. Wanting me. Maybe regretting ghosting me."

"I was shaking my fist at the universe for stopping me from having you that night," Patrick assured me, his hands moving down to cup my arse. "It's been torture, seeing you every day, and knowing I shouldn't let anything happen."

"I'm glad you changed your mind." I pressed my lips to his collarbone, standing up on tiptoe to taste the heat of his skin. Salt, sand, and *him*.

"I'm lucky you're so forgiving." His mouth claimed mine once more. Stumbling, tripping, and making the floorboards creak ominously, we made our way from the stuffy lounge to the cramped bedroom where I had been complaining to my sisters such a short time ago.

"So, how bad is this mattress?"

"Very bad," I said, frowning. "Almost as bad as my pyjamas."

"You'd better take them off then."

"Don't you want to do it for me?" I asked, moving closer to him.

"That would be a lot of fun." Patrick ran a hand up my bare thigh, making my body shiver under his touch. "But I know," his voice was a low rumble, "that you like it when I watch you."

My breath caught in my throat, and I couldn't say a word. How did he know, just from that day at the beach, how much I liked that? Biting my lip, I slowly began unbuttoning my pyjamas, wishing passionately they were at least red satin even if they couldn't magically transform into lingerie.

But Patrick didn't seem to be looking at the shooting stars and anthropomorphised rainbows. His eyes were fixed on me, watching, waiting. "You're so beautiful, Michelle," he murmured. "Show me."

Hot sparks of desire shot through my body, making the heat between my thighs sear. I abandoned the buttons and slipped my shirt over my head, flinging it to the floor.

"Is that what you wanted to see?" I asked, looking right at him. His stare felt like a touch, so intense were those green eyes as they hungrily devoured my body.

"Yes," he breathed. "I've wanted to see you like this for so long. Do you know how many times I thought about it?"

"You really thought about me?"

"You have no idea," Patrick groaned, his hands cupping my arse once more and pulling me down onto the bed with him. "I don't know how I've managed to do anything else, I've spent so much time thinking about you. How do you think I cut my hand?" He held up the bandaged palm, and I brought it to my lips once more.

"I hate to have caused you so much trouble." I looked up at him through my lashes.

"Lies." Patrick's eyes crinkled. "You love that I can't stop thinking about you."

"I thought about you too," I whispered, lips moving over his neck as those big hands moved over my body, touching, testing, finding the places that made me cry out and moan. "I'm still not completely sure you're not a very realistic fantasy."

"Do you need to touch me to make sure I'm real?" Patrick grinned into my skin, and I let out a soft chuckle.

"You do feel very firm," I assured him, my fingertips trailing over the muscles of his back. "I thought about you coming here, kissing me, touching me, showing me exactly what I've been missing."

"And was I good?" Patrick's mouth was a smirk. An actual smirk. The kind you usually only saw on TV.

"So good," I whispered. "You might find it hard to live up to fantasy Patrick."

"Is that a challenge?"

"Definitely," I murmured. "One hundred per cent."

"You should know I rise to a challenge."

"Seems like you've already risen." I slid my hand over his belly and down to where I could see he was hard for me. "Do you want me to—"

"No." Patrick caught my wrist with strong fingers. "Because I can't wait to taste you." And with those words, he flipped me down onto the bed, pressing my legs apart so I was utterly exposed for him.

I let out a cry. "God, Patrick, are you going to—"

But my words were cut off by strong hands on my thighs, holding me in place for him, and those green eyes that I had searched so often were fixed on mine as he licked his lips in anticipation.

"Please!"

"You don't have to beg, Michelle." I could feel his breath on my skin, and then—

"God, Patrick!" My fingers dug into the sheets, and it was all I could do not to buck up into him like some kind of deranged and needy animal. The reality of his mouth on me, tasting me, teasing me, and clearly loving every second of it made my daydreams look like something a nun might have dreamed up by comparison. That wicked tongue of his was driving me perilously close to the edge, and my body was almost convulsing off the bed.

"Just like that!" I cried out. "If you keep doing that, I'm going to—"

But Patrick didn't stop. Didn't stop those dizzying, perfect spirals of pleasure that were taking me right to the edge. Every man I had ever been with before seemed incapable of understanding that the way to make a woman come was to *keep doing* the thing she liked best. But not Patrick. He knew exactly what I needed, and seeing his eyes on me, knowing he was watching me, took me as close to nirvana as a person could get without years of extensive study in Buddhism.

And then my body came apart for him. I was barely aware of what I was screaming as my hands fisted in the sheets, no longer aware of the low thread count or inferior cotton. I was floating, gliding, soaring, ascending through pleasure like never before. It seemed to last forever until, finally, I collapsed down onto the bed, sweaty and breathless.

"Bloody hell, Michelle," Patrick breathed, coming up to kiss me, the taste of me slick on his lips. "That was the hottest thing ever."

"What about that time you were stuck in the desert on *Outback Adventures*?"

"Nope." Patrick shook his head. "You're way hotter. No question."

When his lips met mine, my stomach squirmed and writhed with pleasure. In that moment, it felt like this man – this beautiful, complicated, charming man – was truly mine. That this wasn't a holiday fling, but something real, something I could keep forever.

I was also very aware of how he must be feeling, pressed hard against me. "Am I allowed to touch you now?"

"I might pass out if you don't," Patrick groaned, pressing back into my touch. "I don't think it would be wise to risk it."

"Well, as a qualified first aid officer, I can't allow that. In the interests of safety..." I unbuttoned his fly, his shorts sliding to the floor, and wow, was everything bigger down under? Wait, that was Texas. But I was sure that it should be Australia, because, *damn*.

"What do you want me to do?"

"Well, that does feel amazing." Patrick's mouth was so close to mine that we were almost kissing, even as he spoke. "But when you're ready, what I really want is to see you ride me."

"Yeah," I whispered as fresh heat surged through me. "I want that too. Right now."

I had always been a one-and-done kind of girl when it came to orgasms; I didn't even like to be touched once I had come. But right now, with Patrick? I couldn't think of anything I wanted more.

"Then I'm going to have to find my shorts." Patrick pressed a kiss to my forehead. "Condoms," he added at my mystified expression.

"You came prepared, then?" I teased, watching as his back muscles rippled, his arse firm as he bent over to scrabble in the pocket of the abandoned shorts.

"More like hoping." Patrick stood up, holding the foil packet between his teeth. "Very, very much hoping."

"Good answer," I said, taking the condom from him and ripping it open. Carefully, I slid the sheath over him.

"Safety first?"

"Always," I told him. "I take my responsibilities very seriously."

But all joking was lost as his strong hands gripped my hips, pulling me on top to straddle him. I bit my lip, waiting for the moment he pressed inside me.

"You look so perfect. So beautiful, Michelle." With those words, he eased me down onto his thick length. Almost painstakingly slowly, like he wanted me to feel every inch. I cried out as he spread me open, filled me up, and made me *his*.

Patrick let out a grunt that became a growl, something almost animal, gripping me tighter still as he pushed himself into me. I had never felt so full, or so utterly exposed and *watched*. I began rolling my hips slowly, rising and falling, and making my breasts bounce with every movement.

Another groan became a sigh, and his lips moved over my super-heated skin even as his strong hands guided my hips up and down, again and again. It was like he couldn't get enough of me, even when deep inside my body. I cried out as the fresh ripples of pleasure shot through me.

"I'm seriously close," Patrick breathed against my neck. "But I want you to come again first."

"No, it's fine, I don't—" I began, but then he slipped one hand between our sweat-slick bodies. And *god*, no man had ever touched me like this, never been so utterly insistent on my pleasure when his own orgasm was clearly imminent.

The world became a blur of pleasure, of throbbing rhythm, our bodies moving together, his mouth moving over my skin, and then—

My first orgasm had, apparently, just been the dress rehearsal. This was opening night. And it was an extravaganza; all singing, all dancing, with world-class pyrotechnics. Patrick's groans mingled with my own cries as I squeezed tight around him, determined to grasp every last bit of him.

I attempted to elegantly move my body off Patrick's, but I had to admit it was more of a controlled collapse. I was gasping, breathless, sheathed in sweat, and completely, utterly satisfied.

"Wow," I whispered, looking up into his face. He, too, was breathing hard, his muscles gleaming like he had just been doing something excitingly masculine in his workshop.

"That's a good reaction." Patrick drew my body against his with one strong arm. "And, right back at you. Seriously wow."

I smiled into him, my body feeling pleasantly weightless, not to mention boneless. The lumpy mattress had ceased to bother me.

"I'm glad you changed your mind," I said quietly, running one finger down the side of the handsome face I had come to know so well. "Because if we had missed out on this? That would be seriously sad."

"Eventually I worked out I shouldn't be stupid enough not to enjoy the time I have with you," Patrick said. "It took a little push. From Khalid. And Phoenix, too, if I think about it."

"Speaking of, does that mean you need to run off?"

"I left him a note." Patrick shrugged. "And I've got my phone on."

"He knows you're here?" My eyes widened, but I supposed I shouldn't have been surprised.

"After all the times he's tried to get us alone together, I could hardly keep it from him."

"I'm glad you can stay a while. Even if this mattress belongs on the side of the road."

"I hadn't noticed," Patrick said, his lips brushing against mine. "And it would take a hell of a lot more than a lumpy mattress to stop me from enjoying every moment I have with you before—"

"Before the baggage handlers' union reaches resolution?" I finished, an odd twist in my stomach. I didn't want to think about that, not now. "Who knows when that will happen?"

"Exactly," Patrick murmured, and then his lips met mine considerably less lightly, and all I could do was hope there were more condoms in his pockets.

· ♥ · ♥ · ♥ · ♥ · ♥ ·

Too much light and the sound of rustling woke me, and I blinked awake. Holy crap. Had last night really happened? Had Patrick actually, in real life and not my vibrator-aided fantasies, come over and...?

The presence of one half-naked Patrick struggling back into his shorts would seem to indicate that yes, yes it had.

"Hi," I said softly, sitting up.

"Good morning." Patrick gave me that smile that melted my insides like an ice cream wielded by a cranky toddler on a hot summer's day. "I didn't want to wake you, but I'd better get back. I told Phoenix where I was going, but I don't want him to feel...you know."

"Like you're abandoning him to bang the neighbour?" I supplied. "I think that's the right call."

"You're not just my neighbour," Patrick said, those green eyes fixed on me. He dropped down to the bed, still shirtless, and crawled up to kiss me.

"What am I, then?" A part of me was almost afraid to hear the answer.

"You're Michelle. And Michelle is...a very special person."

And that didn't exactly give me a clear answer about what this was, but I liked to hear it just the same.

"Good answer," I said, letting myself melt into his kiss, heedless of the possibilities of morning breath.

There was a noise outside the bedroom, and we broke apart.

"Yo, Michelle! You should really lock your door!" Abby's voice boomed through the thin walls.

"Maybe it doesn't lock properly," I heard Tessa say.

"Michelle, you need to sue Air BnB if your door doesn't lock!" Abby's voice came through the wall again.

I looked at Patrick, who was frozen above me, and I couldn't help the silent laughter that escaped me, making my whole body shake.

The door opened, and suddenly my sisters were in the room. I yelped and pulled the sheet up while Patrick bounced off the bed so fast he almost hit the wall.

"Oh." Abby, for once, was clearly at a loss for words.

"I see." Tessa was grinning madly.

"Good morning," Patrick said, stooping to pick up his shirt. "I'm just going. Now."

"Good idea," I said, still trying not to laugh. "I'll see you later?"

"Definitely." He nodded and slipped from the room.

I heard the front door actually lock behind him, and then my sisters jumped on the bed.

"You liar!" Abby hit me with a dusty pillow. "You told us he wasn't interested in you! What was that?"

"I wasn't lying!" I protested, trying to protect myself from the pillow assault. "Just as I was texting you guys, he knocked on the door. How was I supposed to know he'd do that?"

"Because he's clearly been into you this whole time!" Tessa was whacking me now. "We could see it!"

"Fine, you were right!" I said, holding up my hands in surrender. "You were both right! Now, will you please let me get dressed before you ask any more questions?"

"Tessa, what do you think?" Abby asked. "Is that a fair request?"

"I'll allow it," Tessa said, still grinning like a demented Cheshire cat. "We came to pick you up for a smoothie, but I think we might need to get you a proper breakfast. I bet you worked up an appetite."

I groaned, but I had to admit it was true. My night with Patrick had left me ravenous.

14 Patrick

I managed to slip my shirt back over my head between Michelle's front door and my own. But that didn't entirely prepare me for Phoenix, sitting at the kitchen table and munching on his peanut butter toast with a bemused expression.

"I guess it went well last night," he said, taking another mouthful of toast.

"Uh, yes," I said, feeling more embarrassed than a grown man should in his own home. "I went to talk to her, and we..."

"I get it." Phoenix nodded. "Mum has lots of boyfriends. You don't have to act like I don't know what happens when someone 'comes over to talk'."

I winced at that. "Sorry," I said. "I know you're not a kid; it's just people get embarrassed talking about this stuff. Even adults."

"Mum doesn't like to talk about it, either."

"But she has talked to you about safe sex and stuff, right?" I suddenly realised it was entirely possible that my sister hadn't given him the talk. "You should know there are condoms in the bathroom cupboard. You're welcome to take some if you ever... I mean, I'll keep restocking them. No questions asked."

Phoenix took another bite of toast. "Uh, thanks. But I know all about that stuff. They made us put a condom on a banana last year at school."

"Right," I said. "I must have missed that one." I cleared my throat. "I know it's kind of awkward, but if you ever need to talk about this stuff... I mean, about girls you like – or boys! – then I'm here. Always. Even if you're not living here, you can call me. I promise not to make it weird."

Patrick appeared to consider this as he finished his toast. "So, is Michelle your girlfriend now? When Mum has someone come over late, he's usually her boyfriend after that."

And shit, I didn't know how to answer. "Well, that's a bit complicated. Because she'll be going back to Glasgow soon. So, we haven't really talked about things like boyfriend and girlfriend."

"But you like her," Phoenix pressed. "And she likes you."

"I think she does," I said, obviously not about to tell my nephew that Michelle had made it abundantly clear that she liked me multiple times last night. "But like I said, it's complicated."

"If she wasn't leaving, would she be your girlfriend?" Phoenix made it sound like that point was important to him.

"Probably," I said. It wasn't like it mattered, really, because she was leaving. But my stomach, squirming with more than just the need to refuel after my considerable exertions, twisted violently on that point. "I haven't had a lot of real girlfriends. Not serious ones. I'm not really into being...committed."

Phoenix nodded, and I noticed he had started to twist his hands together. "You're going to be sad when she leaves, right?"

"Maybe a little," I lied because I knew that it would be a whole lot more than a little.

"Will it still be okay for me to stay when she's gone?" Phoenix asked suddenly, standing up and looking much younger than his fourteen years. "Or do you want me to go? Because you don't like commitments and—"

"That's completely different!" I said, and I took a step towards him before I paused. I should probably have a shower before I hugged my nephew; I didn't want to traumatise the kid any further. "You'll always be welcome here; I want you to know that."

"Okay," Phoenix said and stood there a moment longer. "I'm going to go and play Xbox."

"Good call. I'm going to have a shower."

"Yeah, you probably should." Phoenix gave me a slightly mischievous grin. "Because you stink."

· ♥ · ♥ · ♥ · ♥ · ♥ ·

Khalid: how did it go last night?

Khalid: hello? would it kill you to reply?

Khalid: i'm going to assume it went really well, based on your lack of reply

Khalid: either that or she's murdered you

Khalid: i'll murder you if you don't reply soon

Patrick: it went well

Khalid: ...is that seriously all you're going to give me? DUDE

Patrick: really well. i stayed over

Khalid: i had worked that out. but what happened? did you tell her how you feel about her?

Patrick: we didn't talk all that much actually

Patrick: and definitely not about feelings and stuff. just about how we both want this, so let's enjoy it while we can

Khalid: how could you not talk about feelings?!

Patrick: we were busy <winky face emoji>

Khalid: i'd say that was no excuse but knowing how long you've been into her, it probably is. are you going to talk to her about how you feel?

Patrick: there's nothing to say! she knows i like her, but this whole thing is short term because she literally lives on the other side of the world

Khalid: you should ask her to stay

Patrick: her sisters have begged her to move here. if she won't move for them, she's not going to move for a guy she's known a couple of weeks

Khalid: she would if it's serious

Patrick: it's not serious

Khalid: are you sure?

I was about to reply to Khalid's last message, but instead, I leaned back against my workbench, chewing my lip.

Was I sure it wasn't serious? I was sure that Michelle wouldn't seriously consider leaving her job and moving to Sydney, just for me. She definitely didn't like me that much, and I'd be an arsehole to suggest it.

But was I that serious about her?

"I've got no bloody idea," I told my collection of wood clamps. "How am I supposed to know?"

· ♥ · ♥ · ♥ · ♥ · ♥ ·

"Is it okay if Michelle comes over for dinner?" I asked, leaning against the door frame to what I no longer thought of as the spare room but as Phoenix's room.

"Yeah." Phoenix looked up from the Xbox controller. "Why wouldn't it be?"

"Well, because we're..." I held up my hands. "You know."

"You said she's not your girlfriend." Phoenix didn't pause in his obliteration of zombies. "So, it's not really that different, right?"

"I guess not." It certainly *felt* different, but I didn't know how to explain that to myself, let alone to a four-teen-year-old who clearly wanted me to leave him alone. "We're not going to be, like, kissing in front of you."

"Good," Phoenix said, with a visible shudder at the thought of his uncle kissing anyone. "I don't really want to see that."

"You won't have to!" I assured him. "Anyway, I'll try to make something nice. For dinner, I mean."

"You should get more Tim-Tams," Phoenix said with a little nod. "For dessert."

"Double coat?"

"They're better," Phoenix agreed and then was once more absorbed by the game. Maybe, I thought, I'd get a new gaming system for him. Like a PS5. If I was honest, I wouldn't mind playing it myself. Gaming together would be good for bonding, right?

But then I remembered I didn't know how much longer Phoenix would be staying with me, and the idea of buying a PS5 for myself seemed just plain sad.

When Michelle left, and Phoenix too, my life would be... Shit, I didn't know what it would be. But I didn't like the thought of it.

· ♥ · ♥ · ♥ · ♥ · ♥ ·

"This," Michelle proclaimed, "is a perfect steak."

"Thanks," I said, more relieved to hear that than I wanted to let on. "Steak, I can do. Chicken, fine. Lamb, it's a possibility. But anything that can't be grilled? We're in trouble."

"I'm not much of a cook either," Michelle said, helping herself to more of the salad that had come in a bag, complete with a plastic dressing sachet. "Tessa's a great cook. But mostly, I just pick something up from Sainsbury's on the way home from work."

"What's Sainsbury's?" Phoenix asked, looking up from his steak, which he had wedged between two pieces of crusty French bread. That was mildly insulting to the quality of my steak, but I couldn't blame a growing teenager for wanting more carbs. I had bought more bread since Phoenix had arrived than in the whole previous year.

"It's a supermarket," Michelle explained. "Kind of fancy, but not too fancy. Waitrose is the really fancy one. Like, so fancy that they've got duck liver pâté and artichoke hearts in their Essentials range."

Phoenix snorted at that. "Yuck."

"I like artichokes in salad." Michelle tilted her head as though considering. "But pâté's just gross."

"You're both wrong. A good pâté on sourdough is sublime."

"But you don't eat bread," Phoenix pointed out. "You said it will give you a gut."

"Well, if I did eat bread," I said, "I'd want pâté on it, that's for sure."

"I bet Tessa knows a deli where I could find you a good one," Michelle said thoughtfully. "I'll have to ask her."

I looked up at her, touched that Michelle cared enough about me to try to source a food she personally detested. Did that mean she liked me in a serious way? Or maybe – more likely – she was just that nice. It was hard to tell when a good person liked you. They treated everyone well; it was impossible to know if you were special.

"Uncle Patrick didn't make dessert," Phoenix said to Michelle. "But we got Tim-Tams."

"The best dessert!" Michelle enthused, smiling at him. "I bet that was your idea, right?"

Phoenix squirmed under her approval, but I could see he enjoyed it, and there I went again; appreciating Michelle for being such a damn nice person.

"Yeah," Phoenix said, shrugging. "Can you get them in England?"

"Well, I actually live in Scotland," Michelle explained. "But no, you can't. So, I'll have to eat as many as possible while I'm still here."

Phoenix nodded and returned to his makeshift steak sandwich with gusto.

"Will they be the thing you miss most about Australia?" I asked her. "Or will it be the weather?"

Michelle laughed, her nose wrinkling. "Neither," she said. "You do remember my sisters live here, right?"

"Of course," I said. "Sisters are better than Tim-Tams."

"I might have disagreed with you a few times when we were teenagers, but now I think they're pretty great," Michelle said, cutting another piece of steak. "And, of course, I'll miss the two of you a whole lot."

I felt a tightness in my chest and a lump in my throat that wasn't the result of swallowing too large a piece of meat (I had done that enough times to know). Because I knew, right then, that I'd miss her. Miss her more than I wanted to admit to anyone, especially myself.

Right now, I had Michelle and Phoenix at my table, chatting, laughing, and making my house feel like a home. But they'd both be gone in a few more days, or maybe weeks if I was lucky. This life – with people I cared about around me – wasn't real. It was a life I was borrowing by the chance intersection of aggrieved baggage handlers and my sister inhabiting the excitingly pointy end of the mental health spectrum. I'd be back to normal, with my empty house – despite frequent one-time visitors – and my empty life.

I had never thought of it as empty before. Apparently, I hadn't known what I was missing, and now I did. And that *sucked*.

"Are you okay?" Michelle asked gently, one hand on my arm. "You look like you're off with the pixies."

"Just thinking about a new commission I've got," I lied. "The customer is insisting on mahogany, but I think it would be better in teak. He won't be told, though."

"I see," Michelle said, and she looked at me through her lashes, biting her lip. "That's the only thing on your mind?"

"Of course," I said, reaching out to squeeze her hand.

Phoenix set his knife and fork neatly in the middle of his plate. "I'm done," he said. "Is it okay if I go for a walk and take some photos by the beach? I'll be a couple of hours."

I could have sworn that kid smirked at me.

"That's fine," I said. "Enjoy."

"Save some Tim-Tams for me," he said, disappearing down the hall and out the door.

"Did he just wingman you? Because it seemed like he did."

"Pretty sure he's seen too many movies," I said. "I think he totally did."

"Well, while we've got some time alone..." Michelle looked at me and licked her lips.

And that was enough to quiet the turmoil in my stupid brain, at least for now.

15 Michelle

"You know, if the baggage handlers hadn't decided to stick it to the man, we would never have had the chance to do this," Abby said. "And wouldn't that have been a shame?"

"You know what, Abby?" I replied. "I completely agree."

Abby pretended to faint in shock all over Tessa, making us all laugh. The three of us were seated on the top deck of the ferry that chugged its way from Brekkie Beach to the city every half hour. The sun was bright in the sky, but out on the water, there was a pleasant breeze, and everywhere I looked, views were begging to be photographed. Headlands dotted with multi-million-dollar homes, the city coming up on the horizon with its skyscrapers and gleaming chrome, yachts and motorboats zooming around the harbour, and up ahead, the famous Sydney Opera House and Harbour Bridge, just like in all the postcards.

"We're going to miss you so much," Tessa said, pushing the collapsed Abby from her lap to wrap an arm around me. "I've gotten used to having the three of us together again."

"Don't say that. I don't want to think about it, not when it's such a beautiful day, and you two promised me some seriously amazing shopping."

"And lunch," Abby added. "I booked Café Sydney; best views in the city." She pointed to a tall building that counted as historic by Australian standards, and I could just make out tables and well-dressed diners on the rooftop.

"Wow," I said. "Won't that be expensive?"

"Nothing's too good for you, Michelle," Abby told me firmly. "Today, we're going all out!"

"Shop till we drop," Tessa agreed. "Come on, let's go down so we can be first off. Those clothes aren't going to buy themselves."

And that, I thought, was true.

Two hours later, I was laden with shopping bags, but my sisters were already dragging me into another boutique, and truthfully, it didn't take all that much dragging.

"You won't have this in Glasgow," Abby told me. "The designer creates all the patterns herself, and it's made in Australia."

A riot of bright prints, everything from abstract flamingos to watercolour octopuses, met my eyes. It was overwhelming but in a delightful kind of way.

"I can see you in this," I said, picking up a tank dress with a print of leopard spots and actual leopards and holding it against Abby.

"Yes, leopards suit you, Abby." Tessa nodded.

"Because I'm scary?"

"Because you're fierce."

"Nice save," Abby said, plucking a shirt off the rack and offering it to me. "This could be good for you."

I took the shirt, feeling the delicate silk between my fingers. Bright sunset colours drifted across the surface; oranges, purples, and deep red blending and changing. I bit my lip and put it back.

"You love those colours!"

"It's cute," I said. "But I couldn't wear that to work. I have enough trouble making people take me seriously without turning up in a sunset."

"It's only a bit of colour," Tessa said, picking up the shirt again. "Just try it on; it would look amazing on you. And you don't have to wear it to work!"

"Where else do I go?" I sighed, but I let her give me the shirt again. What would be the harm in humouring my sisters and trying it on?

"I'll start a change room for you!" A perky young woman in a tulip dress printed with pink and yellow balloons approached, forcefully taking the shirt from my hands. "I love this colour story for you, hun! You just sit tight and I'll choose some more things for you."

"You don't need to—" I began, but she had already swooped on Abby.

"And this one for you?" She plucked the leopard dress from Abby's fingers. "I can see you in leopard. It's so your vibe, babe!"

"Apparently, I'm fierce." Abby grinned. "Let her do her job," she whispered to me. "It wouldn't kill you to wear something other than black and grey."

"It might." Tessa pretended to take my temperature. "Are you sure it's worth the risk?"

"I wear colour!" I protested, but it wasn't entirely true. My corporate wardrobe was all muted shades, and it had spilled out into my few non-work clothes. Even my workout gear was funeral ready.

"Go and try it on!" Tessa began to march me towards the changing room. "So we can admire you."

Stepping into a curtained booth, I quickly slipped off my t-shirt dress (yes, it was black) and pulled on the shirt, as well as the yellow linen shorts that the perky woman had chosen for me. I was almost annoyed at how well they fit.

Of course, the changing room didn't have its own mirror, so I was forced to reveal myself to my sisters and was met with wolf whistles from Abby and applause from Tessa.

"Look at you!" Tessa said approvingly. "You look amazing!"

The mirror proved that she was right. The bright colours made my olive skin look warmer and fresher than my usual choices.

"You look like your old self again," Abby said. "You used to love bright colours."

"I still do," I said, running a hand over the shirt. "But they're not practical for my job."

"Forget your job!" Tessa snorted. "I bet Patrick would like you in colours like this!"

"I'd usually say that you shouldn't give a shit what a man thinks about your clothes," Abby said. "Given that most men walk around looking like their mum dressed them. But I gotta agree."

"I think Patrick likes me in less clothing."

"Then we should go lingerie shopping after this," Tessa said brightly. "What are you thinking? Corset? Garter belt?"

"How's it going with Patrick, anyway?" Abby interrupted.

"Good." I shrugged as though it didn't matter. "We're going paddleboarding tomorrow. Well, he's taking Phoenix paddle boarding, and I'm tagging along."

"Not what I meant." Abby waved a hand. "You like him, don't you?"

"I do," I admitted because there was no point in lying to my sisters. They always knew and wouldn't let me forget it if I tried. "He's...amazing. He's set the bar high for when I'm ready to meet the right guy."

"But he isn't the right guy?"

I swallowed. "He can't be," I said. "He lives here, I live in Glasgow. And besides, I'm not—"

"A Partner yet?" Abby finished. "So, the right guy will only appear once you're a Partner? Do they give you some kind of pheromone-blasting beacon so you can attract him?"

"You know what I mean. I have things I need to do before I can..." I shook my head. "You know why it's important to me that I stick to my plan. It's the wrong time for me to meet anyone serious."

"He really couldn't be a serious guy for you?" Tessa pressed. "What if he moved to Glasgow?"

"He's not going to do that, he's got Phoenix! And a whole life here. Besides, I'd never ask anyone I actually liked to move to Glasgow."

"Because of the deep-fried food, or the weather?" Abby joked, but then she looked serious. "I don't know, Michelle. I've never seen you like this about a guy before."

"There's definitely something there," Tessa said. "And it's a shame that you feel like it can't be serious, just because of the timing. I mean, you told him about what happened when you were at kid at school. You haven't told any other guys about that. If you really like him, then—"

"I'm going to buy this," I announced, because I didn't want to hear any more of it. Not when my head was already such a mess. A part of me – an increasingly large part – knew that how I felt about Patrick *was* serious. But I also knew I couldn't let myself give in to that feeling. I had a plan. Falling for some handsome Australian was not part of that plan. So, I just wouldn't let myself fall.

Any harder, anyway.

"Amazing choice!" The saleswoman reappeared. "The shorts too?"

"Yes," I nodded firmly. "The lot."

"You're making the right decision," she told me happily, giving me a totally unnecessary wink.

Well, at least someone thought I was making the right decision.

· ♥ · ♥ · ♥ · ♥ · ♥ ·

"You've all done great today, guys!" The paddleboarding instructor, who was called Mitch, had a permanent grin on his face. He was like a tattooed, dreadlocked golden retriever in his boundless enthusiasm. "We're pretty much done here, so why don't we all head back to the shore?"

"You know, I think this could be my thing," I said, looking over at Phoenix and Patrick. "I'm totally getting the hang of it!" I held up my paddle like a baton, twirling it around in the air, and—

I lost my balance and fell into the water. I came up laughing and spluttering, my wet hair plastered to my face, and saw Phoenix trying very hard not to smile as he carefully paddled himself away from the general disaster zone that was me.

But then strong arms were around my waist. "You okay?" Patrick's breath was warm in my ear.

"I'm fine," I said, suddenly not feeling the cold of the water at all. "Did you jump in just to save me?"

"Seemed like the thing to do."

"You know I can swim, right?" I teased. "I know I'm English, but I can. And I can practically stand on the bottom."

"I know." Patrick tucked my damp hair behind my ear. "But I wanted an excuse to touch *your* bottom. You're driving me crazy in that bikini."

Under the cover of the water, his hands moved over my waist and down to squeeze my arse, pressing my body into his.

"And here was me thinking you just wanted the rush of being the hero," I managed to gasp, even as my body became more and more interested in those hands.

"I could be your hero," Patrick said, his lips so close to my ear I could almost imagine they were touching me. Except, of course, we were in the middle of a paddle boarding class and that would be highly inappropriate.

"We should get out of the water." I sighed, pushing away from him. "Or we're going to traumatise poor Phoenix."

"He seems okay," Patrick said, motioning with his head as he, rather reluctantly, clambered back onto his board. Looking over at the shore, I could see Phoenix talking to a small group of teenagers who had been in the class. He was even...smiling? Smiling and laughing! That was definitely a good sign.

"This is good," I said, pulling myself back onto my own board and feeling less like a mermaid and more like a walrus flopping onto a sun-warmed rock. "He's making friends."

"Seems like it." Patrick nodded, still watching Phoenix on the beach.

As we reached the shore, Phoenix came back over to us. "Keenan – he's the one with the red hair – asked if I wanted to hang out later. Is that okay? He lives near you."

"Sure. So long as hanging out doesn't mean buying drugs, vandalising street signs, and stealing a car."

Phoenix made a face. "He's got a PlayStation and this game where you fight zombies in space!"

"Well, space zombies sound irresistible," Patrick said, his eyes crinkling. "Of course you can go; it sounds like fun."

Looking relieved, Phoenix returned to the group of teenagers, who were probably making fun of the elderly woman in her twenties who couldn't paddleboard for shit. But I didn't mind. It made my chest swell to see Phoenix looking so happy with kids his own age.

"I get the feeling his mum doesn't make friendships easy for him," I said under my breath as I dragged my paddleboard up the sand.

"No," Patrick said. "She... Well, sometimes she likes him out of the house a lot. You know, if there's a new guy. But other times she wants him with her, like an emotional support animal."

"That's rough." I winced. "But he seems to be doing really well here. Definitely happier than when I first met him."

"You think so?" Patrick looked like he wanted to believe it but couldn't be sure.

"Definitely. I mean, who wouldn't be happier living in Brekkie Beach?" As soon as I said the words, I felt a twist in my stomach. I'd be leaving all too soon, back to twelve-hour days, endless rain, and gusty winds that would blow you off your feet. Brekkie Beach was paradise, but it wasn't my real life. I had to remember that.

"Do you think you'll miss it?" Patrick asked, those green eyes fixed on me with an intensity that made me shift under his gaze, but unable to look away.

"Of course I will," I said, my voice low and oddly husky. "I wish..." I shook my head. "But it's not like I can change my job."

"No." Patrick looked away, finally. "No, I know how much it means to you."

"I've put in so much work already," I said, wondering why I felt like I had to defend myself.

"They're lucky to have you," Patrick said. "And you deserve to...". He paused. "To finish your plan."

I forced a smile, but my stomach was doing that horrible twisting, writhing thing again. Every time I thought of leaving Brekkie Beach, my internal organs instantly turned into a pulsating, squirming mass that wouldn't have looked out of place in a cheap sci-fi movie.

But it didn't change the truth. I had to go back to Glasgow, sooner or later. And I couldn't let myself get too attached.

・♥ ・ ♥ ・ ♥ ・ ♥ ・ ♥ ・

Patrick: phoenix is having a zombie-killing marathon with his new friend. maybe I could come over?

Michelle: you should definitely come over. right now.

Before the now-familiar knock came on the door, I had just enough time to change into the last of the purchases I had made with my sisters that morning. I fumbled with the seemingly endless number of straps, and swore over the corset fastenings, but when I looked in the cloudy bathroom mirror?

Yeah, totally worth the effort.

I bit my lip and went to the door. "Patrick?" I had to check. It wouldn't do to answer the door like this to a total stranger.

"It's me."

I opened the door, and...

Patrick was grinning, but then his jaw went slack, and his eyes lit up like a kid from a cartoon spotting an unattended pie cooling on a windowsill.

"Do you like it?" I asked, turning in a slow circle so he could see that while the tight red lacy corset covered my torso, the matching G-string covered exactly none of my bottom.

"I like it." Patrick's voice was husky as he came into the house, pulling the door behind him heavily. "I really like it."

He pressed me against the wall, big hands gripping me through sheer lace and silk, sending sparks of pure want throughout my body and wet heat surging between my thighs.

"I wanted to make the most of the time we have." I gasped as Patrick's lips moved over my neck and down to my collarbone, a trail of grazing stubble, hot kisses, and delicate nips of his teeth that set my body on fire.

I gasped as he picked me up, throwing me over his shoulder like I weighed nothing at all. You really couldn't beat a carpenter's strength. "You're going to make it impossible for me to let you go, Michelle."

I gasped out in pleasure at his words, even as they made my chest tighten and my heart sink. He didn't mean it like *that*, did he?

But as he carried me to the stuffy bedroom with its lumpy mattress, I wished, for a moment, that he did.

16 Patrick

"Is it okay if I go down to the beach?" Phoenix asked, carefully putting his plate and glass in the dishwasher in a move that eluded many grown adults. "Keenan's got some body boards, and he reckons it's a good day for it."

"Yeah, for sure," I said, delighted that my nephew seemed to have found a friend. "Just remember your sunscreen."

Phoenix frowned, holding up one brown arm. "I don't need it."

"Yes, you do," I said. "You can still get sunburnt." That seemed like the responsible thing to say. "And besides, Keenan's a redhead, right?"

"Yeah?" Phoenix clearly didn't see the connection.

"So he *really* needs it," I told him. "Have you ever seen a sunburnt ginger? It's tragic. If you put some on, it'll probably make him feel better about having to wear it."

Phoenix thought for a minute. "Yeah, I guess so. So, if I take the sunscreen, I can go out?"

"And you promise to actually use it," I confirmed. "Go for your life. It's a beautiful day."

Phoenix was halfway out the door when I realised I had let the kid leave without—

"Mate!" I called out the door to my rapidly departing nephew. "Towel!"

Phoenix turned, and he did look slightly embarrassed. "Oh yeah," he said. "I forgot."

"Don't worry about it," I said, giving him the towel. "Forgetting stuff like that's part of being a teenager. I'll be on your arse about taking a jacket with you when it gets cold."

Phoenix paused, holding the towel to him. "Do you think I'll still be here? When it gets cold?"

And I hadn't thought about that. Not really. "I don't know. But you'll always be welcome."

Phoenix squirmed under my attempt to be serious. "Okay," he said. "Thanks."

"Have fun!" I called to his retreating back. "And don't forget to make Keenan slip slop slap!"

"You little bitch!" A howl of frustration met my ears, and I looked over to see Michelle – on her way to the gym if those tiny shorts were any guide – swearing at the cottage's front door.

I leaned against the fence. "What seems to be the problem, ma'am?" I asked, putting on a southern drawl to make her laugh.

Michelle let out a tiny chuckle. "The bloody door won't close properly. I know this is a quiet street, but leaving the front door flapping in the wind is just tempting fate."

"Give me a minute; I'll grab my tools."

"You don't need to—" Michelle began.

But it wouldn't take long to fix, and I could hardly leave Michelle without a working door.

When I returned, toolbox in hand, Michelle gave me a rueful smile. "Thanks," she said. "But it seems like a waste of your skills when I won't be here much longer."

And ouch. Her words felt like a soaring soccer ball had scored a direct hit to my guts. Or maybe my head.

"It will only take a minute," I said, swallowing down the pain of her words. "I reckon it's the hinges. They get loose over time, especially near the beach. The humidity makes the wood swell."

"I see." Michelle stood and watched as I tested the door against the rusty hinges.

"You did break out the lingerie the other night," I said. "So it's only fair you get to see me in full tradie mode. Chicks dig a guy who can fix things, right?"

And that made her laugh, easy and genuine. "That's a stereotype, but I'm not going to deny it," she said. "I once read a romance about this woman who lived next to a whole house full of tradies. Very good with their hands."

"Damn," I said. "Me being just one tradie must be a big disappointment." I let out an unnecessary grunt as I tightened the hinges. Really, they needed to be replaced. But Michelle had said it herself. She wouldn't be here much longer.

"You could never be a disappointment, Patrick," she said, her voice soft. "Um, I should make you some tea. Tradies like strong tea with two sugars, right? And a biscuit?"

"This tradie doesn't. Just a splash of milk for me. And no biscuits."

"Because of your carb thing?"

"Right," I said. "I only eat them on special occasions. Or if I'm very sad."

Michelle frowned slightly. "You're pretty strict with yourself about that, huh?"

"It's no big deal."

"I don't think the odd biscuit is going to make your shape any less appealing." Michelle ran a hand down my chest and over my stomach, as though proving her point. "But I guess I don't know what it's like to have photos of me discussed online."

I didn't know what to say to that, so I just fiddled with my screwdriver in a way that I hoped looked purposeful.

"I'll go and make the tea." Michelle moved past me into the house.

MICHELLE FINCH STICKS TO THE PLAN

I was just screwing the final hinge back into something approximating its correct place in the moisture-ridden wood when I heard Michelle answer her phone inside.

"Hello, this is Michelle," I heard her say, her accent going from broad Birmingham to something posh enough to present a BBC documentary. I wondered if that was because of her fear of people thinking she was stupid. How could she possibly worry about that? Michelle was one of the smartest people I had ever met.

"Really? I hadn't seen the news. So, when—" I felt a clench in my stomach. I hadn't seen the news either, but I could make an educated guess as to what Michelle was being told. "And so how long before I can—"

I set down my screwdriver and sighed heavily, leaning against the doorframe. It creaked ominously, and I stood up. I didn't want to destroy the house, even if demolition would be the kindest option for it.

"I see," I heard Michelle say. "I'll let you know when I get the confirmation. Right." Another pause. "Yes, I'll be able to look at that briefing paper this morning. Of course, no problem."

And then there was more silence. Michelle didn't appear for a few minutes, and when she did, her face was tight and drawn, her mouth screwed up like she had been sucking lemons and hadn't been offered a tequila shot afterwards.

"Um," she began, and she looked at me with a strangely helpless expression. "The baggage handlers' union reached a resolution. So, flights are back on."

"Oh," I said, pretending I hadn't already worked that out. "Well, that's good news, isn't it? You can go home."

"Yeah." Michelle was still clutching her phone to her chest. "Yes, it's definitely good news. And it sounds like my colleague Ash made a mess of one of my projects, so I'll definitely be getting it back."

"That's great." My voice was cheerful but hollow, like a plastic toy with a voice box rattling around in its empty shell. "You deserve to get your projects back. Get your promotion and get that bit closer to making Partner. Your whole plan, right?"

"Yeah." Michelle wasn't quite looking at me. "It will be good."

"Well, I'd better leave you to your workout," I said, putting my screwdriver back in the toolbox and picking it up. "You're going to the gym, right?"

"Actually, I've got to get onto some work now. So I'm across everything when I get back."

"Right," I said. "That...that makes sense."

"Thanks for fixing the door," Michelle said, opening and then closing it. "That works so much better."

"No problem." I forced a smile. "Even though it's just for a couple more days."

"I'm still grateful." Michelle was looking at me like she was about to say something else.

"No worries." I looked away. "I'll... I guess I'll see you later?"

"Definitely," Michelle's voice sounded as forced as my smile felt. "Got to enjoy the time we've got left, right?"

"I guess we do," I said and turned away.

· ♥ · ♥ · ♥ · ♥ · ♥ ·

After cutting a decorative piece of timber to the wrong length for the third time in a row, I gave up and sat down heavily on the same stool where Michelle had bandaged my hand. The cut had healed, but I could still feel the memory of her lips pressed to my palm. No, I couldn't. That was stupid.

But I definitely couldn't concentrate, so I pulled out my phone.

"What's up, dude?" Khalid answered. "I'm bloody glad you called, I was about to lose my shit at this client, and you distracted me."

"Glad to be of service," I said wryly. "So, I just found out Michelle's leaving."

"She's always been leaving."

"No, I mean, soon," I clarified. "The whole baggage handlers thing got resolved. Her flight's on Friday."

"Ohhh." Khalid drew out the word so that it had at least three and possibly more syllables. "Shit, dude. You okay?"

"I'm fine," I said. "Just, you know, I knew she'd leave, but I kind of... I don't know; I still wasn't expecting it to be this soon. If that makes sense?"

"Not really," Khalid said cheerfully. "So, your summer fling's coming to an end, huh? Guess that puts you back on the market."

"I guess," I said. The idea of putting myself back on the market had never been less appealing. What was wrong with me? I had never wanted to be tied down to just one woman, but Michelle had me seriously reconsidering my position on committed relationships. It was just that having one with her was utterly impossible.

"We could hit the clubs on Friday night," Khalid suggested. "Take your mind off it."

"I've got Phoenix," I reminded him, but that wasn't the real reason.

"Of course. Sorry, dude." He paused. "You sound a bit shit."

"Yeah," I agreed. I felt more than a bit shit. Totally shit would be closer to the mark. "I just... I thought I had a bit more time with her."

Khalid hissed out a breath between his teeth. "Dude," he said in a low voice. "You're serious about Michelle, aren't you?"

"No," I lied, even to myself. "I've always known she's going to leave. She's great, but it's never been serious."

"That sounds like bullshit," Khalid told me bluntly. "Complete bullshit. I should have known. You've never wanted to spend so much time with just one woman before. At first, I thought it was just because she was the one that almost got away, but it's not that, is it?"

"I don't know!" I closed my eyes and scrunched up my face. "It's just hit me harder than I thought. That she's leaving. It shouldn't be a big deal; I've known all along. And it's not like I do serious relationships anyway, and I've got Phoenix to think about and..."

"And you still like her more than you think you should," Khalid finished. "Maybe even more than like, huh?"

"I don't know about that," I said quickly. "I haven't known her that long."

"Doesn't matter." Khalid was dismissive. "I was with my ex, Bryan, for two years, and I never got big feelings for him after all that time. But when I met Adam, it was like, bam! Feelings explosion. Shame he turned out to be the human embodiment of a dumpster fire, but you get my point."

"Fine," I said. "But it's not like... I mean, I'll get over it."

"So, you're not going to confess your undying love, beg her to stay, and get down on one knee?" Khalid sounded like he was only half-joking.

"Of course not!" I made it sound like a ridiculous suggestion, but the idea of begging Michelle to stay had definitely crossed my mind. I wondered if there were any words, any combination of letters and sounds that I could string together that might make her consider leaving the job she had worked so hard for so she could... What, exactly? Stay in Brekkie Beach, with me? "She's super focused on her career. She wants to make Partner, it's really important to her. Her sisters have tried to convince her to move here loads of times. Nothing I could say would make her do it."

"Are you sure about that?" Khalid pressed. "Nothing you could say? Not even telling her how you feel?"

"Nothing," I repeated. "Anyway, I don't even know how I feel. I'm not going to ask her to stay when...when I don't know."

"Fine." Khalid sounded resigned to my indecision. "Look, dude, I've got to go and try to finish this mock-up without committing a felony against my client, but call me later, okay?"

"I will."

· ♥ · ♥ · ♥ · ♥ · ♥ ·

I was relieved that Phoenix was at the beach with his new friend when the next phone call came in.

"Hi, Mum," I said, trying to ensure my sigh wasn't audible.

"Patrick." Her tone was clipped. "I'm calling to let you know that Julia's feeling ready to see Phoenix. She'll be coming up on Saturday afternoon."

I noticed but didn't comment on the fact that she told me she was coming rather than asking if it was convenient. My mother never asked.

"Okay," I said, taking a quick breath. "So, Julia's feeling better?"

"Some rest and relaxation were just what she needed, and she's really taken to yoga. The instructor's wonderful. I think it's helped her find a sense of peace and healing."

I couldn't see how Julia, who hadn't had a job besides the odd TV advert in years, could possibly need rest and relaxation, but I didn't say so.

"Is this like when she got involved in that church group with all the power circles?" I asked, wincing at the memory. It was so like my sister to believe, truly believe, that whatever her newest distraction happened to be was the answer to all her problems. If it wasn't yoga, spiritualist groups, or nudism, it was a man. Often, they crossed over.

"Of course not!" My mother was clearly annoyed. "What's the problem, Patrick? Don't you want your sister to be happy?"

"It's not that," I said and chose my next words carefully. "It's just that when she gets a new interest or makes a new...friend, it can be great for a while, but it doesn't last."

"I don't think that's the case at all." We both knew that was a lie. But it was a well-practised one; my mother always defended Julia, no matter what she did or who she hurt.

"Fine." I was willing to drop it. What could I do, anyway? "So, does this mean she wants to take Phoenix home?"

"Are you already sick of him? It's not even been a month! Why don't you want to help your family when we need you?"

"I didn't say that," I said wearily. "I like having him here; he's a great kid. It's just that if she's ready to have him back, I need to make sure he's ready for it. Maybe he could chat to his psychologist about—"

"What psychologist?" My mother demanded. "Who have you been taking him to? I can't believe you'd do something like that without his mother's permission! Who do you think you are?"

And, *shit*. I really should not have said that. "Look, you had me pick him up in the middle of the night when Julia was having one of her meltdowns—"

"Don't say it like that!"

"Well, that's what it was," I said irritably. "And I came. I brought him home. None of you could tell me how long he'd be with me. He's been through a lot. He needed support, and I'd be a shitty uncle if I didn't get it for him. I'm trying to be responsible here."

"Been through a lot? Spending a few weeks at the beach with his uncle is hardly a lot!"

"That's not," I said, more loudly, "what I'm referring to. He's a great kid but he's anxious. And of course he is, not knowing whether his mum will be normal when he gets home from school, or if she'll be sobbing in bed with a bottle of wine and a packet of painkillers, or all over some new man."

"She's troubled!" My mother's voice was rising now. "You've never been kind to your sister, never given her any sympathy."

"This isn't about her," I said. "It's about Phoenix. He's way more anxious than a kid his age should be, and I found him someone to talk to about it. And I'm not going to apologise for that."

There was a silence. It was the closest I had ever come to fighting with my mother. It was easier to let it go, disengage, and end the call. But now, it wasn't just about me. It was about Phoenix.

"I'm not going to tell Julia about this psychologist business," my mother said finally. "It would only upset her."

"Fine," I said. "I guess I'll see her on Saturday, then."

I ended the call, considered throwing my phone at the ground, and then thought better of it. Instead, I went into the fridge and opened a beer. Lunchtime beers weren't appropriate for a responsible adult and were chock-full of carbs, but I felt that, at this moment, I deserved one. Phoenix wasn't here, so I couldn't be accused of being a poor role model.

"Hey, Uncle Patrick!" A bright voice interrupted me, and I quickly hid the beer behind me.

"Hey, dude!" I said, trying to sound cheerful. "And Keenan, right?" The red-headed boy from the paddle-boarding lesson was close behind him.

"Hi," Keenan said, giving me a grin that showed that he had been gifted with braces as well as red hair.

"I wanted to show Keenan the Xbox. If that's okay?"

"Yeah, of course," I said, contorting my mouth into a smile. There was no way I was going to tell Phoenix about his mother's visit, not when he had a friend with him. Not when he seemed so happy. "It's your home too; you can have guests. Are you guys hungry?"

"Nah." Phoenix shook his head. "We went to the bakery. We had, like, four cheese and bacon rolls."

"Six." Keenan nudged him, and they both laughed.

"Sounds like a good feed. You guys have fun, okay?"

The boys turned and made for Phoenix's room up the stairs.

"Your uncle's, like, super ripped," I heard Keenan say admiringly. "I bet he gets tons of chicks."

And that made me chuckle. It was true. But now, there was just one chick I wanted, and she was about to leave the country.

MICHELLE FINCH STICKS TO THE PLAN

· ♥ · ♥ · ♥ · ♥ · ♥ ·

Keenan didn't leave until it was almost time for dinner, and I was grilling chicken breasts (with seasoning now, at least) on the barbecue.

"You can stay if you like," I told him. "Plenty of chicken to go around." I waved my tongs in a way I hoped was friendly.

Keenan looked at the chicken breasts with a distinct lack of interest. "No thanks," he said politely. "Mum would kill me if I didn't come home for dinner."

"No worries." And that wasn't even close to being true. I was, as of this moment, full of worries. I had worries pouring out of my freaking ears. I wished Keenan was staying for dinner. Anything to put off having the discussion with Phoenix that I knew was coming.

When Phoenix had seen his friend to the door, he made his way back outside and plopped down in a chair.

"Good day?"

"Really good." Phoenix nodded to make his point. "It was fun, bodyboarding and stuff. And Keenan liked the Xbox, but he still reckons PlayStation is better."

"It's an age-old rivalry." I turned the chicken, took a breath, and made sure I was actually looking at him when I said the next words. "Your Nan called me today."

"Yeah?" Phoenix seemed to stiffen, his formerly relaxed posture in the chair becoming military-like in its erect precision. "About Mum?"

"She's coming on Saturday to see you. Your mum, that is."

Phoenix took a moment to absorb this information. "She didn't text me."

"Yeah, she's...well, your Nan said she's trying to stay away from technology for a while. Some kind of digital cleanse thing."

"Oh," Phoenix said, looking down at his knees, which I was pleased to see weren't sunburnt. "So, am I going back home with Mum?"

"Your Nan didn't say," I said, wishing I had something more certain to tell him. "I think it's just a visit for now."

"But then what?" Phoenix asked. "Am I starting school here or going home?"

"I'm not sure." I felt utterly useless. "I mean, I'm happy for you to stay as long as...as long as you need to. But it's not really my call."

Phoenix nodded, still looking at his knees. He fiddled with the hem of his boardshorts and then began rolling and unrolling the drawstring. "Mum will want me to come home," he said finally. "When she gets... I mean, when she misses me."

"I'm sure she's missing you right now," I said. "She's just not well. But I'm sure she misses you."

Phoenix continued his rolling and unrolling of the drawstring. "Will Michelle be here when she comes over? Like, is she going to meet my mum?"

Oof, and there was another one of my worries. "Actually, no," I said, trying hard to make it sound like no big deal. "That problem with the flights? It got sorted out. So, Michelle's going home on Friday."

"Really?" Phoenix looked up at me, his drawstring abandoned. "Are you, like, sad about that?"

Was I sad about that? Yes, I was sad. Probably way beyond sad and well into devastated. But I wasn't going to put that on a kid.

"Look, we always knew she'd be going home sometime." I shrugged, making every effort to keep my voice light. "So, it's no big deal."

But even my fourteen-year-old nephew could tell I was lying.

17 Michelle

"I can't believe you're leaving us!" Abby brandished a bottle of wine at me somewhat threateningly.

"I'm going home!" I objected, stepping aside to let my sisters in. "I was only supposed to be here a week and you've had me almost a month!"

"And we're very grateful." Tessa kissed me on the cheek, her arms full of a baking tray covered in foil. "But we're still devastated you're leaving."

"I know." I sighed, taking the wine from Abby and fetching the chipped glasses that had become strangely familiar. The one with a crack at the base was my favourite. "I'm even going to miss this place."

"No, you won't." Abby curled her lip as she inspected the potentially deadly exposed wiring around a light fitting. "But you'll miss being here. With us."

"And Patrick," Tessa added, uncovering the pan to reveal the macaroni and cheese that she had perfected in our teenage years. "I think you're going to really miss him."

I made a noise that I hoped would satisfy them on that point. It didn't.

"You don't think you'll miss him?"

"I mean, I probably will for a bit," I said. "But it's not like—" I shook my head. "I mean, I always knew this whole thing had a use-by date."

"A use-by date," Tessa repeated. "How romantic."

"You know what I mean. Patrick is great. He's really... I don't know how to describe it, but he's just a genuinely good guy. He's smart, funny, and strangely down to earth for a former child actor."

"And he's super-hot," Abby pointed out. "That doesn't hurt."

"And super-hot," I admitted. "Not to mention extremely talented in the bedroom. But, it's not like I..."

"It's not like you what?" Tessa asked, unwilling to let me trail off and refuse to commit to an answer.

"It's not like I ever imagined a future with him," I said finally, putting knives and forks beside the plates. "I mean, I couldn't. Being here has been amazing, but it's not my real life. I need to get back to work, get my career back on track, and then—"

"Then, when you're a Partner, you're allowed to meet someone and maybe take the time to be happy?" Abby finished. "Until then, it's all work and suffering. Just so you can prove that you're worthy when you should already know that you are!"

"I'm hardly suffering," I said, helping myself to a massive portion of macaroni and cheese. Tessa's version included crispy breadcrumbs on the top and the smell could have lured a cheese lover into the seediest of vans and darkest of alleyways. "And yes, I've got a goal. A plan. Because I want to prove something to myself. That's hardly a crime, is it? It would be impossible for me to advance my career and have a relationship. No point trying to have it all. You can't. Not at the same time, anyway."

"I've always thought that was sensible," Tessa said, scrunching up her nose. "But seeing you here, with Patrick, I just think... I don't know, Michelle. I know how important your plan is, and I respect that. But are you sure you aren't making a huge mistake, not trying to work something out with him?"

"There's nothing to work out," I said, taking a gulp of wine. I needed wine; I needed a *lot* of wine. "He lives here. I live in Glasgow. Even if by some insane chance he *wanted* to live in Glasgow – which he can't, because of Phoenix – I still wouldn't have time for a relationship."

"I guess you've decided, then," Abby said, around a mouthful of macaroni. She'd never talk with her mouth full in front of people, but sisters? Sisters didn't count as people.

"I mean, I have to," I said, fiddling with my wine glass. "I've got to go back. It would be stupid to have put in all these years, got this far, and then just abandon it for a guy I don't even know that well. I don't do stupid. And it's not like he's asking me to stay! I have to go back."

"I never said you didn't," Abby said, quirking her mouth. "Sounds like you're convincing yourself."

"I don't need to convince myself. It's the right thing to do."

"But you'll see him before you go, right?" Tessa asked, waiting until she had swallowed. Somewhere along the line, she had picked up better table manners than Abby.

"Why wouldn't I? Believe me, I'll be spending as much time as I can either over or under Patrick until I leave for the airport!"

But then I thought of how I had brushed him aside when I got the news. Because I couldn't bear to be around him, not when I knew that each time that I saw him brought me closer to the last. Still, my sisters didn't need to know that. I had just been...shocked. Yes, that was right. Shocked that the flights had finally been resolved. I'd see him later, I thought. And it would be sexy and delightful and not give me even remotely confusing feelings.

I took another long sip of wine as though that would make the feelings disappear.

"I mean, I can't say I disapprove of that idea." Abby waved her fork. "But you'll still have a little time for us, right?"

"Of course. You two are what I'll miss most of all."

But as much as I loved my two sisters, I was no longer sure if that was true.

· ♥ · ♥ · ♥ · ♥ · ♥ ·

When Patrick asked me to come for lunch the next day, I had accepted. It wasn't like I was afraid to see him.

Except for the part where I was. We had managed to avoid each other since I had got the news about the baggage handlers' union. I had thought he'd text me to come over, but though I had waited until long after my sisters were gone, no text had come through.

And that was fine. It wasn't like I was the only thing in his life. He had custom furniture pieces to build and an anxious nephew to look after. Still, I couldn't pretend I hadn't been disappointed and relieved in equal measure.

But now, apparently, he wanted to see me, so I knocked on the door, a bowl under one arm, and I needed every bit of my self-control to keep my face bright and neutral.

"Hey!" Patrick leaned in to kiss me, but it was only a brief brush of his lips. "Thanks for coming."

"Thanks for inviting me," I said, like we were workplace acquaintances edging towards friendship rather than people who had seen each other naked and crying, though not at the same time. "Um, I brought a salad. A good one, with cheese and stuff."

"Nice!" Patrick took the bowl from me and peered in approvingly. "Come on through to the deck; I've had some lamb on the barbecue since this morning."

"Good!" I said with a little laugh that sounded horribly fake. "I mean, lamb is...good."

'Lamb is good.' Had I really said that out loud? Pathetic.

But Patrick just beckoned me through the house, and I followed, asking myself why I couldn't just be normal.

"Look who I found!" Patrick said, his own voice sounding oddly loud and obnoxiously cheerful.

"Hi Michelle," Phoenix said, barely lifting his head to look at me. He was staring at something on his phone, his legs tucked under him in the chair.

"Hey," I said, smiling at him. "Patrick said you've been hanging out with Keenan from paddle-boarding. That sounds fun."

A shrug. "It's okay."

And wow, we were back to 'it's okay', were we? I looked at Patrick for an explanation, and he shook his head slightly.

"Lamb!" Patrick announced, throwing open the hood of the barbecue. It smelled amazing; fresh rosemary, abundant garlic, and the aroma of perfectly cooked meat. But I suddenly felt like I couldn't eat a bite. My stomach was somewhere between squirming and absent, like it was flickering in and out of existence.

"You've upped your cooking game," I said, searching for something to say. "Look at all that seasoning!"

"I needed to improve. Now that it's not just for me." He looked over at Phoenix, who didn't raise his head. "You like food with actual taste, don't you?"

"I don't mind," he said. "Do you want me to do anything?"

"Uh, the table's set," Patrick said, looking awkward. "So, just sit and eat."

I sat, and Patrick began to carve up the lamb. I'd force myself to eat at least some, I decided, given Patrick had gone to all this effort.

"Why are you leaving?" Phoenix suddenly asked, looking at me with a fierceness you didn't expect to see in such a young face.

"Um..." I began, wondering what the hell to say. "Well, I live in Glasgow. My job's in Glasgow. I was just here to visit."

"And all the flights got screwed up because of that baggage handler's thing," Patrick cut in from where he was carving up the lamb. "I told you about that."

"I know, but—" Phoenix was still frowning. "Your family are here."

I swallowed. "Yes," I agreed. "My sisters are here. And it sucks that I don't get to live in the same country as them because of my job, but we keep in touch all the time. We've got a group chat, and we facetime a lot. We're still really close."

But Phoenix just looked down at his phone again before getting up from the table.

"What's up, dude?" Patrick looked concerned. "Not hungry?"

"No," Phoenix said firmly. "I'm not."

He didn't slam the sliding door as he went in, but the sentiment was there just the same.

"Was it something I said?" I tried to smile, but it didn't feel like much more than a grimace.

"It's not you," Patrick said, sitting down and serving himself a large piece of lamb. "His mum's coming on Saturday, but she still hasn't said if she's taking him home. It's been really hard on him."

"Oh, shit." I closed my eyes for a moment. "That would be incredibly rough."

"Yeah," Patrick agreed. "She's put him through so much, but he loves his mum, you know?"

"I do." My chest tightened painfully because I knew just how that felt. Still loving a parent who had disappointed you again and again. Until you didn't. "I wondered if he was going to stay with you. Permanently, I mean."

Patrick huffed out a breath. "Well, you remember how it went last time that came up."

"That's when she stopped letting you see him, right? She accused you of trying to steal her son."

"Yep. She went ballistic." Patrick shifted uneasily at the memory. "So, when I got the call this time, I knew it must be pretty bad for her to need me."

"I'm so sorry, that's...so hard." The words weren't enough, but I didn't know what to say.

"I just feel bad for Phoenix." Patrick sighed. "Up until then, I saw him a ton. I felt like I could be at least one thing in his life he could rely on. And then he couldn't."

"Poor kid," I murmured. "It's so unfair that he's had to go through all of this."

"Yeah, it is," Patrick said. "So, the truth is, I'd love him to stay here with me. Forever. I don't know if I'd be the best father figure, but I can...I guess I can give him the basics. Routines. Boundaries. Someone to talk to."

"You've been great for him," I said earnestly. "He's so much happier than when I first met him."

"Until today." Patrick raised his eyebrows.

"Until today. But that's not on you. You're a good guy, Patrick. Not many people would just change their whole life to look after their nephew even if they really needed them. And you're good with him, and I can see how much he trusts you. He's lucky to have you. Really lucky."

"Michelle..." Patrick looked at me like he wasn't sure whether to kiss me or just lay his head on my lap and close his eyes. I would have been happy with either option, to be honest. I just wanted to be close to him, to hold this good, kind man against me and—

"You should have some lamb." Patrick put a piece on my plate. "Before it gets cold."

"Right," I said, picking up my knife and fork. "Because lamb is good."

And that was easier to say than any of the other million thoughts swirling through my brain.

· ♥ · ♥ · ♥ · ♥ · ♥ ·

When the knock came on my door late that night, I didn't have to guess who it was.

I opened the door with the word 'hi' in my mouth, but I never got the chance to let it out. Because the moment that weather-beaten door on its no longer loose but still rusty hinges opened, Patrick's mouth was on mine, his hands on my body, pressing me to him like he never wanted to let me go. That part was probably my imagination, but as calloused fingertips pressed into my bare skin, I could believe it.

Maybe I even wanted to.

I let myself melt into his body; our mouths locked together like we were sharing oxygen. And when he lifted me up, my legs wrapped around his waist, tight and vice-like, I didn't say a word. I didn't trust myself not to say something wrong, something that was too much – or too little – and ruin my very last time with him.

As Patrick carried me into the bedroom, the lumpy mattress was the last thing on my mind. I didn't notice the creaking ceiling fan, the ever-present humidity, or how the overhead light flickered every few minutes. There was only Patrick.

Clothes arced gracefully through the air and fell to the ground without a word. Tonight, there was no dirty talk, no teasing. The only sounds were my sighs, my moans, my gasps of pleasure, met by low grunts, sharp intakes of breath, and groans that bordered on growls.

But that didn't stop this from being absolutely perfect. And when Patrick was inside me, filling me up like nothing and no one ever had, those bright green eyes never left my face. Somehow, I knew that wasn't an insult to the bounce of my breasts as I rode him or to the appealing curves of my body.

I knew that it meant something. Something I couldn't name, even if I could have guessed what it was. When his skilled fingers brought me to climax just as he peaked inside me, I called out his name, like a chant, a prayer, or maybe a eulogy.

Because this was the last time.

When it was over, I collapsed into his arms, sweaty and full of endorphins and still unable to say a single word. Patrick held me against him and I drifted into sleep. It shouldn't have been possible the way my brain was buzzing, but a seriously powerful orgasm, it seemed, was more than capable of knocking out even the most persistent of thoughts.

And when I woke late in the night, he was gone.

18 Patrick

"Phoenix?" I knocked gently on the door. "Are you up?"

A grunt from inside the room let me know he hadn't been.

Feeling slightly ashamed, I pushed open the door. "Hey, dude," I said with a bright grin. "Sorry to wake you. I was just thinking, it's a beautiful day. We should go to the zoo!"

Phoenix blinked at me like he thought I might be a particularly persistent dream. "The zoo?"

"I was just thinking about how much you liked it when I took you a few years ago," I said. "And I bet you could take some great photos."

"What time is it?" Phoenix made a grab for his phone. "It's early."

"It is. But if we get there early, before the crowds get in, it will be better. I mean, you could get better photos!"

"Okay." Phoenix put his phone down. "Um, that sounds good."

"Well, I've got your toast on, so when you're ready, we'll get going!"

I left my poor nephew to slowly orient himself to the world, as a teenager awakened before eight in the morning on his summer holiday needed to, and made my way back down the stairs. Maybe I'd make another coffee.

And I definitely wouldn't look through the window at the cottage next door to see if Michelle was still there or if she had already walked out of my life forever.

· ♥ · ♥ · ♥ · ♥ · ♥ ·

"We should go and see the penguins next." I held up a map of the zoo, and pointed. "Or there's the seal show! No, wait, that's not for another two hours."

"Uncle Patrick," Phoenix said, stopping in front of the baboons.

"Yeah?" I paused in my walk. "Oh, you want to look at the baboons? Sure! Who doesn't love a monkey."

"They're *apes*," a man in a puffer vest with a camera worthy of a professional safari photographer informed me. "Not monkeys."

"Right," I nodded. "Apes. Great apes. Apes are great."

"Uncle Patrick, are we here because you didn't want to see Michelle leave?" Phoenix held onto the railing that separated us from our long-lost cousins and didn't look at me.

"Well, I did think you'd like it," I said. "But yeah, kind of. Sorry for waking you up so early. I just..."

"You didn't want to see her go," Phoenix said slowly, watching as a small baboon crept up behind another and picked a flea from its back, popping it into its mouth like a particularly delicious chocolate-covered coffee bean.

"I don't know when her flight is," I admitted. "But no, I don't want to be there when she leaves. I didn't want to do the awkward goodbye thing."

"Or you don't want to say goodbye."

I winced and wished my nephew wasn't quite so insightful. "Maybe," I admitted. "Look, I knew it was never going to be long term, me and Michelle, but..."

"Are you, like, okay?" Phoenix looked up at me then.

"I'm okay," I said quickly and then paused. "Well, I guess I'm not completely okay. But I'm not going to—" I took a breath. "I know your mum takes it pretty hard when she breaks up with a guy. It won't be like that. I just feel..."

"Sad?" Phoenix offered, watching as three of the baboons began to bob their heads at each other rhythmically like they were at their own private silent disco.

"Sad," I agreed. "But you don't have to worry about me. Not like with your mum."

"I know," Phoenix said, but it sounded like he needed the reassurance. "I just wanted to check."

"And I appreciate it," I said. "Look, if you don't want to be here, we can do something else. Anything you like."

"Nah." Phoenix managed a smile. "Who doesn't love a monkey?"

· ♥ · ♥ · ♥ · ♥ · ♥ ·

"We can go and do something else if you want," Phoenix offered as I turned the car down the road that led to my house. And to the cottage next door. "I don't know, the movies?"

"I've kept you out all day already," I said. "It's fine if I end up seeing Michelle leave, and we have an awkward goodbye. I'll cope. I'm an adult, after all."

"Adults don't always cope with stuff," Phoenix said, and that was certainly true in his experience. "I don't mind."

"It's fine," I said. "Anyway, she's probably gone by now. Thanks for keeping me company."

"The zoo was fun."

"Even when that American lady next to us kept talking during the seal show?"

"She was funny," Phoenix said. "Can you believe a dumb animal can do all that? It's gotta be a robot, I'm telling ya!" He did a surprisingly good impression of her accent.

I chuckled at the memory. But then, as I approached the end of the road, I held my breath.

All the lights were out at the cottage, and I knew Michelle was gone. Had she come to say goodbye, I wondered? Or had she thought we had said everything we needed to, without words, the night before? Maybe neither. Maybe she had just glanced at the house and shrugged, thinking only of the life she was returning to in Glasgow. Maybe she didn't think of me at all.

And damn, I was really punching myself in the gut here; it was like an invisible douchebag had a hold of my arm. 'Why do you keep hitting yourself?' he asked, punching me with my own fist. I had to stop torturing myself with what Michelle may – or may not – have thought about me. Wondering if she'd ever think about me again.

Whatever had happened between us, it hadn't been enough to make her consider changing her plans, changing her life. She hadn't done it for her sisters and certainly not for me.

I pulled up in the driveway and turned off the car. Phoenix got out first, still wearing the monkey-shaped hat that had seemed a lot funnier in the gift shop. I sat in the car a moment longer and then told myself to stop being such a sad sack of shit.

MICHELLE FINCH STICKS TO THE PLAN

"Uncle Patrick?" Phoenix was on the doorstep.

"Coming," I said and opened the door for him.

He gave me a look that told me, quite plainly, he was still worried about me. "Do you want to do something else now?" he asked. "We could watch TV?"

It was tempting. Very tempting. I sure as hell didn't want to sit alone with my thoughts. But Phoenix was a kid, not an emotional support teenager. And I wasn't going to let him suffer because the woman I was seeing had left the country without so much as a goodbye.

"Nah." I shook my head. "I should get onto some work in the studio. That bar isn't going to sand itself."

Phoenix nodded. "Okay." He paused and held up the monkey hat. "Thanks for this."

"You're welcome, dude."

· ♥ · ♥ · ♥ · ♥ · ♥ ·

The custom bar did need sanding; that hadn't been a lie. But mostly, I hadn't wanted Phoenix to feel like it was his job to keep me company or cheer me up. Not more than he already had, anyway. Poor kid had done enough of that for his mother; he didn't need to do it for me.

Even though I'd be the first to admit I was in dire need of cheering up.

The whirr of the oscillating sander was usually a sound I found oddly soothing, but this evening, it irritated me. It made me wonder if this was why Michelle had never considered, not even for a minute, staying in Sydney. She was a high-flying finance executive; I was a guy who sanded furniture in his garage and starred in a cheesy TV show as a kid. I had never been ashamed of my job, no matter how hard my mother had tried to make me, but I had to wonder if I wasn't the kind of guy Michelle would let herself fall for.

The image of Michelle, her legs wrapped around some slick arsehole in a suit, rose up in my mind, and I let out a grunt. The sander kicked back, and I swore, turning it off and slamming it to the ground. "Piece of shit!"

"And hello to you too!"

I looked up through my goggles to see Khalid standing at the garage entrance.

"What are you doing here?"

"Well, that's a nice way to greet me!" Khalid made a great show of being offended. "And here was me about to offer you a beer, dickhead!"

"Sorry!" I held up my hands. "I wasn't expecting you."

"Phoenix texted me. He said you might need some cheering up."

A tiny flicker of warmth in my chest. "He did? That's...really good, actually. He told me his psychologist has been helping him with strategies on what to do if someone he cares about is feeling bad, so he feels like it's not all on him. I mean, I was thinking about his mum, but—"

"But he's trying it out on you," Khalid said. "Smart kid. So, I guess you're feeling like shit because Michelle took off, right?"

"Yeah," I admitted. "I wasn't expecting it to hit me so hard."

"But it did. What happened when she left? Did you have some big drawn-out farewell? Did you cry?"

"We didn't really say goodbye. I went over last night, but... Well, we didn't really talk."

"Dude, did you ghost her again?" Khalid demanded. "What the hell!?"

"I didn't ghost her!" I shot back, although now I was slightly concerned that maybe I had. "She didn't say goodbye either. I was out today, so I guess I didn't give her a chance. But neither of us wanted some big awkward goodbye."

"I don't get how you're thirty years old and still so shit at this stuff."

"I've never had to deal with this before!" I protested. "I've never been in the kind of relationship where someone I care about is leaving, and there's nothing I can do."

"So, you do care about her, then. Glad we're admitting that, at least."

"I never said I didn't care, just that it wasn't serious. And it wasn't serious for Michelle. She was never going to consider changing her life to be with someone like me."

"But it was serious for you?" Khalid pressed. "If you didn't have Phoenix, would you be flying to Glasgow right now?"

"She never asked me to," I replied, avoiding the question. "And that would be one hell of a commitment, and I..."

Khalid rolled his eyes. He was very good at it, making a full rotation that could have served as a popular reaction gif.

"If she had? Would you have made that commitment for her? Given up your precious freedom?"

"I don't know!" I threw up my sawdust-covered hands. "No. Maybe! It's... I can't know what might have happened. Anyway, she didn't. And I couldn't have, even if she had. Look, it's probably for the best, anyway, that she's gone. I need to focus on Phoenix and..."

"And?" Khalid snorted. "That's such bullshit." He reached into the bag, pulled out a beer, and offered it to me.

I took it from him and gulped it down, hops and alcohol washing away some of the sawdust (no, I wasn't wearing a mask. Tell Occupational Health and Safety to kiss my arse), but none of the confusing mess of feelings that had me in a chokehold.

"Maybe it is bullshit," I said, mostly to my beer. "I wish she hadn't left. Not yet, anyway. I wish we could have had more time to see if maybe—" I finished the beer and crumpled up the can. "But I can't change it."

"So, what then? Distraction?"

"Yep. Phoenix thinks it's a good idea; he did text you."

"I am the master of distraction." Khalid smirked. "Hey, the man himself!"

Phoenix appeared in the doorway that connected the garage to the house. "Hey," he said quietly. "I hope it's okay that I texted Khalid."

"Mate," I said, my voice thick. It was just the sawdust, I told myself. "It was exactly the right thing to do. Very mature, dude."

Phoenix smiled, raising his chin. "Does that mean I can have a beer?"

I huffed out a breath of laughter. "Nice try."

"Come on, let's go inside," Khalid said, picking up the bag of beer again. "This place is making me sneeze."

"Good call," I said, nodding. "And I think we should get some pizza."

"Doesn't pizza have carbs?" Phoenix asked, frowning slightly.

"I think," I said with a sigh, "that I'm going to need a lot of carbs tonight."

19 Michelle

"Michelle, can I see you for a moment?" Martin appeared in my doorway, hovering like a gigantic and annoying mosquito. If only I could swat him without risking a disciplinary meeting with HR.

"Sure," I said, stifling a yawn. Bloody jetlag. "I was just trying to get on top of the minutes from the meeting with Wind Corp. Seems like it didn't go very well."

Martin slipped inside my office and closed the door. "Not very well, no."

"They weren't happy with Ash's presentation?" Usually, being able to say that would leave me nothing less than gleeful, but glee didn't seem to be filling me right now. Maybe it was the jetlag. I had, of course, come straight to the office from the airport before even stopping at my flat to visit my dead plants.

"They didn't feel he had considered the full implications of those legislative changes proposed at the EU summit. I mean, I'm sure he did his best, but—"

"Martin," I cut in, suddenly feeling bone-weary. "Do you want me to take the project back?"

"Yes!" Martin seemed relieved I had said it. "I was always going to make sure it was handed over to you again. Once you were back."

I hid a snort behind my hand. That was a total lie; Ash must have seriously messed up. I should have been elated at this proof that I was better than Ash, but all I felt was tired.

"And what about the Huberman meeting?" I asked. "How did that go?"

"Oh, we'll be keeping that one with Ash," Martin said airily, flexing his drooping shoulders. "It seemed like they had a real camaraderie. It's a natural fit."

"I see," I said. 'Natural fit' typically meant 'they liked that he's a man, in the way that you're not'. Usually, I'd argue, but... "Well, good luck to him. I'll send him all my notes."

Martin frowned, his mouth falling open. "You will?"

"Sure," I said. "I mean, we're all on the same team, aren't we?"

"Well, yes," Martin said. "But you don't usually—"

"I'll send those files," I said. "Was there anything else you needed?"

"No, no." Martin stood up, chewing his pen in that way that made me want to spray him with water like he was an anxious Maltese Terrier gnawing on my Persian rug. Not that I owned a Persian rug. "It's good to have you back. I hope you enjoyed your holiday because I don't think I can ever let you leave again!" He let out a chuckle that was clearly supposed to be hearty.

"It was a lot of fun seeing my sisters," I said. "But I don't have any future travel plans."

"Well, that's for the best, isn't it?" Martin said, leaving my door open as he left, even though it had been closed before. "Staying committed to your future here. I know how much you want to advance, and I think you've got the potential to go all the way."

It should have been gratifying to hear that Martin thought I could make Partner. It was the most important thing in my life, wasn't it? Being back here was for the best. I knew that. Even if I did miss my sisters.

And someone else, too.

·♥·♥·♥·♥·♥·

It was dark when I left work. Not that that signified much. January in Glasgow was almost permanently dark, and I'd go days without seeing the sun if I didn't have a lunch meeting at some swanky gastropub or trendy fusion restaurant.

The Sainsbury's I passed on my way back to my flat hadn't changed. Not that I had expected it to. It was bathed in warm light, a beacon in the cold, bitter darkness. As I went through the automatic doors, I couldn't help thinking of my grocery shopping trip with Phoenix and Patrick, even though I had been endeavouring not to think about Patrick.

What would Patrick have said about the booze in the supermarket aisles, right next to the Cadbury's chocolate with the ever so slightly different packaging (and a very different taste, if you asked anyone from England)? Would he have had any comments on the 'build your own salad bar' that I eschewed in favour of a pre-packaged option that claimed to be Mediterranean chicken but primarily consisted of wet leaves? Would Phoenix have been interested in the Jaffa cakes, or would he have liked to try the violently orange Irn-Bru?

"Stop it," I muttered to myself as I added milk, organic Greek yoghurt, and, after a moment's consideration, a bottle of Australian Chardonnay to my shopping basket. "Stop it."

"Dinnae talk to yourself, hen," a woman in a puffy coat and knitted hat with bright pompoms warned me.

I blushed and made my way towards the self-checkout at a quick walk. The last thing I needed was the locals thinking I was nuts.

The air outside was bitingly cold, and I shivered even in my thick cashmere blend coat that a saleswoman had promised would keep out even the most persistent Glasgow chill. Surrounded by the ugly apartment buildings, damp, slushy roads, and the sense that it would be dark forever, I suddenly felt just how far I was from Brekkie Beach.

I shook my head quickly, trying to force the thought away. Of course, Scotland in January was nothing like an Australian beachside suburb. Stupid thing to think. As I made my way into my apartment building, which was thankfully well-heated, I firmly told myself that it was good to be home. And it was worth it, right? If I could keep this up for a few more years, I'd finally make Partner. And prove to myself, once and for all, that I wasn't stupid. I was worthy, I was—

"Something," I finished, turning the key in the lock.

"Home sweet home," I said, with an ironic twist of my lips that no one could see. Because it didn't feel like home. Not even close.

My flat didn't look any different. It was small, neatly furnished, and in far better condition than the cottage I had spent the last month in. Dying succulents notwithstanding.

I was tired. Probably somewhere well beyond tired and into such torturous sleep deprivation levels it would count as a war crime to inflict them on another human. But still, I dumped my sad salad on the table, slipped into some workout shorts and made for the one thing in my apartment that did feel like home.

My exercise bike was truly a thing of beauty; a Peloton, pimped out with all the accessories. I had been lucky enough to get it for half the usual price from a New Year's Resolutioner who had told me when I picked it up, 'I'd rather be fat than spend another minute on that bloody thing'. I managed a faint smile at the memory as the screen displayed a perky woman in a tight sports bra, telling me to get ready for the workout of my life.

But even as my feet stepped into the pedals, and my legs certainly retained enough muscle memory to do what was demanded, my brain went straight to Patrick, telling me how he had thought of me on that exercise bike at the gym in Brekkie Beach, watched that bead of sweat fall from my collarbone to sink lower and lower, and how he had longed to chase it with his tongue...

"Fuck this," I said aloud, getting rid of the perky woman with the scary eyes and clambering off the bike. I collapsed onto my sofa, flicked on the TV for background noise, and opened my phone.

• ♥ • ♥ • ♥ • ♥ • ♥ •

Michelle: how's life in paradise? it's freezing here <blizzard emoji>

Tessa: if it makes you feel better, it rained after you left!

Abby: and then it became a glorious sunset

Abby: <picture of said glorious sunset, complete with palm trees>

Michelle: <sad face emoji>

Abby: how are you going, anyway?

Michelle: it's good to be back at work. i've got most of my projects back, except one where the client decided my colleague was a better 'fit'

Abby: let me guess, he's a dude?

Michelle: yep

Tessa: but great that you got your projects back! you thought it might take months

Michelle: yeah

Abby: why no confetti emoji?

Michelle: i'm too jetlagged for confetti. i'm fine, just settling back in after being away so long

Tessa: we miss you already. i went for a walk past your old cottage and felt all weepy

```
Abby:  are  you  about  to  get  your
period?
```

Tessa: ...yes. but still, we do miss you michelle!

```
Abby: of course we do! brekkie beach
is bereft, babe. i hope those arse-
holes in glasgow know how lucky they
are to have you
```

Michelle: <emoji surrounded by hearts> thanks for the love

```
Abby: you sound pretty flat
```

Michelle: i'm seriously jetlagged, how perky do you expect me to be?

Tessa: are you missing patrick? i saw him and phoenix coming out of nick and nikki's. we did the awkward head nod thing

```
Abby: i saw phoenix with some red-
headed kid getting slushees at the
petrol station. so i got a slushie
too. how good are slushees?! i always
forget how good they are!
```

Michelle: slushees are proof that if there is a god, he loves us

Tessa: you didn't answer my question

Michelle: i'm too tired and busy to miss anybody

Michelle: i should go to bed. gotta be fresh for work tomorrow

```
Abby: tomorrow's saturday for you
```

Michelle: since when has that stopped me?

· ♥ · ♥ · ♥ · ♥ · ♥ ·

I turned out the light slipped into bed, still in my gym clothes, and let out a sigh. I had definitely lied to my sisters about whether or not I missed Patrick. I should have been too jetlagged to miss anyone. But I had been missing him since Abby's van had taken me away from Brekkie Beach and towards the airport. Now, back in dark and dank Glasgow, it was only getting worse.

But that would pass. The breakneck pace of my job would take over once more, especially as I edged closer to my annual review and that tantalising glimpse of my next promotion. I'd settle back into my old life. A life I didn't love but could cope with until I reached my goal.

And I'd stop thinking about Patrick. Wouldn't I?

20 Patrick

"Do you know where my blue shirt is?" Phoenix was digging through a basket of laundry, a frown right between his eyebrows.

"Uh, try the clothesline," I said. "You feeling okay?"

"I'm fine," he said, piling the laundry back into the basket. "You didn't get rid of my old sneakers, did you?"

"I think I saw them under your bed," I said. "But why? They've definitely seen better days, dude."

Phoenix looked down at his bare feet, his hands twisting together. "I know. But I don't want Mum to think—" He let out a small sigh. "I think it would be better to wear the ones she got me when I see her."

"You know you're not responsible for your mum's feelings, right? That whole thing you talked about with your psychologist?"

Phoenix made a face. "I know," he said. "I know she's an adult, and it's not my job to manage her feelings. But I haven't seen her in ages, and I just don't want..."

"You don't want her to get upset about something like sneakers when you first see her?" I finished, and Phoenix nodded. "I'd say that was pretty fair. I'm going to shave this morning so your mum doesn't call me scruffy."

Phoenix managed a slight smile. "When do you reckon I'll have to shave?"

"Sooner than I did. I had this super fine blonde bum fluff until I was twenty-two. Very embarrassing."

Phoenix rubbed his upper lip hopefully, as though it might make a full handlebar moustache appear.

"It's going to be okay today," I told Phoenix, even though I wasn't entirely sure of that. "Your mum really wants to see you, and whatever happens, I'll be here for you."

"Thanks." Phoenix was still touching his lip. "I just...I don't know what's going to happen."

"Neither do I. But we'll get through it together, okay?"

"Okay. I'm going to go find my sneakers."

"No worries," I said. "So long as you remember you're not responsible for people's feelings, right?"

Phoenix rolled his eyes. "I know." And that was something very close to a petulant teenage whine; I was rather proud of him.

I ran my hand over my stubbled chin and winced. Yep, I definitely had to shave before Julia arrived. As I made my way up the stairs, I tried very hard not to think about how Michelle had run her hand over my stubbled cheek and whispered how it made her feel when said stubble grazed over her skin.

I really needed to shave.

· ♥ · ♥ · ♥ · ♥ · ♥ ·

After all our preparations and worry about the arrival of Phoenix's mother, it had been rather anticlimactic. Julia had swanned into my living room, the picture of glowing good health in a beaded kaftan and leather sandals. She had hugged Phoenix, kissed me on the cheek, and beamed beatifically at us like the icon of a minor saint.

And then she had taken Phoenix out for a walk, and I had been left alone with my thoughts.

I should have been pleased to see that Julia looked well. But I felt a selfish twinge in my guts. If my sister was well enough to take Phoenix home, I'd be alone.

And even though I had told Khalid that I liked living alone with no one to answer to, no responsibilities, and the ability to scratch my balls whenever the mood took me, it felt different now. I wanted Phoenix to stay. And not just for his sake; for mine. Having an anxious fourteen-year-old in my house made me a better person, apparently. And strangely, a happier one.

But aside from my selfish reasons, I still didn't want Phoenix to go. Sure, Julia seemed to be a beacon of calm oneness with the universe right now, but I knew, realistically, that it couldn't last. As much as I desperately wished it was otherwise, I knew better than to be too hopeful.

How long until my sister turned on her beloved yoga instructor, burning bridges – and yoga mats – and getting herself into a state where she couldn't look after herself, let alone my nephew? And what would happen then? Would Phoenix come and stay for a few weeks, just enough time to regain a sense of normality before he had to return to chaos at home?

But I didn't let any of that show on my face as I welcomed them back inside. "Hey guys," I said. "Looks like you had fun."

"The walk around the headland was very peaceful," Julia said in an exaggeratedly serene voice. "There's a powerful calm that comes from the ocean."

"I think I saw a snake," Phoenix said. "But it could have just been a blue tongue."

"Cool," I said. "Or terrifying, depending on your perspective."

Phoenix chuckled and then looked up at his mother as if for approval. She gave him a radiant smile, and he seemed to relax. And that made my stomach churn again. I could hardly expect a handful of appointments with a psychologist to undo a lifetime of feeling responsible for his mother's ever-changing moods. But I hated to see it, just the same.

"I was going to chuck some steaks on the barbecue for an early dinner," I said to my sister. "I know you've gone vego so I got some big mushrooms too." I held my hands apart to indicate the impressive size of the mushrooms. "Were you planning to stay for dinner?"

Julia looked back at me with green eyes so like my own. "Yes," she said. "I think I'll stay." Then she looked down at her son. "I'm going to help your uncle with the barbecue, if there's something you want to do upstairs."

Phoenix nodded, clearly understanding. "Sure," he said, backing away down the hall. "I won't get in your way."

I wondered how often my sister had said something similar to him when she was 'entertaining'. How many times Phoenix had stayed in his room, guessing at what his mother was doing and trying not to think about it.

"I've got everything ready outside," I said. "If you just want to grab those mushrooms." I pointed, and my sister followed me to the deck.

I carefully laid the steaks on the preheated barbecue, and they gave a satisfying hiss. "This side can be the veggie side," I told Julia. "They won't touch."

But Julia was looking at the bowl of mushrooms. "You marinated these."

"Well, yeah," I said. "Don't worry, I didn't use Worcestershire sauce. I know that's not vegetarian."

"No, I..." Julia gave me an odd look. "That was nice of you."

"Well, Mum said you were vego now." I shrugged. "I wanted you to have a nice dinner too."

"Thanks for that," she said. "I just didn't expect you to be marinating mushrooms for me. Given that the last time we saw each other, I told you to never speak to me or my son again."

I winced. "Well, you weren't feeling your best then," I said, unsure how to handle Julia actually admitting to something she had said in the past.

"Phoenix has been happy here," she said, using a clean set of tongs to put the big flat mushrooms onto the grill. "He didn't say that, exactly. But I can tell."

"Uh, that's good," I said, unnecessarily flicking my own tongs. It sure beat eye contact. "But he missed you a lot. I'm sure he's ready to go home."

Julia made a faint sound, something like a laugh. "I'm not so sure," she said. "He told me you said he always had a home here for however long he needed. Is that true?"

"Well, yeah," I said, pushing at the edge of one steak, though they weren't even close to needing flipping. "But I know you—"

"I know what I said." Julia tucked her long blonde hair behind her ears. "Back then, when Phoenix asked if he could stay, I felt like you were trying to take my son away from me."

"I never meant to do that," I said quickly. "I just care about the kid."

"Then you didn't mean it?" Julia asked. "That he could stay forever if he wanted to?"

"Of course I did," I said. "But I also told him I didn't think that was what you'd want."

"But I think it's what he wants. And..." She nudged a mushroom that was just starting to charr. "I think it's what's best for him."

There was a long silence broken only by the hiss and sizzle of the grill plates, umami scents of meat and fungi rising up in steamy union.

"Okay," I said finally. "I wasn't expecting that."

"Neither was I," Julia said, a wry smile playing on her lips. "But I've done a lot of reflecting. And I think maybe it's time to admit that it's best for both of us, him being here with you."

I grabbed one of the beers left over from Khalid's visit and took a long swallow. "Okay."

"He's growing up," Julia said. "And I need space to find out what's next for me. To build the next chapter of my life. I've got a screen test for a new show about luxury escapes in the Australian outback. They think I'd be perfect! If I get the job, I'll be travelling a lot. So, it would be easier if he was here."

And then I understood. Julia hadn't found some new enlightenment that had made her see that what was best for Phoenix mattered more than what she wanted. Nope. Not this time, anyway. Julia had simply discovered something she wanted more than having her son at home.

I shouldn't have been surprised. But I still felt my chest clench with something between anger and grief.

"I see," I said. "Sounds like a great opportunity."

"This could be a fresh start for me," Julia said, looking dreamy. "A whole new way of looking at my career. I've been trying to be an actress, but what if I was supposed to just be myself all along?"

"It sounds like a great opportunity," I said again. "For you." I flipped the steaks, making sure that the one I had earmarked for Phoenix didn't get too blackened at the edges. He hated that. "And I'm happy to look after Phoenix. For as long as..." I shook my head. "For as long as that's what he wants."

"Phoenix said you were seeing a woman, too," Julia went on, and shit, I wasn't expecting that. "But she left."

"Well, she was just on holiday," I said, clearing my throat. "It wasn't like she left. She was always going to go home. But she was living next door, so we spent a bit of time together and—"

"In that crappy cottage?" Julia shot a disdainful look over her shoulder.

"In that crappy cottage," I confirmed. "She booked it online. The photos were misleading."

"But it's over with this woman?" Julia pressed. "It didn't work out?"

"She wasn't my girlfriend," I said, my voice oddly thick. Definitely just the smoke from the barbecue. "There was nothing to work out. She lives in Glasgow. I live here."

"It never works out for you, does it? You've never been able to keep a woman around."

"I've never really tried to," I shot back, unsure why I was defending myself.

"I guess you're just not a relationships kind of guy," she said, patting me on the shoulder. "These mushrooms are done; I'll call Phoenix down, and we can tell him the good news."

But I was still staring at my steaks which were definitely becoming overcooked. Just not a relationships kind of guy. Was that true?

I couldn't help wishing that I had been granted just a little more time with Michelle to see if maybe, just maybe, I *could* be a relationships sort of guy. Because she was totally worth it.

· ♥ · ♥ · ♥ · ♥ · ♥ ·

When my sister left, I couldn't hold back my sigh of relief. Phoenix was sitting on the sofa, booting up Season Two of

Seinfeld (I blamed Khalid for that entirely), and I sat down next to him.

"Big day, huh?"

"Yeah," Phoenix agreed, his finger hovering on the remote.

"Um, is there anything you want to talk about?" I asked. "You know, like you staying here long term?"

Phoenix shifted. "I didn't think Mum would want me to, but I guess she—"

"Wants what's best for you," I finished. "It was very mature of her, you know, recognising that maybe she can't give you everything you need right now. She loves you so much, dude. And you'll still see her whenever you want."

"You really think that's why she said I can stay?" Phoenix's eyes were wide, and he looked much younger than fourteen. "I kind of thought...maybe she decided she was happier without me."

I didn't think I had ever seen anything so heartbreakingly sad as Phoenix saying those words to me, his young face contorted. My ribcage felt like it was contracting, suddenly shrinking to miniature form around my heart until it felt too tight to breathe.

"Nah." I shook my head and tried for a grin. "That's not it at all. She just wants you to be happy. It's not easy for her, but I know that if she could give you everything you need, she'd want you with her right now."

Phoenix nodded. "Yeah," he said. "I just hope she'll be okay without me."

And my contracting ribcage was immediately overshadowed by a lump in my throat. No, not a lump. A boulder, not unlike the one Indiana Jones was nearly crushed by. And I didn't have Indy's reflexes. I tried to swallow, feeling like I might throw up my steak.

"She will, dude," I said. "She's got your Nan to look out for her. And," I went on, "you can talk to Evan about all this stuff. And how you feel about moving in with me long term. You can totally bitch to him about me; I don't mind."

Phoenix looked up at that. "Yeah?"

"Definitely," I said. "And he can't tell me about it. Patient confidentiality."

"You really think I still need to see him?"

"Yeah, I do," I said. "It's...kind of hard to explain, I guess. But I reckon Evan's way smarter than me. He can help you with stuff I can't, even though I want to."

"Okay." Phoenix looked like he didn't completely understand, but I was sure he would one day. Just like I knew that one day, he'd know I had lied to him about why his mother had decided he could stay with me.

"Are you sure you want me to stay?" Phoenix's face was drawn. "You said that you really like being free and you don't like having commitments and—"

"Phoenix," I cut him off. "It's been fun, not having any commitments or responsibilities. Doing whatever I wanted, whenever I wanted. But the thing is, dude," I took a breath. "I love you a whole lot more than I like doing whatever, whenever. Like, a shit ton more."

Phoenix just looked at me with his wide dark eyes. "Really?"

"Of course," I said. "Besides, you're great company. I reckon I'm getting too old to live alone, anyway. Everyone else my age is settling down."

Phoenix's finger hovered over the remote, and I braced myself for the familiar bass twang of the theme tune, but he paused again. "Do you miss Michelle?"

"Um..." I played for time. "I guess I hadn't really thought about it. We've been busy with your mum coming over, and..."

Phoenix gave me a deeply unimpressed look. "People can think about more than one thing at a time."

"Well, you're not wrong," I said. "I do miss her. More than I thought I would, actually. But it is what it is. She doesn't live here, so we could never have—" I shrugged. "I'll be okay, eventually."

Phoenix screwed up his face. "If you want to have other ladies come over, it's okay," he said. "I can go to Keenan's. He's got bunkbeds!"

I managed to huff out a small chuckle. "I appreciate that, dude, but I don't think I'll be in the mood to meet other ladies for a while."

"Can I still go to Keenan's sometimes?"

"Yeah," I said. "Of course."

Satisfied, Phoenix finally pressed 'play', and I was greeted by the familiar sight of George venting to Jerry, awaiting the inevitable interruption by Kramer.

Maybe a show about nothing could take my mind off Michelle.

For a little while, at least.

· ♥ · ♥ · ♥ · ♥ · ♥ ·

After many, many episodes of *Seinfeld*, I realised I was falling asleep on the sofa, and Phoenix was already passed out and drooling onto the leather. "Dude." I nudged him. "Time for bed."

"Don't want to go to the zoo," he muttered, waving me away.

I had to smile at that. "Not the zoo, dude. Just your bed."

With some effort, I managed to get him upright and half-steered, half-carried him to bed. Turning out the light, I looked at my nephew's peacefully sleeping face and felt a swell of something like parental pride. Phoenix was going to be okay. I'd make sure of it.

Me, on the other hand? I stomped up the stairs to my bedroom, losing my jeans and shirt, and fell face-first onto the mattress. I checked my phone for the time. Shit, it was after two. And I had a message.

For a moment, my heart swelled at the possibility that a new message, at such an odd time of day, might be from Michelle.

But when I clicked it open, I found it was from an unsaved number.

```
You up? xx PS - it's Stevie. Hope
you haven't forgotten me <winky face
emoji>
```

As it turned out, I had forgotten about Stevie. It came back to me slowly. Stevie. Stevie with the cute black bob and seriously scary talon-like nails (my back had taken quite the beating). I knew exactly what a 'you up?' text meant, too.

But as far as Stevie was concerned, I was not up. I deleted her text quickly and then sat and stared at my phone, scrolling through the few messages I had exchanged with Michelle. Would it be weird if I sent her a text now, just checking she had arrived home safely? Letting her know that Phoenix was going to live with me permanently? Would she even reply if I did?

And why – *why* – did it feel like the walls and ceiling might crumble and crush me in my bed if I did text, and she never replied. If she never again acknowledged my existence or what had happened between us.

I dropped my phone to the ground with a clatter.

"Oh, *fuck*," I swore, holding my head in my hands. "I think I'm in love with her."

21 Michelle

It was late, it was dark, and I felt like absolute shit. Plenty of people felt that way in winter in Glasgow, but I hadn't felt like this *before* I left for my holiday in Brekkie Beach. So why did I feel it now?

There was an obvious answer to that question, but I was choosing to ignore it. Maybe, I thought, it was being back in the office. After a month away, maybe I had forgotten what utter dickheads I worked with. Perhaps it would take a while to numb myself to once more being surrounded by idiots, like Scar in *The Lion King* had once lamented (he was always my favourite). But it was worth it, right? A few more years of dickheads, and I'd be a Partner. More reasonable hours, better projects, and tons of money; I'd be the queen of the dickheads.

Like a spectre, Patrick's face swam up in my mind with that blazing Australian smile, telling me I deserved to be happy right now. But he was wrong. He had to be. Because if I did deserve to be happy now, I was doing a totally shit job of it.

I had received a rare compliment on my presentation from one of the top suits, been given another plum project right in front of Ash and heard the words 'additional bonus for exceptional performance' today. Still, it wasn't enough. Before, those things would have kept me going through the long hours, the endless backstabbing, and the bad joke that was Martin's management style for months. But now, the glow had lasted mere minutes, and I was back to wondering...

...could I really keep doing this?

And if I couldn't, what had changed? What had made the life that I had been willing to accept to get what I wanted go from bearable to completely torturous?

"Oh *shit*." I stopped dead in the footpath, right in front of a noisy pub full of people having a much better time than me. "I think I'm in love with him."

Immediately, there was a cheer, and I looked around to see three middle-aged men huddled together, smoking pungent cigarettes. "Good on yer, lass!" one of them called to me. "You go get yer man!"

And if this was a rom-com, I would have started running to his house. But Patrick was on the other side of the world.

And I didn't have a clue how he felt about me.

· ♥ · ♥ · ♥ · ♥ · ♥ ·

I was on my fourth coffee of the morning when the email came in. Realising you're in love with the man you left a world away really screws with your circadian rhythms. I had been tossing, turning, wondering what the hell I should do, and occasionally getting up to stress cycle all damn night. Even with carefully applied makeup, I looked like a panda with a drinking problem.

Mid-slurp, I clicked open the email and almost spat my coffee out. Not quite, though; I couldn't waste the caffeine.

Dear Michelle,

I hope this finds you well. We met at the Women in Finance Conference last June. I was impressed by the way you spoke about the impact of a changing legislative environment on long-term forecasting within the energy sector.

You mentioned that you'd requested a Sydney transfer at your firm, so I thought you might be interested in our job opening for an experienced Analyst at my consultancy.

Attached is the job description. Based on your experience, I think you'd be more than capable of meeting the requirements.

If you'd be interested, please get back to me by the end of the week.

Best,

Marcia Jenkins

It wasn't the first email like that I had ever received. Not even close. I started to worry if I went a whole month without someone trying to poach me.

But it was the first time I had felt an ache low in my stomach as I read, and a powerful urge to reply 'Yes, please consider me!' at the same time. I remembered Marcia well. A short, red-headed woman in high-waisted polka dot trousers and a teal blazer, she had stood out amongst the sea of grey suits. I remembered she was sharp, astute, and had spoken candidly about the difficulties women faced in the finance industry.

I set my coffee down and stared into the murky brown depths, willing the coffee to tell me what to do. The position wasn't a promotion. It was a sideways step, and into a smaller firm too, which might mean a pay cut. And I'd completely lose my chance at becoming Partner at a Big Four firm by the time I was thirty-three. Completely and utterly. Could I do that? Lose my chance to prove myself, like I had always said I would?

But my fingers itched just the same as I stared into my coffee as though scrying into a crystal ball.

"Fuck it." I began to type a reply.

•❤•❤•❤•❤•❤•

Michelle: so i have some news

Tessa: what is it?
Abby: are you pregnant?!

Tessa: why would you think she's pregnant?
Abby: because that's what tons of shagging can lead to!

Michelle: i'm not pregnant
Abby: good! so what's the news?

Michelle: i got an email about a job in sydney

Michelle: ...and i sent in an application

Tessa: oh my gosh
Abby: no fucking way!

Abby: i can't believe it! i've been telling you to change jobs forever! i never thought you'd do it with your whole plan and everything

Tessa: that's wonderful! we get you back!

Michelle: i just sent an application! i don't even have an interview yet

Abby: of course you'll get it. they came after you. they want you!

Tessa: does this mean you're coming back? when?
Michelle: i don't even have an interview yet, remember?

```
Abby: but assuming you do get it,
you're coming back?
```

Michelle: maybe. i guess. i don't know yet

Tessa: <confetti emoji>

```
Abby: <gif of Michael Scott from The
Office dancing>
Abby: but what made you change your
mind?
Abby: wait i can guess
```

Michelle: i just can't keep doing this job. being in brekkie beach was so good and coming back here made me realise how miserable this life is. maybe it's not worth it just so i can become a partner by 33

Michelle: and it's not like being a partner will change what happened when i was a kid, anyway

Tessa: you deserve to be happy now!

```
Abby: this has nothing to do with
patrick?
```

Michelle: about that

Michelle: i think maybe i made a huge mistake walking away from him. i know i said i'd wait until i had achieved everything i wanted to before i met someone

Michelle: but i don't think i'll ever meet another patrick

Michelle: and i don't want to take the chance of missing out on the one guy i've ever felt like this about

Tessa: i knew it! i knew you were serious about him! oh my god, you're totally in love with him!

Michelle: i have no idea how he feels about me

Michelle: i might come back and he's like...nah, that was just a fling

Michelle: but even if that does happen, i'll be with you two and have a job that doesn't consume my whole life. that's still worth it, right?

Abby: of course it is!

Tessa: i don't think he's going to say that! i've been telling you he's serious about you since he asked dylan for that photo

Michelle: maybe. if not, you two better have the tequila and angry girl music ready

Abby: i've always got tequila ready

Abby: but i don't think we're going to need it

22 Patrick

"You're still sad about Michelle," Phoenix said, wrinkling his nose at me.

"Um, maybe a little," I said, wincing. "But what makes you say that?" I thought I had been doing an excellent job hiding the fact that I had worked out I was in love – and had no idea what to do about it – from my nephew.

Apparently not.

"You're eating toast," Phoenix pointed out, and I dropped the toast guiltily. "Which is carbs. And you haven't worked out since she left. And we haven't walked down to the café, either."

"You noticed all that stuff, huh?" It made sense. A kid like Phoenix would be hyper-aware of behavioural changes after all those years of his mother's mercurial moods.

"Yeah," Phoenix agreed, nodding. "So, I think you're really sad about Michelle."

"I'm sorry, dude," I said, looking at my abandoned toast. "I didn't mean to make you worry."

"I'm not really worried." Phoenix shrugged. "I know you're not going to do anything bad. Not like Mum. But shouldn't you, like, do something?"

"Like what?

"If this was a movie, you'd go to Glasgow," Phoenix told me. "And wait outside her apartment with flowers and a poem or something."

"I think that's pretty creepy outside of movies. Real life doesn't work that way. Michelle made a choice to go back to Glasgow. If she had wanted something else, she would have told me."

Phoenix wrinkled up his nose. "Really?" he asked. "I dunno. Did you tell her that you wanted her to stay?"

"Not exactly," I said. "I mean, I didn't want to make her feel bad about leaving. It just... We never really talked about what was going to happen next."

"You don't know if maybe she did want to stay but didn't think you wanted her to," Phoenix said, far too astutely. "Mum got an audition for this movie once, and she made me read the lines with her. The man and the woman saw each other again after breaking up ages ago."

"And?"

"And she asked him why he left, and he was like 'I didn't think you wanted me to stay', and she was all, 'I didn't know you wanted to'. Mum was, like, full-on crying and everything," Phoenix said, miming tears. "But she didn't get the part."

"Right," I said cautiously, seeing where he was going with this.

"So maybe it's like that with Michelle. You just never told each other how you felt."

"Well, to be honest with you, I didn't really realise how I felt until she left," I said, resting my head in my hands. "I don't have a whole lot of experience with relationships."

"I know," Phoenix said. "Mum says you have lots of one-night stands because you don't want to be committed to a proper relationship."

"Ouch," I said. "I mean, she's not wrong. Not exactly, anyway. I never really met someone who I wanted a proper relationship with."

"But you do with Michelle," Phoenix said. "Because you love her."

I took a breath. "I think I do, actually. My timing sucks, huh?"

"Why?"

"Well, I shouldn't have been thinking about Michelle at all," I said, frowning. "Because I have you to think of."

"I reckon you can do both. I'm not a baby. I can look after myself."

"I know you can," I said. "But I want to focus on looking after you. Anyway, she's gone now, so it doesn't matter."

"We're not going to Glasgow to get her back? Are you sure?"

"We're not going to Glasgow," I said firmly. "Well, probably not, anyway. It's too crazy. And she wouldn't even want me to do that. I don't think so. Well, maybe. I don't know.

Phoenix snorted. "Okay. But if you change your mind, I could hold up one of those antique speaker things for you."

"Antique speaker? Wait, you mean a boombox?"

"Yeah." Phoenix nodded. "There's gotta be one of them."

"I'll let you know," I said drily.

· ❤ · ❤ · ❤ · ❤ · ❤ ·

Stalking is a strong word. And so I absolutely wasn't stalking. I was just making sure I was down at Nick and Nikki's every day at the same time I had seen Michelle there with her sisters. Tessa and Abby were Brekkie Beach locals; I was bound to bump into one of them sooner or later.

"Can I get another iced chocolate?" Phoenix asked, looking up from his phone. We had been camped at one of the small tables and seated on old milk crates for almost an hour, and my legs were starting to cramp.

"Sure," I said, handing him my debit card. "And grab a coffee for me too. I'll have a—"

"Double shot flat white," Phoenix finished. "I know."

"Thanks, dude," I said. "We won't stay much longer; I know it's boring."

"I don't mind," he said. "But is it okay if I go and meet Keenan later? His cousins are coming over, and they're bringing a PS5!"

"That's got to beat retro gaming, huh? Of course, you can go."

I smiled as Phoenix made his way up to the counter, holding my debit card like it was his own. He had come a long way.

After this coffee, I'd give up for today. Endlessly good-natured as Nick and Nikki were, I was sure they didn't want Phoenix and me taking up a table for so long. Usually, it was impossible to go anywhere in Brekkie Beach without bumping into an acquaintance or someone you'd rather avoid. But now, when I desperately wanted to bump into Abby or Tessa, they seemed to have disappeared into the void.

But then—

"Hey, it's Phoenix, right?" I looked up and saw a tall man greeting my nephew. "I'm Dylan. The guy who took those photos down at the beach?"

Dylan, I remembered, was Tessa's boyfriend. I could only hope that Tessa herself was somewhere close by.

"Hi," I said, standing up and making my way over. "Good to see you again. I'm Pat—"

"Mate, you don't need to remind me!" Dylan's face split into a grin. "I was the one getting starstruck when I met the legend of *Outback Adventures*. How've you been?"

"Uh, well," I began. "Good," I lied. "I was hoping to have a word with Tessa if she's around?"

Dylan didn't look all that surprised. "She should be down in a few minutes. She asked me to order for her; she's just finishing up a phone interview with some reality TV star."

At my mystified look, he explained. "She's a ghostwriter. And it's pretty amazing how she comes up with a whole autobiography for celebrities who are only twenty-five."

"Right," I said, remembering that Michelle had explained that to me. "She did your dad's autobiography, is that right?"

"Yep!" Dylan was clearly pleased I had remembered. "That's how we met, actually. I was—"

"Sorry, sorry, that took longer than I thought!" Tessa came hurrying into the coffee shop, her hair tossed up in a bun. "Please tell me there's a very large coffee with my name on it coming soon."

"There surely is." Dylan pressed a kiss to the top of her head. "Tessa, you remember Patrick, right? Michelle's...friend?"

"Patrick!" Tessa's eyes went wide at the sight of me. "Hi! How are you?"

"Uh, okay," I said. "I was actually hoping I could have a quick chat with you. About—"

"About Michelle?" Tessa cut in, looking almost breathless with excitement. "Yes! I mean, that would be fine."

"Phoenix, do you want to see some photos I did for the Sydney Festival?" Dylan asked my nephew loudly. "Over here?" He pointed to a table some way from where we had been sitting before.

And thank goodness my nephew had social skills because he nodded, leaving Tessa and me free to talk.

Or, at least, try to talk. When we sat down, I stared at the old industrial spool masquerading as a table and wondered how I could begin what I had to say.

"So she got home safely?" I asked finally. "To Glasgow, I mean?"

"Uh, yes," Tessa said, her face showing that she didn't think I had wanted to speak to her only about Michelle's flight. "She said the flight was long but fine."

"Right," I said. "Well, that's good. And she's well?"

"No health complaints that I know of," Tessa said, hiding her mouth with her hand. I could see that she was trying not to smile like she knew something.

"Right," I said again. "The thing is— Look, I know you're Michelle's sister, and you can't tell me anything she's said to you. I'm not asking you to do that."

"Good, because I never would."

"This is just a hypothetical thing," I said, swallowing hard. "But I was hoping we could keep this discussion just between us. For now, anyway."

"Of course." Tessa sat up straight. "Do you want me to swear on my mother's grave? She's not dead, but if we're doing hypotheticals, I don't suppose that matters."

I managed to laugh, despite feeling like an entire wasp's nest had taken up residence in my stomach and was buzzing angrily, demanding to be freed.

"Okay," I said. "The thing is, I just wanted to ask if hypothetically a guy she had been seeing was to hypothetically fly to Glasgow and ask her to reconsider everything in her life to come back to Sydney and be with him, would she find that creepy, or would it be acceptable under the circumstances? Just hypothetically speaking, of course."

Tessa made a sound from behind her hand like the squeak a rubber chicken might make when attacked by a Border Collie.

"Hypothetically," she drew out the word in her accent so like her sister's. "I think she'd absolutely love it. I mean, you know she loves romance novels, right? And that's straight out of the romance playbook, the guy making the big gesture to get the girl back."

"So, hypothetically, you think Michelle might be okay with a guy she was seeing showing up in Glasgow and making some sort of...declaration?"

"I think she'd be very okay with it," Tessa said, and then her mouth squirmed like she wasn't sure whether she should keep speaking. I waited, crossing my fingers under the table because, apparently, I was twelve.

"But speaking purely hypothetically, I'd tell the guy not to book tickets to Glasgow just yet," Tessa said, tilting her head to one side.

"Oh." All of the softly unfurling tendrils of hope in my chest wilted like they had been blasted with industrial-strength weed killer. "Okay. Well, if that's what you think, then—"

"No, it's not—" Tessa let out a sigh. "Damn it, I shouldn't be telling you this, but she's flying back to Sydney next week."

"She is?" I half stood up and then sat back down again, the milk crate pressing a diamond pattern into my arse. My insides were such a confused mass of competing emotions that my body didn't know how to process them.

"She's got a job interview with this small Sydney firm," Tessa explained. "But I'm sure she'll get it."

"So, she's not coming back because of...a guy she met?"

Tessa pursed her lips once more, and I held up my hands. "Right, I know. Sisterly cone of silence."

"Afraid so," Tessa said. "But you know she's never applied for another job, right?"

"Because of her plan to become a Partner by the time she's thirty-three. Once she's done that, she'll have time for relationships and stuff."

"Exactly," Tessa said. "But she just applied for a new job now, so..." She looked at me as though willing me to make the connection.

"What you're saying is..." My tongue felt thick in my mouth. Michelle was coming back. She was actually coming back. After all these years, Michelle decided to leave the job that kept her in Glasgow and make a new life in Sydney. My existence had to have something to do with that. Right?

"What I'm saying is, I think you'd better be in International Arrivals at three o'clock next Tuesday. Just in case you bump into anyone you know."

"I can do that. I... Thank you."

"Please don't thank me!" Tessa held up her hands. "And don't tell her I said anything!"

"I won't," I promised. "Um, I'd better leave you to your coffee."

"Looks like those two have plenty to talk about." Tessa nudged me and pointed to where Dylan was showing Phoenix something on his MacBook.

"Brekkie Beach has been really good for Phoenix," I said. "I guess maybe it can change people."

Tessa gave me a knowing look. "Maybe it can."

And that was enough to give me hope that on Tuesday at three o'clock, my heart might not be shattered in the International Arrivals lounge of Kingsford Smith Airport.

23 Michelle

Tessa: we're here to meet you! have you landed?

Michelle: just landed. coming through customs now. i always worry i've accidentally packed 10kg of cocaine and several firearms and just forgot about them. see you soon if i'm not hauled off by the feds

Tessa: <laughing emoji>

I smiled at my phone as I slipped it back in my pocket. I hadn't been able to sleep much on the flight, but I didn't feel tired. I felt gritty, dehydrated, and vaguely disgusting, but not tired. I wasn't quite excited – there was too much anxiety for that – but I was full of adrenaline just the same, knowing that I was on the verge of changing my life forever.

In one way or another.

The customs officers waved me through without a second glance, and the sniffer beagles didn't come anywhere near me, proving I had not, in fact, packed any cocaine.

So, all that was left to do was make my way down the winding path, tugging my suitcase on its neat wheels, towards my sisters' arms. Once I was back in Brekkie Beach, showered, changed, and definitely after I had brushed my teeth, I could think about going to see Patrick. First, I'd have to plan out what the hell I was going to say.

As I turned the corner to a sea of faces, I tried to pick out the two dark heads of my sisters and listened for Abby's voice, which certainly had the ability to carry across a crowd. But I couldn't see them.

When I reached the bottom of the walkway, I looked around, frowning. Tessa had told me they were already there. What, had both of them needed to pee at precisely the same time? I wouldn't put it past them, but—

"Michelle?" A familiar voice, but one I had absolutely not expected to hear.

I stood there, dumbstruck and blinking. It really was him. Or them, rather. Patrick and Phoenix were standing in front of me. Patrick was holding an enormous bouquet of roses and looking at me like he, too, had been struck dumb.

"Hi," Phoenix said, raising a hand.

"Hi," I managed to say. "You're here. How did you know I was coming?"

"We, uh, talked to Tessa," Patrick said, shifting the roses in his arms uncomfortably.

"You talked to Tessa?" My heart was beating so fast I was surprised it didn't propel me several feet off the floor like I was powered by a tiny engine.

"Yeah," Patrick said. "Uh, these are for you." He thrust the roses at me, and I took them, cradling them awkwardly between my handbag and passport wallet.

"I'm going to go and get doughnuts," Phoenix announced loudly. "And coffee." With that, he disappeared through the crowd, leaving Patrick, me, and the enormous bunch of roses alone.

"Hi," Patrick said, taking a step closer to me. I wished I could smell the familiar scent of his skin; salty air and clean laundry, but the smell of the roses was completely overpowering.

"Hi," I said softly. "You knew I was coming back."

"Well, I talked to Tessa," he said. "Because I wanted to ask her – just hypothetically – how you might feel if someone – like me, for example – came to Glasgow and asked you to reconsider your whole career and plan for your life, to be with him."

"You were seriously thinking about coming to Glasgow?"

"Only if Tessa thought that, hypothetically, you might be okay with that," Patrick said, his eyes fixed on me like I was the only person in the crowded, noisy airport. "And

MICHELLE FINCH STICKS TO THE PLAN

she said you might be, but I shouldn't book a ticket because you were coming back. Just for a job interview, that's all she said. And I told her I wouldn't tell you about this, so, uh, my bad."

"I won't say a word," I promised. "You were really going to come to Glasgow? For me?"

"I was." Patrick nodded. "And I was going to ask you if you'd consider leaving your job and moving to Sydney, and changing everything about your life, just so..." He paused and took a quick breath. "So we could give whatever started happening between us a real chance."

I made a sound somewhere between a cry, a yelp, and a sob, hugging the roses to my chest and brushing my chin with the wet petals. "But you...you don't like commitments."

"But I want this commitment. Because I..." He squared his shoulders, his eyes fixed on mine. "Because I love you, Michelle. And I've never said that before because I've never felt like this about anyone. And I know it's a lot and that my life is complicated with Phoenix, and you've got your career, but I had to ask if there's a chance you felt like this could be the real deal. Because I do."

I dropped the roses. And my bag. And my passport wallet, which wasn't wise. But I dropped all three and flung myself into his arms like I needed him to carry me out of croc-infested waters.

"Patrick, I—" I began, but I realised I was speaking primarily into his shirt. I lifted my chin to look at him, very glad those strong arms were still around my waist, holding me up. Otherwise, I was sure my body would have taken a liquid form and melted into a slippery mess all over the floor.

"I love you too," I whispered, and the words came out easily because they were absolutely true, and I had been waiting, just waiting, to be able to say them. "And I definitely, absolutely know this is the real deal."

"Are you sure?" Patrick let out a shocked half laugh.

"Very sure." I nodded and then kissed him hard and firm, just to ensure he believed me. I could have kissed him for hours, I thought, as our lips moved together, my body melting into his. Maybe even days. But we were in the middle of International Arrivals, and at some point, I would need to retrieve my belongings and stop acting like the end scene of *Love, Actually*.

"The reason I applied for the job," I told him breathlessly. "It's because of you. I wanted to come back, and I thought, even if you didn't want this—"

"I really do."

"But even if you didn't," I went on. "What you said about not waiting to be happy, just to prove to myself I wasn't stupid? That I deserved to be happy now? I...I knew I couldn't cope with my life the way it was, doing that job, living that way, not after being here with you. It wasn't enough anymore. Besides—" I gave him a rueful smile. "I thought, if I was nursing a broken heart, I'd need my sisters a whole lot closer than a twenty-eight-hour flight away."

"I can promise pretty definitively to never break your heart," Patrick said, squeezing my hands in his. "Never, Michelle."

"And I'm never going to leave again," I said. "Well, actually, that's not completely true. If I get this job, there might be travel from time to time, but—"

"But you won't be leaving me. There's something else I need to tell you. And I hope it doesn't change your mind about wanting to be with me."

"What? You're not polyamorous, are you? Or about to get a neck tattoo? Or join a cult?"

Patrick snorted. "None of the above," he said. "It's Phoenix. He's going to be living with me permanently. I'll tell you the whole story later, but his mum came to see him, and she decided he should stay with me."

"That's great news!" I said, feeling a fresh bubble of warmth rise up in my chest. "I'm so relieved. I hated to think of him going back to his mother after everything you told me."

"I guess it means I'm kind of like a dad now," Patrick said. "Or at least a guardian. Are you okay with that?"

"Patrick," I said, one hand on his face. "The fact that you're the kind of guy who would do that for his nephew is one of the reasons I fell for you. And besides," I said, "dads are totally hot."

"Please don't tell me you've got a daddy kink." Patrick made a face.

"Would that be a dealbreaker?"

"For anyone else? Yes. For you? I'd make it work."

"Excuse me, are you the guy from *Outback Adventures*? Can we get a selfie?" A young couple I vaguely recognised from my flight had stepped over my abandoned carry-on luggage and were looking at Patrick with eager faces.

"He sure is," I said. "I'll take the photo."

And so, I stood there, clutching a stranger's phone in my hands, and took a photo of the man I loved, putting on a big smile for his fans but still looking right at me.

"Thanks," the woman said, taking her phone back. "Are you his girlfriend?"

"Yes." Patrick put one arm around me. "Yes, she is."

"Oh, that's nice," the woman said while her partner struggled with the suitcases. "So lovely."

When she was finally dragged away, I looked up at him. "Girlfriend?"

"Is that okay with you?"

"Very okay."

Then an open box of doughnuts was thrust in front of me. "Do you want one?" Phoenix asked, his mouth half full of something with violently green icing.

"Definitely," I said, taking one from the box. "And coffee! Phoenix, you sure know the way to a woman's heart."

"The flowers were my idea," Phoenix said proudly, and then he saw them on the ground. "Didn't you like them?"

"I do!" I said, quickly bending to scoop them up. "I just got a bit excited and dropped everything."

"Are you guys happy now?" Phoenix looked at Patrick for confirmation.

"Very happy." Patrick selected a sugar-covered jam doughnut. "These are happy carbs!"

"It's a special occasion, then?" I couldn't resist teasing him.

"Very special."

· ♥ · ♥ · ♥ · ♥ · ♥ ·

I couldn't keep the smile – which was probably a maniacal grin – off my face as Patrick's SUV took me away from the airport and towards Brekkie Beach. When the 'Welcome to Brekkie Beach' sign appeared, I felt my heart surge, and squeezed Patrick's hand.

"Welcome home," he said, turning into the street where my booking at Brekkie Beach's most horrible cottage had led me to the man of my dreams.

"I think it is," I said softly. "I just didn't know it until I left."

Patrick looked over at me with a soft, fond expression. "All that matters is that you're here now."

A cough from the back seat. "Is it okay if I go over to Keenan's? And sleep over?"

Patrick let go of my hand as he parked the car in the driveway. "Sure, dude," he said. "I got a big pack of those chips you like. Why don't you take them with you?"

"Cool," Phoenix said, and then he looked at me through the rear-view mirror. "I'm glad you came back, Michelle."

"Me too," I said. "Really glad."

As I got out of the car, the smell of salt, sun, and sand hit my nostrils like an overwhelming sense memory, and I leaned against the door for a moment, feeling something close to teary.

"You okay?" Patrick asked, his big hands on my shoulders. "You're not having second thoughts, are you?"

"Definitely not," I told him, wiping my eyes. "I'm just happy."

"Didn't realise you were a happy crier." Patrick wiped a final tear away with his thumb.

"Neither did I," I admitted. "Maybe I haven't been happy enough to need to before now."

And then Patrick kissed me, pressed against the sun-warmed side of his SUV, right there in the driveway. His lips were soft, graze of stubble on my skin as my body melted into his, desperate to be close to him again, to make up for the lonely nights spent apart.

"I'm off to Keenan's," Phoenix's voice interrupted us, and I looked over to see him with a backpack slung over one shoulder and a huge bag of chips in his hand. "See you tomorrow? I'll text before I come home."

"Have fun, dude!"

"I'm pretty sure he's trying to *Parent Trap* us again," I said, a smile playing on my lips. "He's way too good at that."

And I wanted nothing more than to let Patrick carry me into the house and press me against every conveniently flat surface, but there was something else. "How is he?" I asked. "Really?"

Patrick sighed and took my hand as he led me into the house. "He's good, I think. You know, he was the one who suggested we should fly to Glasgow so I could try to win you back. He was going to hold the boombox."

I laughed. "He's such a great kid."

"He is," Patrick agreed, pulling me down close to him on the sofa, one strong arm wrapping around me. "But everything he's been through with his mum? It doesn't go away overnight. He's going to keep seeing Evan. The psychologist, that is."

"That's good." I rested my head on Patrick's shoulder. "And I think you're right. It's great that he's going to stay here, and you've been awesome for him, but he's been through a lot. He's still going to see his mum, right?"

"Yeah, of course," Patrick said. "She's managed to score a gig hosting this luxury outback travel show, she thinks it could finally be her big break. And that's—" His face contorted. "That's why she said he could stay here. Because she'll be busy travelling and filming."

"Ouch."

"He doesn't know that's the reason," Patrick said. "Not yet, anyway. But he'll still see her when she's in Sydney and spend some weekends there. You and I can still have a bit of privacy."

"Privacy is good," I said, pressing a kiss to Patrick's cheek. "But even if that wasn't the case, I'd still want this. With you. Because I love you."

"Michelle..." Patrick's voice was husky. "I know you've just been on a plane for twenty-eight hours. You're probably exhausted, and you want a shower, and I should just let you sleep, but—"

"I do want to sleep," I told him, my mouth ghosting over his neck. "Afterwards. And yeah, I really do need a shower. But not," I paused, "alone."

"I'm so on board with this plan," Patrick whispered, leading me into the house and up the stairs.

"I'm sorry I'm so gross," I said when the bathroom light showed me that, wow, those dark circles under my eyes were very prominent, and my messy bun, while practical, certainly wasn't the most flattering of hairstyles. My leggings and t-shirt covered the least sexy bra and undies

I owned. "I have this outfit packed that I was going to wear when I came to see you. Little red dress, lingerie. The works."

"Michelle," Patrick said firmly. "You couldn't be more beautiful to me than you are right now." He stripped off my t-shirt and ugly bra so quickly that I didn't even have time to be embarrassed, and my leggings and comfortable but unflattering undies hit the floor soon after.

Big hands moved over my body, cradling, stroking, caressing, and I was already gasping before I managed to turn on the shower. I slipped my hands under his t-shirt, fighting to pull it over his head, and Patrick just chuckled as he helped me.

"You get under the water," he said, guiding me towards the warm spray.

I stepped under the water and sighed. The water seemed to be doing more than washing away the recycled air and stench of hundreds of people in a metal tube. I had never been religious, but at that moment, it felt like a baptism, my old life falling away, and I was reborn into something entirely new.

I rubbed my face, and when I blinked, Patrick had joined me, his long, lean body pressed against mine under the water. Our lips met under the warm spray, bodies pressed together, and I let myself melt into him. My body was tingling, sparks erupting under my skin as I kissed him, as those strong, calloused hands moved over my body like he wanted to map every dip, every curve, every hollow.

"I love you," Patrick murmured, his lips brushing my ear. "So much. I never thought I could feel like this about anyone, and you just..." He looked down at me, and I could see the truth of his words in those bright green eyes. "I never had a chance with you."

"I'm pretty sure it was all over for me when you asked me to dance," I whispered, fingers toying with where his wet hair reached his neck. "Even after you ghosted me."

Patrick let out a chuckle, water droplets spraying from his lips. "Good thing you rented the worst cottage in Brekkie Beach, then."

"Mm, I should send the owners a thank you note," I said. But then I thought of the front door that wouldn't lock, the lumpy mattress, and the death-trap stairs. "Or not."

"I don't think they deserve it," Patrick said, picking up the washcloth and liberally applying an organic body wash that claimed to be made right here in Brekkie Beach.

"Are you going to wash me?" I asked, half-laughing, half excited at the idea.

"Yes." Patrick was completely serious, and it sent a thrill of fresh heat through my body. "Every bit of you." A quick brush of his lips, and then he gently began to move the cloth over my neck and shoulders, taking infinite care.

I let out a low moan as the cloth moved lower, and he traced around my breasts, dragging the soft fabric slowly. "Patrick!"

"I'm not done," Patrick chided me, moving down to my belly, my hips.

When he dropped to his knees, pressing the cloth up my thigh and towards where I really wanted him, I almost lost my footing. I was close to crazy with desire for him, and I couldn't take much more.

"Michelle?" He looked up at me, wet hair plastered to his face, green eyes fixed on me like I was the answer to his every prayer, the subject of every daydream (not to mention wet dream).

"Yeah?" My voice was a husky gasp.

"Spread your legs for me."

I managed to comply, flattening myself against the shower wall, and—

I cried out as he pressed his mouth between my thighs, his tongue moving over me in confident, dizzying spirals. My hands fisted in his hair, and I was squirming, writhing against the glass as he worshipped me with his mouth, strong hands gripping my hips.

"Patrick, I need—" I began. "I want you. Right now."

He looked up at me, lips glistening, eyes blazing with desire. "Yeah?"

"Please."

"You never have to beg." Patrick got to his feet, turning off the shower stream and kissing me again, deep and urgent, the taste of me mingling on our tongues. "Come here."

I had no idea what he was planning, but I let him guide me out of the shower and to the basin, right in front of the mirror. Unlike the mirror in the cottage, this one was clear and bright, and I could see my body with Patrick behind me, glistening and wet.

"Here?"

"Here," Patrick agreed, rummaging in the drawer of the washstand for a condom. "I want you to be able to watch this. You and me, together."

I made a sound that wasn't a word because I couldn't form words. Nothing even close. All I could do was grip the washstand and spread my legs. When I felt him press against my entrance, I let out a cry. But one strong arm wrapped around my waist, holding me steady.

"I love you so much, Michelle." A rough whisper, right in my ear, as he pressed inside me, filling me up as I clenched tight around him, desperate to feel every bit of him. I gasped at the feeling, gripping the basin and very much hoping it was sturdy.

"I love you too."

"Look at yourself." It was almost an order. I lifted my head, gasping at what I saw. My body, still slick from the shower, with Patrick, wrapped around me, ecstasy on his face as he moved inside me. The sight of our bodies locked together was overpowering, intoxicating, and I was surprised I managed to keep breathing. "You're so beautiful."

I managed something between a moan and a shout, our eyes locked together in the mirror. I knew I couldn't last much longer, not like this, not when I had spent every moment we were apart desperately wanting to feel his body on mine, claiming me for his own.

When Patrick reached down to touch me, never breaking that rhythm inside me as he did, my body spasmed in his arms. Stubble on my neck, hot breath in my ear, and I began to shake, right on the edge.

"Do it for me," Patrick whispered, and I did. Lights – fireworks, maybe – exploded behind my eyes, and I was helpless in his arms, shaking and shivering as climax overtook us both, our bodies locked together.

As we stilled, I could see us in the mirror. Two people, one blonde and one dark, wrapped around each other and unable to stop smiling.

"Best shower ever?"

"I hope not." Patrick put a thick, crisp towel, dried in the salty air of Brekkie Beach, around me and wrapped me up like a burrito. "I reckon we could do even better, with practice."

"Practice sounds good." I allowed Patrick to lead me from the bathroom to his bed, where I gratefully sank down onto a mattress that wasn't at all lumpy. Despite the debauchery of our recent actions, I felt clean and fresh as I snuggled into him, my towel falling away, so our bodies were pressed together.

"Well, I hope so." Patrick tucked one damp lock of hair behind my ear. "Because I'm really hoping you want to move in with me. Well, us. Phoenix too."

I just stared at him for a moment, open-mouthed. "You want me to move in with you?"

"Yeah," Patrick said. "I really do. But I understand if that might be a bit much, you know, with Phoenix being here. But he's keen on the idea. He thinks it would be good for me to have some company, so I don't cramp his social life." Patrick raised his eyebrows, grinning. "But I understand if it's too soon or too weird living with a fourteen-year-old, so—"

"I want to move in," I said quickly, not wanting to leave a single doubt in his mind. "I don't care if it's too soon. It feels right. Completely right."

Patrick's face broke into that brilliant smile that so many people knew, but only I got to have lavished on me like this. "Good," he said. "Because I really don't want to let you go. I made that mistake once, but I'm a fast learner. I'm not going to do it again."

"I won't let you," I said, running one hand over his face and staring into those big green eyes. "And you know that once I set my mind to something, I'm very determined."

"Just one of the many things I love about you."

24 Patrick

"It's nearly six," I said, looking at my watch. "Do you want to come for a walk?"

"Sure, Uncle Patrick," Phoenix said, his voice heavy with teenage sarcasm. "Do I need to wear a lead?"

I narrowed my eyes as though assessing him. "No, so long as you promise not to take a dump on anyone's lawn. We don't want child protective services on our arse."

Phoenix laughed, and together, we walked the familiar path down to the small jetty where the ferry from the city docked. The air was fresh and clean, with a slight breeze bringing the smell of salt water towards us.

"So, how's school going?" I asked. "You settling in okay?"

"Yeah, pretty good. Keenan's in most of my classes, so that helps. My woodwork teacher asked about you today."

"Oh really?" I raised my eyebrows. "Is he a fan of *Outback Adventures*, then?"

"Nah." Phoenix shook his head. "That's what I thought he would say, but he asked about your furniture. He reckons he's seen you at the timber yard."

"Well, it's nice to be known for something I've done as an adult for a change. Did you tell him you've been helping me out?"

"He guessed." Phoenix shrugged modestly. "I was the only one who already knew how to use a table saw."

"Nice." I gave him an encouraging nod. "So, you'll be top in that class. No pressure, though!"

"Evan says I shouldn't put too much pressure on myself," Phoenix told me. "Like, when I'm making friends, I don't have to just go along with whatever they want to keep them happy. We've been practising what to say and stuff."

"Yeah? That sounds helpful."

"I think so. Evan reckons I'm making progress, so that's, like, good, isn't it?" I could hear the note of pride in his voice.

"Definitely good," I agreed. "Look, there's the ferry." I pointed, though the ferry wasn't exactly easy to miss.

"I think Michelle's waving."

"She is." I waved back as the ferry drew closer. We made it to the jetty just as the ferry docked, and Michelle jumped off, smiling as she made her way to us.

"My boys! You know, I'm still in awe of the fact that I get to go to work on the ferry, with all those beautiful views of the harbour. Beats my commute in Glasgow."

"Plus, you get to work from home too," I said, raising my eyebrows. "That's gotta be a bonus."

"Oh, it is." Michelle beamed. "Especially since two very thoughtful men ensured I've got the nicest desk in Sydney."

Phoenix grinned and ducked his head.

"So, how was work?" I asked as we turned to go back up the hill. "Still learning the ropes?"

"I think I've pretty much got it now. The work's the same, really. But the office culture took a bit of getting used to. When people ask me how I am, they're not trying to find a weakness to store up for later exploitation. I think my colleagues actually like each other; it's weird." Michelle put on an exaggerated face of shock.

"Amazing," I deadpanned. "I'm not sure I believe it."

"And how was school, Phoenix?"

"Good. But I had maths today. We just started statistics, and it's kind of hard."

"Oh really?" Michelle looked eager. "Can I look over it with you? I'd love to see how they're teaching it."

And that, I thought, was very clever of her. Offering to help Phoenix while making it seem like he'd be doing her a favour. I could see that she never wanted him to feel like he was stupid, like she, however wrongly, once had.

"Yeah, sure," Phoenix said, then he looked up at me, inclining his head. I knew what he was thinking.

"So, they're happy for you to work from home three days a week?" I asked, trying to sound casual.

"Yes, but I'm not sure if I will," Michelle said. "If I work from home that much, my work stuff will take over the living room, and that's not fair on you two."

"Actually," I said, nodding at Phoenix. "We've been thinking about that. I just submitted an application to the council for planning permission to build an extension. So, you could have your own office."

"No way!" Michelle's eyes went wide. "You don't need to do that!"

"But I want to. Besides, I've applied to stick on a rumpus room too, and I reckon we could have an epic gaming set-up. Phoenix is keen."

"It sounds cool," Phoenix confirmed.

"And it will add value to the house," I said, nudging Michelle. "Surely a financial analyst can't disagree with that."

"You've got me there. And it does sound awesome."

"More space is definitely a good thing," I said. "Now that we're a family of three."

"Are we a family?" Phoenix looked up.

"Yeah, dude," I said as Michelle squeezed my hand. "I reckon we are."

"That," I said approvingly, "is one fancy salad." The fancy salad was in honour of the very first barbecue – I couldn't bring myself to say dinner party – that we were hosting together. And maybe it was sickeningly domestic, but I was enjoying myself just the same.

Michelle looked up from where she was scooping pomegranate seeds from the red fruit. "Yep," she said. "Turns out when I'm not working insane hours, I actually have time to make salads that don't come in plastic containers. Who knew?"

"I'm impressed. And very glad that you're not working insane hours." I leaned over the bench to kiss her.

"Well, I found something that mattered more than becoming a Partner by thirty-three," Michelle said, leaning her forehead against mine. "A lot more."

"Pretty sure you're still going to be a Partner soon. Your new boss thinks you're amazing. Because you are."

Michelle smiled in pleasure. "When I don't have to spend half my time dealing with backstabbing co-workers, I'm more efficient. And it's a nice change to actually like the people I work with."

"No regrets, then?"

Michelle snorted. "None at all. I just wish I had made the change sooner, you know? I could have done it years ago!"

"But then we might not have met. And that would be a tragedy."

"Agreed." Michelle wiped her hands on a tea towel and came out from behind the counter to wrap her arms around me. "I don't think I'd be this happy without you. In fact, I know I wouldn't."

I kissed her again, and it was the kind of kiss that could have become much more if we didn't have guests arriving in a matter of minutes.

The doorbell rang but was immediately followed by the sound of the door opening. "That must be Khalid." I stepped away with regret. "Because he never waits for me to let him in."

"Yo!" Khalid himself appeared in the kitchen. "What's up, party people? That is a *nice* salad." He leaned over to inspect the salad and then kissed Michelle on the cheek. "I bet you're responsible for this. Patrick is useless in the kitchen."

"Hey, I've been marinating the meat!" I said, pointing to the tray on the bench where a deboned lamb leg was smothered in garlic and rosemary. "I'm not completely useless."

"No, you're not." Khalid gave me a genial grin. "That's why I only brought bread today."

"Bread?"

"You can never have enough bread! Especially now that the big guy has relaxed on his whole 'no carbs' thing." He pulled a sourdough loaf from his bag. "Anyway, where's Phoenix?"

"Either obliterating zombies or watching *Seinfeld*," Michelle told him. "And we can blame you for at least one of those."

"I'm not apologising for introducing the young man to classic comedy."

Before I could disagree – not that I intended to – the doorbell rang again, and Michelle went to let in her more polite sisters.

"Let's get this party started!" Khalid rubbed his hands together. "Everything needs to go out on the deck, yeah?"

"Thanks," I said. "Then we can do the manly thing and stand by the grill."

"It's what men do."

A few hours later, we were all pleasantly – or overly – full of lamb, sourdough, and Michelle's fancy salad.

"Lamb is good," Abby declared, patting her stomach. "Nice one, Patrick."

"Glad you liked it. Does anyone want more, or is it time for dessert?"

"You made dessert?" Khalid raised his eyebrows.

"Made is probably too strong a word," I admitted. "But Phoenix and I put Tim-Tams and strawberries on a platter with our very own hands."

"Sounds like a winner." Tessa nodded approvingly. "But first, could we get a picture with everyone?"

"That sounds like my cue." Dylan stood up. "Michelle, get nice and close to Patrick. Show us how much you like him."

Michelle snuggled into my side, her head resting on my shoulder. I inhaled the sweet smell of her hair and half-closed my eyes, enjoying the last of the evening's setting sun.

"You're squinting," Dylan told me. "Come on, everyone, look happy!"

And I was happy. Very happy. But I couldn't help thinking about what was hidden behind my least favourite oscillating sander in the garage. A box containing a ring that came with a question. *Do you want this, forever?*

Call me crazy, but I had bought the ring just a week after Michelle had returned to Brekkie Beach. I was sure it was the right thing; more certain than I had ever been of anything. All I had to do now was wait for the right moment to ask.

Epilogue: Michelle

One year later

"I swear to god there were not this many buttons when you tried this thing on in the shop," Abby grumbled as her fingers worked over my back.

"It fits, doesn't it?" I asked, feeling a sudden rush of anxiety. "You can do it up?"

"Of course I can." Tessa put a hand on my arm. "Fits like a dream. A dream with a lot of buttons."

I let out a breath of relief. "Good. I don't want to walk down the aisle safety-pinned together."

"No chance of that," Abby said. "Okay, that's the last little sucker!" She stood back, clapping her hands triumphantly. Then she let out an ear-piercing wolf whistle.

"You look so beautiful," Tessa confirmed. "Come on, look at yourself!"

And I did. My dress – a tight, fitted mermaid style – hugged my curves, and with my hair in loose curls swept to one side, I felt like an old Hollywood starlet.

"Wow!"

"Patrick is going to lose his shit when he sees you," Abby said, wrapping an arm around my waist.

"Definitely," Tessa said, nodding with satisfaction. "Most beautiful bride ever. It's official."

There was a soft click and then another, and I turned to see Dylan smiling as he snapped away. "All three of you look amazing," he said. "Just pretend I'm not here."

"You can say Michelle's the most beautiful today," Tessa told him. "It's her wedding. She gets to be the most beautiful."

But Dylan just laughed. "I'm not saying a word."

"Smart man." Abby nodded her head approvingly. "Okay, we've got one stunningly hot bride ready to go. Let's get you married, girl!"

· ♥ · ♥ · ♥ · ♥ · ♥ ·

Eucalyptus trees towered overhead, the winding Hawkesbury River was majestic, and the song of birds echoed in the breeze. I had readily agreed for our wedding ceremony to be held where *Outback Adventures* was once filmed, but when the time came for me to get out of the car and make that long walk towards Patrick, I didn't give a shit about the natural beauty surrounding me.

All I could see was Patrick. I knew he was standing with Khalid and Phoenix, his best men, but they, too, were a blur. My eyes were fixed only on him in his tailored grey suit and white shirt, open at the collar. His sun-bleached hair was artistically tousled, and those green eyes looked right back at me like we were the only two people in existence.

When I reached him, Patrick took my hands in his and squeezed, giving me a tiny wink. Hours later, Abby told me that I did a beautiful job of repeating my vows, loud and clear, but I was scarcely aware of the words I was saying as I looked at the man who was about to be my husband. When the celebrant told me we could seal the deal with a kiss, Patrick leaned in, wrapping one arm around my waist to tip me right back.

When the kiss broke, a roar of applause greeted my ears, and I was grinning so hard my cheeks were painful as he led me down between the rows of guests, my hand tightly held in his.

"Aren't you glad you didn't wait until you were a Partner to be happy?" Patrick whispered, his lips ghosting over my ear.

"Oh, I think I'm a partner after all. Your partner."

"Good answer," Patrick said, squeezing my hand. "Very good answer."

· ♥ · ♥ · ♥ · ♥ · ♥ ·

Like all good wedding receptions, ours was a babble of noise, music, and laughter. Voices raised, bright smiles, glasses in hands.

I was in the middle of a fascinating conversation with Khalid concerning a missing pair of underpants, an overflowing communal washing machine, and a very open-minded couple from Florida when Patrick approached me. "Look," he said, nudging me. "Our sisters are getting on."

I followed his gaze and saw Abby deep in conversation with Julia, showing her something on her phone. Abby had her finger pointed, a clear sign she was Making A Point.

"I'm pretty sure she's bullying Julia into hiring her," I warned. "Does Julia need her house organised? Because she's going to get it."

"You know, I think she does." Patrick squeezed my hand. "It could be a good thing!"

"Where's Phoenix?" I scanned the room, looking for my...step-nephew? That was a horrible phrase. Phoenix was just Phoenix, a young man who I cared a whole lot about. "Is he checking out Dylan's equipment again?"

"Actually, I just saw him and Keenan sneaking beers from an empty table. I guess it's okay; he'll be sixteen soon."

"I was doing worse at sixteen," I said, tilting my head. "What do you think, Khalid?"

"I think sneaking a beer at a wedding is a rite of passage," Khalid said. "We'd be doing him a disservice if we stopped him. Anyway," he rubbed his hands together, "when are you two stepping out? I want to dance!"

"Pretty much now," I said as the music died down and the MC tapped the microphone.

"Break a leg!" Khalid whispered and gave us a double thumbs up as Patrick took my hands and led me to the centre of the room.

As Ella Fitzgerald crooned from the speakers (we did not, as Khalid had suggested, have our first dance to the *Outback Adventures* theme tune), I let myself relax into Patrick's arms.

"Having fun?"

"I am," I said. "I'm kind of looking forward to when you and I get to sneak off, though."

"Me too." Patrick's lips met mine for just a moment. "Although Abby did warn me not to drink too much, or I'll never be able to undo all your buttons."

"Oh, so you're planning to come home with me?" I teased. "You're not going to go off to get me a drink, and then I'll never see you again?"

"Michelle!" Patrick was laughing as he dipped me low in his arms. "I think you know me better than that."

"I do," I said, leaning up to kiss him to the delight of the watching crowd. "Besides, you couldn't get away from me if you tried. Brekkie Beach is a small town."

"With a very limited number of Air BnB options," Patrick smiled that still-dazzling smile of his.

"Thank goodness for that."

About the Author

Rita Harte is a romantic comedy author who likes to write books with big laughs and big feelings. She firmly believes that characters struggling with mental health, family drama, and painful pasts deserve a fabulous happily ever after.

Living in sometimes sunny Sydney, Rita is powered by caffeine, loud music, and the loving support of her family.

Printed in Great Britain
by Amazon